To my
friend
Dianne —

The Morphine
Murders

LJ King

Enjoy!
LJ King

ISBN 978-1-937520-88-5
Published by
First Edition Design Publishing
April 2012
www.firsteditiondesignpublishing.com

The Morphine Murders is a work of fiction. Names, characters and events in this book are fictitious. Any similarity to real persons, living or dead, or events is entirely coincidental and not intended by the author.

First Edition: May 2012

The Morphine Murders / LJ King – 1ˢᵗ ed.
ISBN 9781937520892 Hardcover
ISBN 9781937520908 eBook

Library of Congress Cataloging-in-Publication Data
2012938285

ACKNOWLEDGEMENTS

There are so many special people that continue to support and encourage me on this journey that I'd have to write another book to include everyone and fully express my gratitude.

Thank you to my mother for all her love and support during this project and throughout my entire life. Thank you to Victor Besson and Shannon King who were my very first editors. Thank you to Chris King for keeping my secrets, which included this book for a long while. Thank you to Robin Gortler and Michelle Terry for not falling asleep while I blabbed on and on about my book and the process. Thank you to Steffi Joerg who does fall asleep when I talk to her but who supports me with great enthusiasm. Thank you to JJ, my constant four-legged companion. Thank you to Julie Mosow whose professional editing was invaluable and taught me a tremendous amount. Thank you to John "J.P." Cardone and James Wassick for providing the endorsements for the back cover. Thank you to Robert Asma for his unwavering confidence in me and for promising to help market the book. Now you have to. Thank you to Karl Brosky for dealing with two crazy authors at the same time and always encouraging us. Thank you to Kerriann Flanagan Brosky for trying to warn me about the insanity. Thank you for sharing the ups, the downs, the research, the celebrations, the hurdles, and our memorable adventures. We're in this together all the way, beach girl.

Thank you to everyone for reading *The Morphine Murders*.

CHAPTER 1

Raina tensed as Tyler embraced her with a tenderness that contradicted his strength. He brushed his fingertips along her cheek and swept her dark hair from her face. She felt their hearts pounding against each other while he held her to his chest, placed his hand at the back of her head, and kissed her for the first time. Raina relaxed into his arms. Together they reclined onto the couch, still entwined and engaged in their kiss. She opened her eyes and focused beyond Tyler to the high ceiling of his living room. It seemed so far away, as did Danny, her boyfriend.

The thought of Danny burned her already flushed face. Raina put her hands flat against Tyler's chest. His warmth heated her palms, making her hesitate. She wanted to pull him back to her but instead watched him move away without any resistance.

"I should go," she said.

She adjusted her tank top and pulled her hair into a clip. Tyler followed her to the door as though nothing was wrong. For a moment, they gazed at each other, momentarily allowing their passion to erase all other thoughts. She squeezed his hand and headed to her car, already anticipating the awkwardness when she saw him at work the following day.

She sped away with the convertible top up. As his house disappeared from sight in her rearview mirror, her phone rang.

"I know, I know. I'm late for DB Night," she answered.

"More than an hour late," Sloan said.

Monday nights were always DB Night, dead body night, always at Sloan's house and always included dinner and half a dozen crime shows on television.

"I'm on my way. I'll explain when I get there," Raina said. How? How was she going to explain?

As she drove, Raina struggled to sort out her feelings. Her relationship with Danny was serious, and she cared for him deeply, but lately it had become stale. Raina had been planning ways to shove it out of its rut. Kissing Tyler was not on that list.

The car engine idled while Raina spoke into the voice activated intercom and waited for Sloan to let her in. Custom iron gates separated and disappeared into the landscape. Up ahead she saw Sloan's backlit silhouette standing in the entranceway, hands on her hips, as though she were poised for an interrogation.

"How are you feeling?" Raina asked.

Sloan cradled her abdomen. "She's kicking a lot today. Here." She took Raina's hand and placed it against her side.

They entered through the center hall and went straight downstairs to the media room. Its design included acoustical insulation, which had noise-dampening properties, but it was Raina's silence that made the room noticeably quiet.

"Have a seat, take a slice," Sloan pointed to the pizza box, "and tell me what's wrong."

"What do you mean?" Raina asked, trying to stall.

"How long have we been friends?"

Raina rolled her eyes, but this was their routine when Sloan was making her point. "Since grade school when you investigated the stolen brownie from your lunch and interrogated me."

"Then you know I can tell when something's wrong."

The tilt of Sloan's head and the lift of her eyebrows left Raina no choice. As long as Raina had known Sloan, once she locked onto something she wouldn't let go.

"It's Tyler. Really, it's Danny and me. It's kind of all of us. We kissed. We didn't plan it, but it felt good. Then I freaked." The words flew out of her mouth.

"All of us? Who kissed?"

Raina clarified and recounted the evening's events. It had begun with an innocent enough dinner. The time from dinner to the kiss was mostly a blur, but she remembered that moment in full detail. The feather-light pressure of his mouth on hers, teasing her, taunting her, and lingering against her lips, was clear as day.

"What are you going to do now?"

"It can't happen again," Raina said quietly and wiped a tear from her cheek.

Sloan's maternal instincts shift into high gear. Sloan hugged her and used her best calming voice. "It will be okay."

It didn't feel like it was going to be okay. There was no denying her attraction to Tyler. "But it's purely physical."

In her head, though, she wasn't so convinced. And then there was Danny.

Anticipating his caffeine fix, a man tapped his fingers rhythmically on his leg while waiting in line at Naturally Sweet, a newly opened bakery. There was a young, blonde woman behind the counter who caught his attention. He noticed her voice at first, but it was her manner and the way her lips came together and parted as she spoke that kept him entranced. He thought it was sweet when she handed a cookie to a well-behaved child who stood patiently next to her mother and thoughtful when she circled a coffee cup lid twice to be sure it was closed securely. Then a sudden tremble in her grip caused coffee to spurt up through the lid. Had she had that all along? He hadn't noticed. Something stirred inside him.

The line of customers crept forward as he studied her. He was sure that she had noticed him too from a series of quick glances towards him between customers. From behind, another woman tapped him on the shoulder with her newspaper. He ignored when it brushed against his ear, but woman's raspy voice followed the tap, "You're next. Move up."

Without acknowledging the woman behind him, he stepped to the counter where the object of his attention smiled at him and asked for his order. An odd feeling of comfort flowed through him. He returned the smile.

"Regular with a drop of skim milk and one sugar, please," he said and then moved down the counter to the register.

After serving him, the woman checked her watch and disappeared into the kitchen. He scanned the few tables for an available seat. There was only one vacant, and it was directly beneath the television mounted in the corner. As he walked towards it, the local morning news was on. He stopped, leaned against the window, and watched. When his coffee had begun to cool and the blonde hadn't come back to the register, he dumped the rest of his coffee in the trash and planned to return earlier the next day. He noted the time. It was just after ten.

"Hello?" he heard as he pressed the remote to unlock his car. When he turned, the woman from the bakery was jogging right toward him.

"Can you help me?" she asked, exhaling.

"Sure," he said without hesitation, positive that she had fabricated an excuse to talk to him. "What can I do?"

"My car won't start."

He tried to appear calm as his heart beat faster. "You have AAA?"

She pursed her lips and shook her head.

"I can give you a ride if you like."

She checked her phone. "If you wouldn't mind, it's only two minutes away."

He opened the passenger door for her, and she slid into the black leather seat in his Mercedes. There was little conversation between them as he drove. He decided he was wrong about her making an excuse to talk to him and wondered why she had accepted a ride from a stranger. A cab or a co-worker could have driven her. Why did she trust him? He had noticed her wedding band when she rested her hand on the center console a minute before. Why didn't she call her husband?

"Turn left up there at the stone-front house," she said.

He nodded and made the turn.

"Right here on the right. This is it. Thanks so much for driving me." She quickly unbuckled her seatbelt and started to open the car door.

It was too quick, and he didn't want her to rush off. "Beautiful house," he said.

"We bought it from the same people we bought the bakery from," she said.

He assumed that she was referring to her and her husband. There was no need for her to ram the existence of her husband down his throat. He hadn't alluded to anything besides helping her out, which had been at her request.

She got out of the car and leaned through the window. "I really appreciate the ride. I wouldn't have been able to make my afternoon appointment without your help."

"I can take you there. I'm not late for work yet."

"Thanks, but no." She gestured towards the two-car garage.

As she moved away from the car, his body tensed, and he wiped his palms against the sides of his pants. Each time she had spoken, he had focused on her lips, watched them move, and listened to her soothing voice. It calmed him. He didn't want the feeling to end, so he tried to come up with a way to keep her engaged. Then he saw it. Thanks to a lazy delivery person, a large box had been left half way up her walkway.

"Let me carry that for you," he said, pointing at the box.

She accepted his offer. It was simple, genuine, and so easy. He was in. As she hurried up the path to the house, he grabbed a small, canvas bag from under the front seat and looped the handles over his wrist to keep his hands free. The box was addressed to an M. Levy.

She fumbled with a ring of keys before finding the right one. Once inside, he placed the box on the slate floor of the entranceway and surveyed the house: antique furniture everywhere, hand-sewn carpets, and walls full of original art. There were so many things that it was hard to focus on them all. She dropped her bags on a bench in time to greet an excited puppy that jumped up on her.

"He's such a mush," she said.

As she bent down to pick up the puppy, he plunged a needle in the back of her neck. She instinctively reached toward the source of the sting, but her knees buckled, and she collapsed. Halfway to the floor, he caught her. He took the woman in his arms and carried her up to the second floor to find her bedroom. Her body hung over his arms. The young puppy whimpered, unable to climb the stairs and follow.

Her blonde curls cascaded over the pillow as he carefully laid her body on top of the silk comforter. Her hair was soft against his hand as he gathered it together, tied it, and laid it over the front of her shoulder, careful not to touch her breast. He adjusted her position. Her eyes were closed, and her make-up shimmered in the late morning sunlight. The slap from the latex glove against his skin set a routine in motion. With precision, he inserted an IV needle into her arm, connected a bag to the tube, and released the drip.

He sought the comfort of an overstuffed chair while he watched the woman lie there peacefully, and waited. The puppy had settled down, leaving the house placid. Occasionally he heard a car drive down the block and listened carefully to make sure it wasn't unwanted company. In between, his thoughts focused on the woman. He was saddened that he would never again hear her voice or feel her touch.

Her breathing slowed and finally ceased. He kneeled down on the floor at the edge of the bed and pressed his warm lips to her cooling forehead.

"No more pain," he said.

CHAPTER 2

Officer John "Hawkeye" Lorenzo of the Suffolk County Police Department had responded to a routine noise complaint in an upscale suburban neighborhood. They were popping up all over Long Island, all the same with new homes and devoid of large, old trees and character. A neighbor had reported excessive barking at the Levy house, and upon his arrival, the dog was still at it. No one answered when he rang the doorbell. He peered through the window. The mess inside the house suggested an invasion had occurred. Things were strewn everywhere.

"Weird. There are no exterior signs of a break-in. All the doors and windows are secured, and no marks from a forced entry."

"Probably a domestic dispute. I see it all the time." A stocky officer with a crew cut slipped in front of Hawkeye, pulled his sleeve over his fist, and broke the window next to the door. "No big deal. It was just an automatic door lock, no deadbolt," the officer said.

"I could've done that," Hawkeye said.

"Could've but didn't."

A second later the alarm sounded. The piercing siren drew the attention of the few neighbors left inside their homes, and they joined the rest on the street. The officer cleared the broken glass from the frame with his jacket, climbed inside, and unlocked the door. Through the blaring siren and the barking dog, they saw the call indicator light on the house phone blinking.

"Got it," Hawkeye said.

He hopped over a pile of books, grabbed the receiver, and asked the security company on the other end to disarm the system. Another pair of officers arrived and searched the house. Hawkeye followed the officers into the room where they had found a woman on the bed, on her back. He felt for a pulse, but there was none. He radioed it in.

"Clear," an officer yelled out, referring to the rest of the house.

"Hawkeye, fill me in," Detective Murphy said as he hit the top of the stairs.

"The body still needs to be officially identified, though she fits the description of the homeowner according to the neighbors. Marlo Levy, married. Husband's out of town. M.E. is on his way. The main floor of the house was ransacked, but the second floor looks untouched, well, except for the vic. There's no visible cause of death: no blood, no weapon, nothing."

Murphy didn't offer a theory. "Continue to question the neighbors and find out what kind of people the Levys' are. And, do your thing."

"Will do."

Hawkeye was happy to perform for anyone that might see his "thing" as a future asset to the Detective Squad, as he did. During his teenage years, Hawkeye had learned that he could read people in an unusual way. Minute facial tics and reactions enabled him to see their otherwise hidden emotions. Some thought it was due to his unusual eyes, so dark that they appeared black.

Hawkeye checked on the street from the bedroom window when he heard a commotion. There were a dozen civilians, an ambulance, two squad cars, and a bit of chaos. The neighbors were speculating together in small groups peppered around the property's edge. One was arguing with an officer.

"One strange thing," Hawkeye said to Murphy.

"Yeah?"

"The alarm was set."

Murphy followed Hawkeye to take a look at the system. It was a sophisticated one, either commercial or highly customized.

"Seems like overkill for this house," Murphy said.

"You're the technological expert."

Murphy's assessment stuck in Hawkeye's mind.

The M.E. arrived, with his newest student, half an hour after they requested his presence, and Hawkeye led them upstairs to the body. Dr. Garza was short, overweight, and his growly voice matched his rough face. He instructed his trainee to hand him the thermometer. After he pierced the body and pushed the thermometer into the liver, it produced an ambient temperature reading.

Dr. Garza addressed his trainee without eye contact, "What does that tell us?"

"Sixty-six degrees, which is about the temperature in this room. The A/C probably slowed down the change, but we can't tell for sure, so it's probably more than a day since she died," Garza's assistant said.

Garza didn't respond to confirm or correct his calculation. Hawkeye stood back and tried not to be obvious as he observed the exchange.

"What's with the lack of bedside manner?" Hawkeye asked Murphy.

"He wants to guarantee that his students come to fear him during their rotation. He thinks they'll be less trouble for him in the future. But with his twenty-plus years on the force, they also learn a great deal. It's a love/hate thing."

"Doesn't look like that from where I stand."

The Homicide Division as a whole regarded Dr. Garza as a highly skilled, extremely intelligent ass.

While Hawkeye and Murphy were finishing their McBreakfast the next morning, Murphy got a text on his cell phone: *autopsy results are in from yesterday's body – Garza*. They shoveled in the rest of their food, tossed the trash, and went to the bottom floor of the building where they found Garza in his lab, a brightly lit, spacious area where some of the equipment had been updated, and everything was meticulously neat and clean, probably sterile. It was Hawkeye's first time in the morgue. He shivered.

"Tore you away from your high tech toys two days in a row?" Garza said to Murphy.

"Yep, low manpower's forced me to pound the pavement with the rest of them. I forgot how damn cold it is in here," Murphy said.

"Feels good compared to the heat outside," Hawkeye said.

"Hey, Detective," Garza said, standing over the corpse. "Look at the screen." He pointed to a tiny needle mark in the victim's arm.

Hawkeye stood across the table from the other two, sure that Garza's use of the word detective had been chosen to address only

Murphy as the higher ranking officer. Towering over Garza, Murphy hunched down to view the screen, which showed Garza's arthritic finger enlarged to the size of an arm. Garza pointed to what looked like a crater with mountains of dried blood around it. Shifting his focus back and forth between the screen and the arm on the table, Hawkeye realized the needle mark was undetectable to the naked eye. Even the dried blood was invisible when he turned back to the vic's un-magnified arm.

"So maybe she donated blood recently," Hawkeye said.

Garza looked up at Murphy, "Maybe she did, but that doesn't explain the extreme amount of morphine I found in her system. Cause of death: morphine overdose."

CHAPTER 3

"Be careful with my niece," Raina said as Sloan navigated her belly into a dark, cavernous booth.

They had met for dinner at Applebee's to satisfy Sloan's latest craving for greasy, fried food.

"She's fine, Aunt *Lorraine*," Sloan said.

"Only my grandmother gets away with calling me that."

"Okay *Raina*, are you feeling better today?"

No, she wasn't feeling better. It had been two days since Raina and Tyler had kissed, and although she appreciated Sloan checking on her, she hadn't figured out her own feelings. How could she explain them to Sloan?

"Trying not to think about it, thanks. How's Paul?"

"He's basically taken over designing the baby's room, and he's got the owner of Elite Designs working on it. Chad comes by his office with fabric swatches, paint colors, and even tiny designer outfits. The room's coming along perfectly."

"That doesn't sound like Paul," Raina said.

"Well, babies change people. You'll see some day."

Raina nodded, but those words made her stomach twist. Someday, she thought, was a long way away. Sloan continued to report on all things baby until the waitress came by and took their order.

"Make sure it's hockey puck done," Raina said to the waitress after ordering a blue cheese, mushroom cheeseburger.

"Well done it is," the waitress said.

"Don't forget the extra sour cream for my chicken quesadillas," Sloan reminded her for the second time. "Bring the boneless buffalo wings with it."

The waitress made a check mark on her pad to indicate that she had the details of their order under control and walked away.

"What are you doing with all your spare time now that Paul's taken over baby preparations?"

"Believe it or not, I miss the job. How's Murphy doing?"

"Danny says he's amazing."

"Better than I was?"

"You trained him as your replacement. Danny gives you a lot of credit for that."

"It didn't take much. That kid came with unbelievable computer skills. He has the same mind as I do, it's a little creepy. I mainly taught him department protocol, and he caught right on to that." Sloan paused. "You know he calls me every so often with a question. It makes me feel useful."

"You could have stayed with the department until closer to her birth date."

"Don't start. You know this is how Paul wants it. Anyway, what happened when you saw Tyler in the office?"

"He wasn't in, but nothing's going to change," Raina said, hoping it would be true.

"So, you're going to pretend it didn't happen?"

"No."

Pretending it hadn't happened wasn't an option with the visual of it continually looping in her head. Denial wasn't working either. Raina felt the emptiness bubble in the pit of her stomach.

Sloan dipped a wing into the sauce. "I hope you know what you're doing,"

Raina didn't. Muted police sirens played from the bottom of Raina's handbag, conveniently interrupting the conversation. She pulled out her phone and glanced at the screen while she stuffed fries into her mouth.

"Now you're letting Danny's call go to voicemail?"

She had intentionally avoided him as much as possible the past couple of days.

Sloan's concerned expression only upset Raina more when she listened to Danny's message. She held the phone to her ear, "What are you wearing, Babe? I want to take it off."

"Danny wants to come over," she interpreted with a worried smile. "I guess I can't put off seeing him forever." Raina pushed her plate to the center of the table and watched Sloan reapply her lip gloss. "Ready? By the way you barely put a dent in the extra sour cream you harassed the waitress about."

"Yeah, let's go," Sloan said. "And I didn't harass her."

It was already dark when they said their goodbyes. Raina glanced into the backseat of her car then slipped inside and locked the doors. The ride home was torturous, full of guilt marinated in regret and disappointment. She felt sick.

As Raina drove around the last corner, she saw Danny in his black Denali parked in front of her house. It triggered a wave of panic from head to toe. She ordered herself to relax and breathe, and then she remembered how happy she had been when he had picked her up for their first date. Sloan had met Danny on the job two years earlier and pegged him as a perfect match for Raina: handsome, smart, single, gainfully employed, and sometimes even funny. The Denali had been brand new then, and she had always been happy to see it.

There was no way out of it. Sitting in the car wasn't going to solve anything. Danny would begin to wonder what was going on. As she gathered her belongings from the trunk, Codis, her black Doberman Pincher, stood on the love seat in the window of her Cold Spring Harbor home. He wagged his rear end in anticipation of her arrival and his dinner.

His name stood for Combined DNA Index System, a national DNA database. Raina had changed it from an acronym to appease her brother, Shane, who lived in Florida near their parents. He expressed his distraction by the all caps name in her regular emails to him.

The house had an attached two-car garage, taupe clapboard siding, large, framed windows, and was always meticulously landscaped. In contrast to the organized mess inside the house, the property outside could have been photographed for any home and gardening magazine.

By the time she got to her front steps, Danny was out of his truck and there, waiting. She diverted her glance away from and slid the key in the lock, dropped her bag inside on a pile of magazines, pulled him inside, and shut the door.

"Nothing's going to happen. We're right here," Danny said and tapped his gun.

"I know," she said and twisted the knob to secure the deadbolt. "Did you eat? I just had dinner with Sloan, but there's some of your leftover prime rib in the fridge. I can microwave a potato to go with it if you're hungry."

I should have brought home Sloan's leftover sour cream.

Danny moved through the piles of papers, stacks of clean, partially folded laundry, and over the carpet peppered with dog toys and made himself comfortable on the couch. Raina left him there while she buzzed around the house performing her evening routine.

"Madison around?" Danny called to her.

"No, she's somewhere exotic posing for some noted fashion photographer."

"She's never here. Why doesn't she just get a storage space rather than your house?"

Madison was Sloan's cousin, and the rent helped pay the mortgage. Raina had taken over the house when her parents retired and relocated to Florida, but it hadn't come free and clear.

When she saw Danny seated on her couch with his big, brown eyes, she put down a stack of mail and joined him. It was always his dimples and his inviting smile that made Raina forget everything else. He opened his fist to expose a small, light blue box with a white ribbon. Her heart skipped a beat. She was afraid it was going to stop altogether from the extreme range of emotions that boomeranged through her.

"What's this?" she asked, staring at the unmistakable Tiffany box.

"Open it," he said.

In one motion, she pulled the white ribbon and flipped off the top to reveal a signature Tiffany bracelet. She didn't waste any time clasping it onto her wrist.

"Just because I can't always spend a lot of time with you doesn't mean I don't want to," Danny said.

Oh my god, what have I done?

Raina rose up on her toes, laced her fingers behind Danny's neck, and kissed him. She felt his muscular chest press against hers and his arms hold her tight. His words echoed in her head. She peered over his shoulder at her wrist newly adorned with his gift. It would become a constant reminder of her guilt, her own personal albatross.

CHAPTER 4

Raina arrived at work the next morning determined to prove that nothing had changed between her and Tyler. Without stopping by her office to settle in, she marched straight to his. Her determination floundered when she bounced inside his doorway only to find him deep in conversation on the phone. He didn't seem to notice her until she waved to him, and he acknowledged her with a slight nod.

He hates me.

Their kiss flashed in her mind. *Mission Prove Status Quo* was a failure as evidenced by his lack of response.

There had been immediate chemistry when, three years before, Tyler Jenkins was recruited from another mortgage lender by their boss, Harvey. She and Tyler had flirted innocently and worked together as a successful team since, but she was afraid that was all ruined now. How had she lost control? Her life was in disarray, and she was to blame for all of it. Had she ruined two relationships with one kiss?

She rushed to hide in her office where tall, black file cabinets lined the walls behind and to the side of her desk. There was an organized mess, much like her home, with additional files stacked on top of the cabinets in various heights. Loose papers poked out from between the manila folders. She pushed a pile to the side of her desk to create some workspace, and she glanced at the list of missed calls on her desk phone. Five were from Harvey. She punched in his extension, but he didn't pick up.

"Raina Prentiss!" Harvey bellowed from the other side of the wall.

Raina strolled into his office to see what he thought was so urgent. He was pacing the length of his office, stopped when he noticed her, and sat down. Harvey kept his chair as low as it would adjust and still he maintained his power position higher than anyone seated across from his desk.

"What are you looking at? I know I need to cover the grays," Harvey said.

"You look fine."

"I'm only thirty-two and shouldn't have this much."

"You're thirty-five, and you look fine. What do you need?"

His attention moved to his cell phone. Raina stood and waited for an answer while he typed on his phone. He barely stopped franticly depressing buttons long enough to ask her for copies of various lease agreements, agreements that were, as he well knew, in her office.

Raina forced a smile. "Sure, I'll be right back with them."

Why does he always do that? And why am I perpetually surprised?

After taking care of Harvey's request, she returned to her mission with renewed resolve. This time she would get Tyler's attention long enough to get a sense of his feelings. She sat in one of the two cushioned chairs across from his desk. In contrast to her office, Tyler's was neatly organized with cleared surfaces. His calculator lined up perfectly with the keyboard on his desk. Sales awards hung level on the walls along with his degree from Penn State. Raina noticed these details for the first time as she sat preparing for what she would say.

"How's Jean doing?" she asked when he finally ended the call. She hoped that it was not necessary to discuss the kiss in order to evaluate his feelings about it.

Jean was Tyler's wife and had been hospitalized in a coma a week earlier. The doctor had determined that she had had an aneurysm. Without a specific trauma, drug abuse, or high blood pressure, the cause of it was unclear.

"This morning the nurse told me that Jean was feeling pain during the night. She'd been tightening her face. They settled her down before I arrived," Tyler said.

He needlessly straightened a few pieces of paper at the side of his keyboard.

"Pain's not good." That was the only thing Raina could come up with to say, and she immediately regretted her lack of compassion.

"In a way it is. They said it means that part of her is functioning. It's small, but we have to take what we can get until she wakes from her coma. It's been two weeks, you know."

She knew.

Unable to imagine his pain, she searched for something better to say. "I'm sure Jean knows you're there with her every morning and every night. Do they know if she understands what's going on or what you say to her?"

"They don't know," Tyler said, struggling to maintain his composure. "They keep trying different therapies and test after test, but they can't really give me any answers. The doctors say they can't know if there's any brain damage until she wakes up. I keep talking to her and hoping."

Raina reached across the desk and touched Tyler's hand. Tyler seemed to accept it for the gesture of comfort it was intended to be, but Raina felt the electricity between them and wished she hadn't done it. She couldn't take it away yet. That might expose her regret. So many other thoughts whirled around inside Raina's head, too. She was happy that things weren't too outwardly awkward with Tyler, glad that he was focused on his wife, and only mildly disappointed that he didn't seem to be pining for her touch again.

Raina was also worried about Jean and frustrated that the general medical consensus was to wait and see. "Well, tell her she's in my prayers, and I miss her."

"Come see her again soon," Tyler said.

"I will." She took her hand from his and returned to her office to call Sloan.

"He doesn't seem to care," Raina said.

"Who? About what? " Sloan asked.

"Tyler."

"You did say you were going to talk to Danny." Sloan paused. "My brother's calling. I'll call you back."

"Sloan, I need you to get down to the precinct right away to bail us out," Michael spoke so fast that his words were almost undecipherable.

"Which precinct, what happened?"

Michael and his friend, Charlie, had been enjoying their last summer break from Long Island University, lounging poolside at

Michael and Sloan's parents' house. In the fall they would be seniors, and then it was off to the world of employment. They had become bored and decided to go target shooting. The plan had been to stop for coffee and head to the range. The plan had not been to wind up in jail. They had taken the baby blue convertible Jaguar with the top down and headed for the nearest 7-11.

Michael counted four customers in the store, five if you counted the baby in the stroller with its young mother. She was at the counter paying for her milk with cash and trying to comfort her crying baby with a rock of the stroller. A uniformed cop poured coffee into a paper hot-cup at the coffee island. An expensively suited businessman with graying hair waited for the clerk to finish with the young woman and sell him lottery tickets. The jackpot was up to seventy-four million dollars according to the animated red lights on the sign behind the register.

"Dude, I'm going to the bathroom," Charlie said.

"Wait 'til we get to the range," Michael said.

"I can't wait."

"You're such a girl."

"I'll be right back," Charlie said as he turned his head to find the bathroom.

Michael reached forward to grab him, and his jacket pulled away from his body and revealed the gun. As the officer walked towards the register, sipping the overfilled cup to avoid spillage, he spotted the gun and dropped his coffee. He unsheathed his gun, and the boys froze in place. He tilted his head to get his mouth near his shoulder and radioed for backup. The bells crashed against the glass as his partner swung the door open. He stood with his gun drawn, spattered coffee at his feet. After the boys were secured with handcuffs, the officer reached inside Michael's jacket and took the revolver.

"Have a permit for this?" the officer asked. He held the gun by the barrel, pointed down.

Michael did not. "Not with me."

It was his father's gun, and the permit was locked in his father's safe, so he and Charlie were taken to the precinct for processing. The boys sat uncomfortably in the back of the police car. Michael watched the computer screen on the dashboard through the metal grate and hoped his parents would never find out about his arrest. Charlie stared out the side window. Since the only crime committed had been

Michael's illegal possession of a fire arm, Charlie was released. Michael was granted bail and was held in custody until Sloan arrived with the funds to pay it. Otherwise ride-less, Charlie waited for Sloan as well.

Michael sat on a bench alone in a room. There were no metal bars for him to clang his mug against, just a solid door with a small window. Confined and on the verge of losing his freedom, he waited. After an hour, boredom set in. He paced. He retraced his morning and how one move had sent it spiraling down in an instant. He wondered how prisoners avoided insanity. Maybe they didn't. Jail seemed like a perfectly solid deterrent to him, yet the prisons were packed. Certainly he never wanted to be even this close again.

After forever and a ton of paperwork, they released Michael. As he entered the reception area, Michael was blinded by a sudden flash of light.

"Kodak moment, dude," Charlie said.

"That better not surface on the Internet."

Michael knew from Sloan's face that she was annoyed. "Let's go," Sloan said.

"Wait a minute," Michael said. On the way to the door, he stopped to talk to the desk officer. "My gun."

"According to the records that's not your gun. Mr. Miller can come to claim it with his registration," the officer replied.

This threw a wrench in his plan to get through this experience without his parents finding out. He had to come up with some version of the story that painted him as the victim. It was the deep disappointment that his mother would feel that affected him the most. His father would be angry, but Michael knew that would subside over time.

"You took Dad's gun? Are you crazy?" Sloan waited fruitlessly for an answer, then gave up. "Get in the car."

"How's Raina?" Michael said.

"Check with Danny."

"One day she'll realize I'm the one for her and dump him."

Sloan ignored him.

"Stop by the 7-11, so I can get dad's car."

"You took his car too?"

"Stop there, okay?"

"Fine," Sloan answered, "but how do you plan to get his gun back?"

Michael winced.

CHAPTER 5

The sound of the mid-day newscast was muted on the television that hung behind the hostess at the counter. Above the stream of closed captions, a local anchorman with product-filled hair sat up straight behind his desk reporting on a woman that died from a drug overdose. With a pleasant expression plastered onto his face, he relayed his sympathy to the victim's family.

"She left behind a husband and three, grade school-aged boys."

A drug abuse hotline phone number flashed on the screen, partly hidden by the closed captions, as the anchorman urged anyone who had a family member in need of help to call.

A man seated at the counter watched the report while he waited for the waitress to deliver his bill. He shook his bent knee up and down, rocking on the ball of his foot, heel raised, and darted his eyes back and forth at the patrons around him. When the bill came, he slapped down a small stack of bills and left the diner in a hurry.

He slammed the car door and took off across two lanes of traffic before turning onto a secondary road. Driving along a quiet residential street, he slowed and scanned the area. The surroundings gradually transformed. Houses were built closer together, and there were more people out and about. He steered over to the curb in front of a three-story house. The engine idled while he watched a woman in the car in front of him fiddle around with something. He pulled an envelope from the mailbox at the end of the driveway, flipped it over to the addressee, and shoved it back in. The woman paid no attention to him and headed to the bottom floor apartment. He crossed the lawn and came up behind her. She had her key in the door and was balancing two supermarket shopping bags between her arm and raised thigh.

"I'm looking for Mr. Thomas," he said.

She glanced at the empty driveway. "I don't think he's home."

"Perhaps you could take down my name and number and give him a message from me?"

The woman exhaled. She left the key in the lock, pushed the door open with her shoulder, and used both hands to give him the bags to hold. Without taking a step inside, she reached through the front doorway and swiped a pad from the table. Before she turned back, he had dropped the bags by the side of the entrance. From there he could see the entire studio apartment.

"I –," The drugs took effect so quickly that she couldn't finish her words.

Her featherweight body went limp. He held her with one arm and dragged her three steps over to the sofa. It took little effort to lift her body onto it. He set a pillow under her head and placed her arms at her sides. It was safe to leave her there while he went to his car, but he pulled the door closed without engaging the latch. On the way back in, he put her bags inside her apartment. With his canvas bag clutched under his arm, he kicked the front door closed, and it swung back open. It wouldn't catch, so he leaned her packages against it.

He used his gloved hands on her cheek to shift her head a small degree to one side. Tilting his head, he examined the angle of hers and shifted it again, and again. Glass clinked in the bag when he pushed aside the vials in order to retrieve his supplies. He raked his fingers through her hair, then stroked it from the ponytail at her neck down to her chest. With the IV in place, he sat on the floor next to her and wrapped his arms around his folded legs. The old wood slats creaked as he rocked back and forth while the intravenous drip affected her death.

"I needed you," he sobbed. "Why didn't you see that? Why didn't you stop?"

The sun had already begun to set when Danny arrived at the scene. The area was taped off, and Hawkeye was inside, involved in a serious exchange with a civilian.

When it seemed that the conversation had fizzled, Danny motioned Hawkeye over. "What do we know so far?"

"9-1-1 received a frantic call from a woman, apparently the mother of the two kids who found the body. The brothers were riding their bikes and saw an open door. Kids being kids, they rode up to the entrance and peered inside, and you can guess the rest. As far as I can see, nothing was touched. There's no blood or sign of struggle. The mail on her table is addressed to a Philomena Ciantos."

"M.E. here yet?"

"Should be soon."

"Did any neighbors give you anything useful?"

"Just spoke to the one so far. Says he doesn't know the girl and didn't see anyone around. I knocked on the door upstairs. No one's home." Hawkeye turned his head when the M.E. pulled close to the house.

Danny nodded, pointing Garza in the direction of the door, and followed him in. "There's no obvious sign of foul play, but I'm thinking you can spray her arms with luminal to check for blood."

"Will do."

Danny compared the similarities of this murder to the last. There were no weapons left at the scene, no viable motive, no forced entry, and no leads. If there was a connection, he had to find it quick. He hovered over the body while Garza examined it.

"I feel like I was standing over this same body a few days ago. It's too big a coincidence not to be the same guy," Danny said.

"There's blood trace on her left arm, but don't jump the gun. I'll know more when I get her on the table," Garza said. "Hey," he addressed his assistant, "get the stretcher and a bag from the truck, and let's get her back to the morgue."

Tony, Garza's newest trainee, stood up from the body and, in his rush to follow direction, kicked over the bottle of luminal. It was capped, so there was no spill, but that didn't detract from the tension. Garza glared as Tony picked up the bottle, placed it back in the kit, muttering apologies, and headed towards the truck. He loaded the body. Garza cleared the scene for investigation, and the CSIs entered the apartment.

"Get me the report as soon as possible," Danny said. He walked outside and dialed Raina.

"How's my favorite lieutenant today?" she answered.

"Working. Can I take you to a late dinner tonight?"

"A homicide makes you think about food…and me?"

"I gotta go. Dinner?"

"It's already late, you know."

He knew, but seeing this victim did make him think about Raina. A tinge of sickness sat in the bottom of his stomach. He didn't quite understand it himself.

"I should be able to get to you by nine," he said, knowing that nine-thirty was probably more accurate. Nine sounded better.

"Okay, see you then."

Danny returned to the victim's apartment already crowded with two CSIs and an officer. He watched over the investigators as they dusted for prints, ran lights across the room looking for blood trace, and inspected the windows and doors for forced entry.

The driveway was blocked by a large sedan that pulled up to the tape. A short, elderly couple emerged from it gingerly. The man was yelling about rights, how he knew his, and that a warrant was needed to enter his house. Danny went to attend to them.

"Please calm down for a minute," Danny said. "Are you the owners of this house?"

"Your officers are trespassing on my property," the grey haired man insisted.

"We're the Thomases," Mrs. Thomas said.

"Sorry about the commotion, but a woman was found dead in the lower apartment." He paused for a moment to let his words register and then continued. "What can you tell me about her? Do you know of any reason why someone would want to kill her?"

"Oh my goodness, Philomena!" Mrs. Thomas cupped one hand around the other, placed them against her chest, then dropped her chin to meet them.

"Did she have many visitors?" Danny asked.

Mrs. Thomas took a minute to calm down, then heeled to the severity of the situation and regained control. She confirmed the victim's identity, and that the victim had been renting the apartment from them for about six months. During that time, she had been a very quiet tenant. She also mentioned that the deceased had had a few men over from time to time.

"One man at a time, not a few men together. She wasn't *that* type of girl," she said.

Mr. Thomas cut in. "Stop talking, you don't know what kind of girl she was. You're wasting the officer's time. Go inside and make some coffee."

"Actually, she's very helpful. What she's told me could help find the person who did this. And, it's Lieutenant Smith."

"Sorry, Lieutenant. I can answer your questions. And you…," Mr. Thomas turned to face his wife and, with a stern look, waited for her to obey without completing his sentence.

"Dear, I'm home all day, and I see her come and go, and sometimes she stops to talk to me when I'm outside gardening." She looked toward Danny through her gold-wired frames. "She was very sweet. She never mentioned any trouble with a man, or anyone. She was taking nursing classes at a local college while she worked her way through school. She brought more men home than I liked, but they were always quiet. I wish I had been around to see who was with her when she, when he, when it happened," Mrs. Thomas continued as her husband boiled with anger.

"Go inside and make my coffee. Now!"

Danny hooked the pen under his finger holding the notepad to free one hand and reached into the back pocket of his jeans. "My card. If you think of anything else, please give me a call - anytime." He handed her the card and returned his attention to the husband. "Mr. Thomas, did you see the men Philomena brought home? Did any of them stand out?"

"I'll tell you that girl had nothing to offer a husband after parading those men in night after night," he answered.

"That might be, but she didn't deserve to die. So, is there any information you can share that might help?" Danny asked.

"I don't think she knew these guys. Never seen the same one twice."

"Did you notice how they were dressed? Type of cars they drove? Anything?"

"Last man I saw was tall like you, same buzzed hair, too," Mr. Thomas said.

Danny accepted the man's description and the accompanying nasty tone as his way of exhibiting his resistance to help the police.

"Okay, thank you. We'll be in touch if we have any more questions for you." Danny noted Mr. Thomas's contact information and handed him a card as well, "Just in case you think of something."

Something, anything, he begged to himself.

CHAPTER 6

Raina pushed around some make up, her wallet, and tissues and searched inside her bag to retrieve her cell. The sirens played. Danny was running late but would be on his way shortly, he said, and he should be there about nine-thirty.

It wasn't a surprise at twenty to ten when he still wasn't there, so she called Sloan. By the end of the arrest story of Sloan's trouble-magnet brother and his friend, Raina had laughed numerous times.

"Michael has no luck," Raina said.

"No luck, dumb friends, stupid ideas. Speaking of, Michael is still hoping you and Danny will break up," Sloan said.

"Really? I thought he'd given that up by now. Tell him he'll have to wait at least one more day. Danny's on his way over now."

"It's practically ten," Sloan said.

"I know. Don't get me started."

"Paul's waiting with the movie paused. Considering my hormonal outburst this afternoon, I don't want to upset him again."

"What happened?"

"Nothing really. One minute I was fine, the next I was in tears, hysterical, and I didn't even know why. I was ranting about something stupid. Paul didn't know what to do with me. He said I wasn't even making sense, so now I'm trying to be extra nice to him. How about lunch on the beach tomorrow?"

"Beach? Definitely. Say hi to Paul for me."

Raina checked the time again as her stomach growled. If Danny didn't show up soon, she'd have to eat something without him. This happened all the time. At the beginning of their relationship, she had been excited no matter how late he showed up. These days it was more frustrating. Something at work always kept him longer than expected. Worse were the times when he cancelled after an already long wait. It was his job, it was part of what she had to accept, and there wasn't much she could do about it.

When her phone finally rang again, she was disappointed that it wasn't Danny's ringtone.

"Darling, forget the lemon Chanel. I want the champagne-colored Armani. You know the one? Over one shoulder, gathered top. And I need it by Thursday, remember?" Madison was calling from Vegas to change a shipping order she had placed earlier.

"I remember. No problem." Raina only vaguely remembered the dress, but she would find it.

"*Ciao.*"

On occasions like this, Raina reminded herself that Madison was almost never in the house, and the rent money made it possible for her to live without the constant stress of meeting her financial obligations. Someday, she hoped, she and Danny's income would be combined, and they would live comfortably and happily ever after.

The sound of a car woke Raina from a light sleep on the couch. If it wasn't him, she was done for the night and going to bed hungry. It was him. She grabbed a light sweater from a pile in the corner, and her bag, told Codis to be a good boy, and flew out to the car.

Danny grabbed her by her long, dark ponytail, gently jerked her head back, and kissed her. She melted into his kiss. At moments like that, he was foremost in her thoughts, and all the cons of their relationship seemed benign.

The truck doors locked as Danny accelerated, and Raina settled in for the short drive. Her one block town, lined with quaint stores and restaurants, bustled during the day, but nothing would be open at such a late hour. Danny drove them to a local Italian restaurant in the next town, one of the few that was still open, and they were seated in a booth.

"Sorry I was late. Another homicide, and it's just the beginning of summer. You know how long those calls can run."

Raina knew.

"I left Hawkeye at the scene to coordinate with Murphy back at the station."

"Which one is Hawkeye?"

"Really dark eyes, he swears they're purple. Nice guy though."

"Sloan was just asking about Murphy. She misses the work. I think she's bored to tears doing nothing."

"He's at least as good as she was. Half the time I don't know what he's saying."

"Interesting way to measure how good he is."

A short, stout waiter interrupted them politely and asked if they were ready to order.

"Give us a couple more minutes, please," Danny said.

"Okay, but the kitchen is ready to shut down. Don't take too long."

The waiter took a few steps back and waited. Raina pulled a piece of bread from the basket, slathered it with butter, and devoured it in record time. As much as she wanted to hear about the homicide, she wanted to get her dinner ordered, so they could bring it sooner rather than later. Danny had pulled out his reading glasses and was buried in the menu. They reminded her of his age, forty-one, six years her senior. The only time she thought about it was when he used those glasses.

"You're not having your usual?"

"Linguini and meatballs? Good idea," he said and nodded at the waiter.

"Make it an order for two," she said to the waiter. "I feel like sharing tonight," she said to Danny and glanced at the time. Midnight was not far away.

"Perfect," he said.

"Anything to drink?" the waiter asked. "We have a nice house wine."

"That okay with you?" he asked Raina. She nodded.

"Tell me about the case."

"What a pair the landlords were," Danny said. "You would have slapped the old man."

"Why? What did he do?"

"He wanted his wife to shut up and make him coffee. Like a good wife," Danny said and waited for her reaction. Then he reached for his phone.

"Saved by the bell," she said.

He answered it on speaker, grinning at Raina. "Smith."

"It's Garza, another morphine overdose. No other tracks on her body. No defensive wounds. No other apparent cause of death."

"Thanks for the heads up." Danny snapped his phone shut and focused on Raina. "Some similarities between this murder and the one from a few days ago. They might be connected."

"Like what?" Raina asked.

"Both died from a morphine overdose, but neither had any drug paraphernalia. If it had been a self-induced overdose, there would have been needles and drugs near the body. My guys searched the whole house and found nothing. Not even a prescription bottle in the medicine cabinet."

"So it was murder," she said.

"Seems that way, they did call homicide."

"Ha-ha. What about the differences in the cases?"

"The first victim's house was torn apart, like someone was looking for something specific. The furniture was ripped open, and things were thrown everywhere. The second place wasn't disturbed at all."

She knew he was telling her more than he should. None of these details would have been released to the press who were always hovering for a story.

"What else?" She continued *her* investigation.

"What I can't figure out is a motive."

"Was anything stolen?"

"Nothing reported. There were also no signs of forced entry into either vic's home."

The waiter delivered dinner to the table, and they paused their conversation while they shared their meatballs. The kitchen staff had split the order evenly, but after Danny scoffed down his portion, he snaked his fork across the table to Raina's plate and stabbed a meatball. During the silence, Raina's mind drifted to the long list of things she needed to accomplish the next day. When her mental list rounded to work, Tyler naturally entered her thoughts. Danny's presence didn't abate that, but she kept her eyes on her plate until those thoughts were temporarily banished.

"Any dessert?" The waiter's voice snapped them out of their individual thoughts.

"No thanks, just the check," Raina answered. "You didn't want dessert, did you?"

"I want you for dessert," Danny answered with his dimpled smile.

Raina smiled back, and they headed to the parking lot. She noticed the drop in temperature and slipped on her sweater before she climbed into his truck. He stroked her hair away from her face and gave her a sweet kiss. She kept her hand on his leg, and the headlights lit the way.

Codis greeted them. Danny pushed him away with one hand and pulled Raina closer with the other. He scooped her up into his arms and kissed her. She twisted and reached for the keypad to set the alarm. He shook his head as the tone sounded and then carried her to her bed.

It didn't take long for their clothes to come off and blend into one pile on the floor. He ran his hand up the outside of her leg, crossing over the top of her thigh, teasing her as she leaned against the bed. Then he climbed on top of her, and she guided him inside. He slid in and out and reached down with his hand until she quivered with delight.

She relaxed, feeling fully satisfied as he kissed her neck, and then twisted for him to lie back on the bed. Raina maneuvered on top with him still inside her, arched her back, and pushed her hips back and forth. Her hands pressed against his chest. She curled her fingers, digging her nails into him.

"Oh yeah," Danny groaned.

When he finished, he moved to his side and pressed against her from behind. He lay there for a few minutes, then rolled over.

"Babe, you would have loved the dog at the first vic's home. Luckily, one of the neighbors took him. They said they'd hold onto him until the husband returned from his business trip." He paused. "We verified his alibi, so he isn't a suspect."

"Are you sure he's okay?"

"Doubt it, he just lost his wife."

"I meant the dog."

CHAPTER 7

The quiet rhythm of the rippling waves and the heat of the sun lulled Raina into a meditative state. She and Sloan were planted on West Neck Beach, a small stretch of naturally rocky beach nestled on an inlet of the Long Island Sound, five minutes from Raina's house. It was a relaxed way to start to the Memorial Day weekend.

When the sun had moved positions, Raina woke feeling disoriented. She squinted at the brightness and rose up onto her elbows. After she regained her bearings, she turned to Sloan who was engrossed in the pages of her book. "I fell asleep," Raina said.

Sloan held her place with a bookmark. "Paul called. Maybe my phone woke you up. Sorry."

Raina was hungry. She straightened her legs and pushed her heels into the rocky sand as she reached into her beach bag for the Fritos. Crunching away, she wondered what she would do that night and if Danny would be around to do it with her. With a double murder on his plate, who knew when she'd get to see him again. Or maybe he was getting bored with the relationship. She spun her Tiffany bracelet.

"Danny's working two cases and thinks they might be connected," Raina said.

"You mean one killer?"

"Maybe, that's what he's trying to figure out."

Raina shared all she knew, and together she and Sloan applied their theories. It was all speculative, nothing substantial enough to share with Danny.

"How's work going?" Sloan asked.

"Same, Harvey's driving me crazy as usual."

"That's not really what I was asking."

"Tyler?"

"Yes, Tyler."

"I'm not sure that kiss meant anything more to him than comfort in a moment of weakness," Raina said.

He hadn't mentioned it since. Part of her was relieved, but a bigger part felt rejected. That latter part generated most of her guilt. She rationalized that if Danny had been giving her what she needed, maybe that kiss would have never happened. Blaming Danny wasn't going to make her feel better beyond that moment, not even at that moment.

"Is that what you want it to mean?" Sloan asked, saving Raina from walking the tightrope of her own thoughts.

"What are you saying?"

"You know what I'm saying. You just don't want to think about it."

"I can't even go there in my mind."

Raina wished that were true. She had gone there many times. If that kiss meant nothing to him, what did he think of her? Did he even think about her? Were his feelings so strong for her that he couldn't address them? Where did that leave her with Danny? That's where her focus should have been, on Danny.

"I know it must be eating you alive. I want to help. Maybe talking about it would make you feel better," Sloan said.

Raina knew that no matter how she spun the situation, it was wrong. Whether it meant something or not, it was still wrong. For distraction, Raina skimmed the newspaper. When she came across the notification of the burial for the first victim, she had an idea: *Mission Funeral.*

"Sloan, we should go to the funeral."

"What?"

Their conversation was interrupted by the piercing screams of a child. "Give me back my shovel!"

Raina twisted and watched as a little boy ran down the beach after a girl, followed by a woman who was trying to control them. The woman yelled, the girl screeched, and the boy cried.

"That's going to be you soon," Raina said.

"Not my kid, she'll be perfectly well behaved. Let's go."

They were back in the driveway of Sloan's Lloyd Harbor home in less than ten minutes. Raina opened the passenger door and admired the front yard bursting with color. She had trouble remembering all the designers that filled Sloan's closet, but she could tell you the name and care details of all her friend's plantings.

When the front door swung open, Trace, Sloan's six-month-old Pomeranian puppy, greeted them. He had been aptly named for trace evidence found at a crime scene. During one DB Night a while back, they had decided that they would name their future dogs after one of their favorite pastimes.

"How did you get loose?" Sloan widened her stance, bent down, and scooped up the puppy. "Paul!"

When Paul didn't answer, they walked around the corner to inspect the crate and were surprised to see the den in disarray. The front of the sofa was scratched open, the carpet edges were frayed, and the items from the end table were strewn across the floor. Raina picked up a small crystal vase and a candle and returned them to the table.

"I need to call Danny."

"It's a mess, but there's no crime," Sloan said.

"Just listen," Raina said and hit speed dial.

She didn't give him a chance to speak before she did. "It was the dog!" she said.

"What dog?" Danny asked.

"The dog from the crime scene. Was it in a crate or confined somewhere?" she asked.

"He was loose. Why?"

"I know what happened," she said. "The puppy got loose in the house and destroyed it. Furniture is one giant, stuffed dog toy or a release for a bored, hungry, and probably scared puppy."

"Holy shit, you're right! Good job, Detective Prentiss. The first vic's home was *not* disturbed by the killer. It was the dog."

Raina got off the call and helped Sloan clean up the mess as best they could. Sloan held the puppy in one arm and closed the door behind them.

"We'll deal with that later. Come see what Paul's done to the baby's room," Sloan said.

Raina followed her up the eight-foot wide stairway that curved around to the second floor landing. She slid her hand up the iron railing as she ascended. The chandelier had become level with them, and she imagined how labor intensive it must be to clean it. The poor cleaning woman, she thought. They turned a corner at the top of the stairs and strolled toward the end of the hallway.

"How are you going to keep the baby from falling down the stairs?" Raina asked.

"The whole house will be baby-proofed before she arrives."

"Maybe you should have puppy-proofed the house."

"Not funny," Sloan said. "Don't worry, Aunt Lorraine, the baby will be safe."

"Can you stop calling me that? She'll call me Raina like everyone else."

Sloan opened the door and presented the nursery. The walls were painted a soft, mossy green, and there was a bookcase that matched the wood floors. The shelves were already filled with soft, plush animals and children's books. A musical mobile hung from the ceiling and in the center of the floor was an area rug covered with pastel-colored fish. The closet was filled with a tiny-sized wardrobe. The only thing missing was furniture...and the baby.

"We hired an artist to paint an underwater scene on that wall." Sloan pointed to the wall without a window.

As she stood inside the nursery and listened to her pregnant friend go on about baby this and baby that, Raina thought about having a family of her own. With the relationship mess she was in, that might never happen. Sloan was right. She needed to speak to Danny, and soon.

CHAPTER 8

Hawkeye hiked down the narrow corridor to his sergeant's desk after being summoned without an explanation. The bright ceiling lights enhanced the dirt and the dull color of the paint. At the doorway of the office, he saw not only his sergeant, but the lieutenant, Danny, sitting there as well. Was he in trouble? For what? It had to be for breaking the window at the Levy house. What else could it be? And it wasn't even his doing. Images of terrible outcomes flashed in his head.

"Sirs," Hawkeye greeted them.

"Officer, please sit down," Danny said.

Hawkeye braced himself mentally. When a ranking officer referred to him that way, he meant serious business. Hawkeye's read on Danny's face was serious but not negative, although his sergeant's face showed possible hesitation. Hawkeye wasn't sure why the two didn't match.

Danny explained, "I'll get right to the point since we don't have much time. This case has become top priority, and I'm down two detectives for the remainder of the month. Your sergeant has agreed to loan you to the Detective Squad for the next four weeks. You're already familiar with preliminary information on the case. I need you to read through the files tonight and report to me in the morning."

"Yes, sir!" He signed for possession of the case files on the two victims and raced out.

As soon as he stepped outside the precinct doors, he pulled out his cell phone and called his wife, Kathy. "The Detective Squad recruited me!"

When he got home, Hawkeye relayed the details of his temporary appointment while he ate his dry, chicken dinner. Then he took the case files to the second bedroom, which they used as an office. Well, he referred to it as an office; she insisted it was the guest room. He studied every written detail, memorized each photo, and made a list of the similarities and differences until he knew everything about the two murders inside and out. Hours had passed. His cell phone rang as he closed the folders.

"Hi, Lieutenant. I've been through every shred of information. I understand that the first vic's husband is returning from overseas tomorrow."

"He's not a suspect, Hawk," Danny said.

"I know his alibi was confirmed by multiple sources, but wouldn't he have more information about her life, and maybe who might want to kill her, than neighbors?"

"Good question. He might, but often spouses know less than neighbors, especially ones that travel a lot. Join me when I interview him tomorrow."

Excitement overcame Hawkeye. This was his first homicide case and a big step for his career. He bounced into the living room to share the news, but Kathy was asleep on the couch. Instead, he sat beside her and clicked the remote.

Raina tried to enjoy the live toe-tapping, head-bobbing music playing from the Jones Beach band shell while she and Danny sat on the boardwalk and gazed out over the Atlantic Ocean.

"That's an Eric Church song, but it's not him," Danny said.

"Eric Church?"

"He's —"

"I know who he is. I didn't know you knew country music."

Danny gave her a mysterious look, and Raina let that conversation end. As she considered how best to bring up the future of their relationship, she fidgeted next to him on a cement bench on the boardwalk. Danny climbed behind her and pulled her back against his chest. His warmth penetrated through her. When she was finally relaxed, Codis barked and galloped off after something on the sand. It was too dark for her to see what. Just when she was sure Danny's thoughts were on work, he kissed the back of her neck and then put his arms around her. She pressed into him, and he tightened his arms.

He's relaxed. Now's a good time to talk to him. Raina's mouth did not open. *Speak.*

Instead, she rested her hand on his knee. It took her a while but she finally spoke, "I saw the progress on the baby's room today at Sloan's. It started me thinking."

Danny didn't respond. She rolled her right shoulder against his chest, twisting enough to see him. A deep inhale brought in the sea air. Her hope was that her segue would be a smooth one, but his silence threw off her rehearsed conversation and sent her straight to the point without a plan.

"We have to talk about the next level in our relationship," she said.

She felt him cringe. "Meaning what?"

She turned around and faced him, but it was too late. His cell phone had begun to ring. She exhaled as he answered the call on speaker.

"Smith."

"There's a David Levy in the waiting area, and he's demanding to speak to someone about his wife's death. The sergeant told me to call you," an official voice crackled through the poor cell reception.

"I'm on my way."

"10-4, sir."

"I'm sorry, Babe. Duty calls," Danny said.

There was a valid need for him to go, but it still pained Raina to know that he was glad to escape. He kissed her again, got up, whistled for Codis, took her hand in his, and led her in the direction of the parking lot. Flowers and plants, which she usually stopped to admire, spilled over the edges of the wide walkway, but instead of looking at the greenery, Raina pushed herself to re-start the dreaded conversation. As the words formed in her throat, Codis bounded towards them holding his head up proudly and showing off something in his mouth. It was moving.

"Ew! A rat!" Raina said. "Drop it!"

The high pitch of her voice forced Codis to reluctantly open his mouth and let the rat drop to the ground. It scrambled away into the darkness.

"Good boy." She shook off her disgust long enough to give him the proper praise for responding to her command.

As the beach receded behind them, Raina sent a text to Sloan while Danny called the precinct and gave them clear instructions on how to keep Mr. Levy calm until he arrived. Then he alerted Hawkeye to the earlier-than-planned interview. Twenty-one minutes of exceeding all speed limits, and they were at the precinct.

"Stay in the car with the dog," Danny said as he whipped into a spot and turned off the engine.

Raina heard him but had other ideas.

Hawkeye had arrived before Danny and had tried to calm down the victim's husband to no avail.

"My wife is dead, and nobody is doing a fuckin' thing about it!" David Levy yelled at the desk officer.

"Mr. Levy?" Danny introduced himself. "I'm so sorry for your loss." He paused for the sake of sincerity. "We're investigating the unfortunate death of your wife. Please come this way where we can sit and talk."

Levy pounded his closed fist against the side of the sergeant's desk and followed Hawkeye into the interview room. Danny hung back and gave some instructions to one of the officers before joining the other two men. Levy sat while Danny stood angled behind Hawkeye, establishing his hierarchy in the room.

"I want the asshole that did this punished. Where were your guys when some prick broke into my house and fuckin' killed my wife? And what the hell are you doing about it?" The vic's husband punctuated his rant with another pound of his fist.

Hawkeye gave his condolences and then began to question him.

"Now I'm a suspect?"

"Sir, you came down to see us. Was your wife usually home during the day?"

"What?" Levy said

"Sir, did your wife use any drugs?" Hawkeye asked.

"My wife wasn't a goddamn drug addict!"

"Did she have any injury or illness that might have required prescription drugs?"

"No fuckin' way. My wife was healthy."

"Sir, your wife died of a morphine overdose, and we believe it was murder. Do you have any information that could help us?" Danny asked.

"I'm not doing your goddamn jobs for you, and I'm not getting any answers from you either. I'll be back with my lawyer," he said as he shoved off the chair and stormed from the room.

The force of his swing slammed the door against the wall. The pale blue paint was chipped, and the plasterboard was dented where the doorknob had hit the wall many times before.

Danny turned to Hawkeye. "Everyone grieves differently. He's looking for someone to blame, and his guilt at not being there to protect her has evolved into blaming us."

"I feel bad for him," Hawkeye said.

Danny shook his head. "Leave your feelings out of the job, or you won't make it to pension."

"He didn't kill his wife, but he knows something," Hawkeye said with a confidence that seemed to set Danny off-kilter.

"How can you know that?"

"When he thought he was being accused, anger was the only thing in his eyes. His forehead was tense, but his jaw wasn't. His body showed all the confidence of innocence, but when he was asked about the drugs and any related information, his whole stance changed."

"I didn't see him readjust his stance."

Hawkeye dreaded having to explain himself to a new person. He assumed Danny had known about the origins of his nickname from his Sergeant. Obviously not. Now he had to explain again. It usually took a lot of convincing and endless teasing before people accepted his ability.

"It's always been this way. I can see the most minute facial and body movements. Think of me as a human lie-detector."

He didn't need his special skills to read Danny's face. Like most people, Danny doubted what Hawkeye was saying was true. They parted without further discussion on the subject.

Hawkeye hurried outside in time to see Levy leave the lot in his silver BMW. He trailed him for a couple of miles until the BMW stopped in front of an old bar named Kelly's. Levy didn't order a drink. He walked straight into the back room and out of Hawkeye's sight, so Hawkeye sat in a booth, ordered a burger, and nursed a seltzer with lime while he noted details on his pad. What he couldn't write was the reason why Levy was there. No other person went back through that door, and no other person came out. While Hawkeye waited, he took note of the vertical, old wood moldings that had been carved with initials and had blackened over time. The wood floors were worn across the main path from decades of use. He shifted his knee back and forth until Levy reappeared without an apparent reason for being there in the first place. Hawkeye dropped his head in an attempt to go unnoticed. After Levy breezed by, Hawkeye poked his head through the door to the back room and saw nothing but empty furniture. He threw a twenty on the table and sprinted to catch up to Levy. He saw the BMW's lights flash on, and Hawkeye tailed Levy home. After another hour, Hawkeye accepted that there was nothing else to see and drove home for a few hours of sleep before he had to be back at roll call. He stared at the ceiling conjuring up all kinds of crazy ideas as to why Levy went into an empty back room on the way home. He kept coming back to aliens. Boy, did he need sleep.

CHAPTER 9

Too much time had passed for Raina to remain content in the truck, so she went inside the precinct. A friendly officer greeted her, and they struck up a conversation until the loud voice from the other side of the wall drowned them out. They listened to the exchange between Levy and Danny.

The vic's husband stormed by Raina and the officer without raising his head, but they had heard his fury and weren't upset for the lack of acknowledgement. A cop had rushed passed them next. Danny lagged behind before he entered the main entrance area.

"What are you doing in here?" He didn't wait for a response. "I need to get something from my desk."

Raina followed him down the hall toward his office but was distracted by the case board hanging in the open area. She stared at the photos on the boards. There was no blood and guts like she had seen on television. The women were not mutilated, mangled, or otherwise defaced. It was their translucent, almost bluish tone that indicated they were dead. That, and that their photos were hanging in the homicide room. Raina wasn't sure how she felt. The fact that she wasn't queasy or emotionally affected in some way disturbed her. The room had a stale smell. It was bright and harshly lit, devoid of compassion. As she stood looking at the various crime-scene photos, she noticed a similar manner in the way the women had been posed.

Danny popped his head through the doorway. "Let's go."

"Wait, come here and look at this," Raina said.

"You shouldn't be looking at those pictures. You're gonna have nightmares."

She knew that was probably true, but it was too late. The photos were already ingrained in her head, and she was excited about what she thought she saw.

"Look at these two pictures." She pointed towards two photos on either end of the board.

"What about them?"

Raina unpinned the photos of the first victim and her crime scene and replaced them back on the board in a vertical line. Then she did the same with the second victim, hanging the victims' photos side by side, and being sure to align the same angled shots together, while Danny stood and waited for her explanation. The two victims were in almost exactly the same position. They were both lying on their backs with their heads on pillows. That was obvious. However, they each had their heads tilted slightly away from the edge, and each had her arm closer to the edge, propped up. One victim's arm was on a pillow, and the other victim's on a folded blanket. With one victim on a couch and one on a bed, it might have been a hard similarity to spot.

"Maybe coincidence, but I doubt it," she said.

"Very observant, Babe," Danny said. "Why do you think the killer did that?"

"Well," she immediately started to recall details from fictional killers on television, "he's posing them to recreate something from his past, probably his childhood, something that severely scarred him psychologically."

"He?"

"Most serial killers *are* males."

"Now he's a serial killer?"

"One more kill by the same guy and he's defined as a serial killer," Raina reminded Danny.

"Let's get past his gender and back to an explanation for why."

"You're the detective."

Back in Danny's SUV, Raina thought about resurrecting the conversation that never really happened, but she chickened out. Danny pulled into her driveway and left the truck idling as he escorted her to the door.

"You're not coming in?"

"The more I think about it, the more I think you really have something with the positioning of the bodies. I need to get back to work and see how that can help us find him."

She smiled. "Sure he's a guy? The bodies were placed very carefully, almost like dolls."

"Not funny, babe."

The next morning Raina dug through her closet for the black sweater that completed her outfit. She found it pressed tightly between two others in a stack of clothes piled high on her dresser. As she slipped on the final layer of her ensemble, she heard the door. For once she hoped it wasn't Danny. She hesitantly opened the door.

Sloan raised her eyebrows and scanned Raina from head to toe. "Who died?"

"Marlo Levy, remember? I'm attending the funeral."

"I thought you were kidding, but apparently I was wrong."

"How many times have we seen it? The killer attends the funeral either to mourn or get some kind of gratification."

"Only on TV. Have you lost your mind?"

Sloan entered cautiously and held her pastel shopping bags out in front of her to protect her belly as Codis jumped to greet her. Sloan placed her bags on the only available spot – the couch. She moved closer and inspected the dining area.

"You're creating your own police case display? You've got a map, even a timeline on your wall. You *have* lost your mind."

"Remember the first victim and the crime scene details?"

"Pretty much." Sloan didn't stop scanning the wall to look at Raina. "Does Danny have the puppy info on his wall too?"

"Every piece of information is important, and I was the one that figured out the puppy trashed the house," Raina said.

"I remember."

"What I can't determine is how the alarm was set when the cops arrived at the scene. How is that possible?"

"Can it be set online?"

"I don't think so. At least my service doesn't offer that option."

"What about the system records? Doesn't the system track it?"

"Oh yeah!" Raina held up her hand, grabbed her phone, and dialed Danny.

"Smith."

"Sloan came up with an idea."

Danny listened while Raina recounted the circumstances of the first murder.

"And when your guys broke into the house, the alarm went off. How did it get turned on? If the woman let the killer in, he killed her, and left, how was the system armed? Maybe the husband came home?"

"We already verified his alibi: out of town on business," Danny said.

"Well, if the victim wasn't a victim and killed herself, she could have set the alarm first, but there was no evidence of suicide."

"And your idea?"

"Sloan's idea. Have the alarm company read the system and see who set the alarm."

"How would they know?"

"If they used a remote, it registers with the serial number like mine."

"And if they used the keypad?"

"Depends on the system. You said it was a sophisticated one. A code probably has to be entered to arm it as well."

"It's worth a try, thanks, gotta go," he said.

Sloan seated herself by the bags and pulled out a dozen tiny outfits. She held each one up as Raina ooh'd and aah'd. *Mission Funeral* was foremost on Raina's mind. The clothes were adorable, but she had important work to do. Baby-time ended when they heard the ringtone set for Danny. Raina hit the speaker button.

"We'll have to wait until tomorrow to get the home security company on the phone, only the central monitoring call center is open, and the operators don't have access to that information. Call you later, Babe."

Raina sighed, "Okay."

"I did some digging last night, hacked around," Sloan began hesitantly.

Raina's eyes were wide with excitement. "Something relevant to the case?"

"Not really."

"You're using your detective voice. Is this like the time you nearly got everyone in trouble for penetrating a federal network?"

"I *was* a detective, and not really."

This time Sloan hadn't been caught, at least not yet. Danny had loosened the reins when he learned how much information Sloan could get. There was only that one time when they were almost suspended from the force.

The funeral was scheduled to begin soon, and Sloan was dragging things out, prolonging her report. Raina gestured towards the time.

Sloan continued after a pause, "Ah, well, I found a random police record on Tyler."

"Tyler!"

"Paul has taken over baby preparations, and Murphy almost never calls me for help anymore, so I'm bored. You've been spending a lot of time with him, and I...."

Raina cut her off, "Just tell me."

"When he was fourteen, he was arrested for stealing a car and street racing. No charges were pressed. As far as I can see, he stayed out of trouble after that."

"Fourteen? How did you get into a minor's record? It had to be sealed, especially if there was no conviction."

As she heard her own words shoot out of her mouth, she felt a strange sense of relief. Grand theft auto seemed to pale that one kiss.

"It was a long time ago, Raina. Don't take it so seriously."

The ride to the cemetery gave Raina enough time to listen to a few songs on the radio and bring her focus from Sloan's discovery back to the case. She remained in her car by the gravesite, slipped on a pair of big, round sunglasses, and studied the attendees. Mostly in pairs, family and friends arrived and lingered quietly around the coffin, sharing hugs and sentimental touches. In the programs she loved, the killer was always there alone, standing right behind the immediate family, looking on emotionless. His shifty eyes were the tell that alerted law enforcement agents to his presence. As far as Raina knew, no cops were assigned to attend. It was up to her. She prepared a response in case someone knocked on her window and questioned her. Her glasses would hide the absence of tears, and she would reveal her inability to deal with the loss of a close friend. They would understand. She was costumed appropriately and wasn't disturbing anyone. If she was addressed, she was convinced that plan would work. *Mission Funeral*, though, was harder than Raina had imagined. No one was posed like on television. There was no one whose face stood apart from the others with bright colored glasses, an unusual cane, or an old-fashioned hat. No mourners made uncomfortable movements or had clear looks of satisfaction painted on their faces.

Instead of giving up, she took pictures of the crowd and wrote down as many details as she could. The list included the number of people, men vs. women, couples, and everyone's approximate ages. There wasn't much else to see besides people dressed in black. Her imagination took over when boredom set in. What if the man walking by was the killer and was there for a quick view of his accomplishment? What if the man holding his elderly mother's hand had brought her there to get her twisted approval? What if?

When the priest began to speak, Raina decided that her character would find the strength to join them. She took very small, careful steps up the shallow incline. Her stomach tightened as the faces came into focus. She positioned herself in the back, across from the family. There she would be able to go unnoticed and spot the shifty-eyed stranger.

The plan went awry when the service ended, and she hadn't identified a suspect. No one departed alone, was isolated from the group, took off in a different direction, or lingered by the grave after everyone else was gone. This time, the unidentified subject had eluded her, but she would file her notes and photos for future use.

All of the case details bounced around in Raina's head like a lotto ball machine in action as she drove away from the cemetery. Something clicked. She called Sloan.

"Hey, I was thinking," Raina began.

"Here we go. Did you find the killer at the funeral?"

"Danny told me that this new cop thinks there's a connection between the first vic's husband and her death, but they confirmed he was out of town when she was killed. Think you can find out where he works and where he went?"

"What do you think? Employment's easy. Travel's even easier. Give me an hour."

CHAPTER 10

He drove furiously, jerking the wheel and jamming the brakes until he nearly hit a teenager with a dog. With the leash in one hand, the teen pounded on the hood with the other. The tires screeched as he drove off and barreled around the corner, and the teenager disappeared from the rearview mirror. His head swiveled from side to side and searched the area. As he hit the brakes to watch a woman walk up her driveway, a bottle rolled off the newspaper on the passenger seat. The shade of a dense, old oak tree transformed the woman into a dark, indistinguishable figure.

"That's not her," he said aloud.

He continued on. Three blocks west, he spotted another woman get out of her car wearing a baseball cap. As she came around the back and reached into her trunk, her short, dark hair poked from the bottom of her cap.

"Not her."

The tires burned rubber marks onto the street. His only concern was to find her. He needed to find her.

Movement behind a "For Sale" sign caught his attention. He slowed the car again and shifted his position to see further up the walkway. The front door to the house was wide open. Inside, a woman was moving about. He circled the block. On the second time around, he stopped in front of the house where the sign hung from a wood post in the lawn. The door was still open. He could see the woman's fit shape from behind, and her blonde hair was neatly clipped behind her head.

"That's her." His agitated state subsided.

What he guessed were a pair of potential buyers exited the home and drove off. He started up the driveway and heard her on the phone.

"Hey, it's Briana. No, the owners won't be back until late tonight. They were away for a few days. I prefer it that way. You know how homeowners don't know which features are selling points." She paused. "Yeah, like the marks on the kitchen wall where they measured Johnny Junior's growth. It's sentimental only to them. To a potential buyer it means the added cost of a paint job."

He stood on the top step. The house was in pristine condition, well-staged, and perfectly clean. He could see her as she sat on a stool by the counter, organizing paperwork from her briefcase.

He gently rapped on the door and entered the house.

"Hi there, are you interested in the house?" she asked.

"We might be."

Briana introduced herself, handed him a sheet of paper on a clipboard, asked him to complete a short form, and offered him some cookies left over from the open house.

"I'm sorry, I already dumped the coffee. I was about to close up."

"Do you want me to come back another time?"

"No, no. Here." She directed him to the form. "I like to get an idea of what my clients are interested in. This way I can point out features of this house and show you other homes that meet your needs and desires."

"You know with all the identity fraud these days," he started to say.

"Let me show you the rest of the house, and I can get an idea of what you're looking for that way," she said.

"Perfect." He abandoned the form on the countertop, keeping his canvas bag tucked under his arm.

As she led him through the first floor, she described the benefits and amenities and told him about all the fancy details. He was quiet.

"How many bedrooms are you looking for?" she asked.

"It's me and my wife. We need an office, one for a guest room. I suppose three."

"This one has four."

Briana glanced back at him a few times.

"Planning for any children?" She stopped and turned around to face him. Her jaw dropped when she saw his hand raised. It was curled into a fist, and he held a needle with his thumb on the plunger.

Instinctively she raised her arm to block him. He grabbed her wrist and held it tight. She kicked him in the shin with force, but it only inflicted enough pain to anger him, not to release his grip.

"Ow! Son of a bitch!"

She screamed. He twisted her around, secured her, and placed his hand over her mouth. She kicked and scratched and squirmed, and tried to yell through his hand, but he held her tight. She dug her nails into his hand. When he gained sufficient control with one arm, he jabbed the needle into her neck. Moments later she slumped over, and he carried her into the fourth bedroom. He went back to the landing to retrieve his bag, which had dropped to the floor during the struggle. His shin throbbed. As he began the IV drip, he pressed the heel of his hand against his leg to relieve the pain.

He shifted the position of her head.

"Why did you do this to me? I tried to help you stop. Didn't you care?" With two fingers, he readjusted the angle of her head, tilting it slightly to one side, and fixed her hair until everything was just right.

Danny received the call. A couple had returned from vacation and were horrified to find their Real Estate Agent dead in their house. The first officer to the scene had sent a picture to Danny's phone. This murder was definitely connected. Her position, her hair. Danny glanced in his rearview mirror as he drove to the crime scene. He was sure that he was being followed and assumed it was the press, but he was too anxious to get to the scene to take the time to lose the tail. Garza had already confirmed morphine overdose as the COD when Danny arrived. Hawkeye was with the homeowners. They weren't suspects. Their alibi had already been verified by the bed and breakfast upstate where they had vacationed.

The CSIs searched for prints, fibers, fluids, or anything else that might have been left behind by the killer while Danny stared at the body. His stomach clenched. There was a pillow on the floor next to the bed, most likely it had been propped under her arm and had been knocked off. Her arm hung off the side of the bed. Raina was right. The positioning was the same, but why? Raina was also right about a potential serial killer. This was the third murder. And there was sufficient cooling off time between the three – the basic definition of a serial killer.

"This could be the break you need. This one fought back. Look at the defensive wounds on her arms," Garza said.

"Look at her finger nails," Tony said quietly as he pointed to her wrist with his gloved hand.

Danny squinted as he leaned over to take a closer look without touching the body.

"Skin under her nails," Tony said.

"Let's get her back to the morgue. We can collect the skin and get it to trace," Garza said.

Danny was uncomfortably ecstatic when he saw that the victim had defensive wounds. Finally a mistake, something that might be useful. Danny and Hawkeye had interviewed neighbors, friends, and families of the other victims but were unable to find a motive or a suspect. They didn't have enough to profile the killer.

"How long before the DNA is run for a match?" Danny asked.

"Under the circumstances, we'll request a rush from the lab," Tony said.

"Just do your job, and I'll do mine, Tommy," Garza said.

"It's Tony."

"Shit, Garza," Danny said. "This kid's with you every day, and you still don't know his name?"

Tony headed to the truck for the gurney. When he returned, Garza was as cold to him as the dead body.

"How much longer you have with Garza?" Danny asked Tony.

"Two more months, then I rotate."

"The kid keeps a calendar in his room and marks off the days," Garza said.

"Can you blame him?"

Danny surveyed a CSI as he took pictures of the body and the room while Tony stood by. Danny waved Hawkeye over. He wanted him to see the defensive wounds before Tony zipped the bag.

"I'll get the photos and reports to you ASAP. The sooner you get this guy off the streets, the better I'll feel leaving my wife at home," the CSI said.

"Thanks," Danny said.

Tony pushed the gurney outside, with Danny close behind, where they were bombarded by press, cameras, and microphones. Tony tried to shove through with the body, but Danny had to step in and move the crowd back. With the press present, Danny and the department were suddenly under a lot more pressure. They would either become the heroes or get slammed with the blame.

"Morphine again?" one reporter yelled.

"Is she blonde?" asked a blonde woman.

"How old was she?"

"Do you have any suspects?"

"Was she married?"

"What do you plan to do to protect the citizens of the community?"

Danny gritted his teeth. "We won't have any details until after the autopsy."

His answer didn't satisfy anyone. They moved in closer, all in one motion like a swarm of killer bees threatening pain. Danny was more annoyed than intimidated. He motioned for two additional officers to keep them back. The press spread out on the block questioning neighbors until they spotted the CSI team exiting the house and closed back in around them.

"Did you find any blood?" a reporter asked.

Danny could only see the reporter's spiked hair over the crowd.

"Any fingerprints?"

"Is there any evidence that will help find whoever did this?"

"Can you tell us anything?"

"Why is it only blondes?"

The officers kept them under control long enough for the M.E.'s truck to pull away and the CSI team to pack up. Danny ordered the two officers to stay put until the press left.

"Try to keep them from harassing the neighbors too much," he said.

Danny ignored a call from his boss.

CHAPTER 11

Danny was relieved that he had made it back to the precinct without the press, but it brought him no closer to finding a suspect. For what seemed like the millionth time, he sat in the open area and stared at the case wall. He felt like the press was closing the walls around him, the brass was sucking the oxygen from the room, and if he didn't get the killer off the streets soon, he'd suffocate.

"Hawk, check for recent police reports on stolen drugs," Danny said.

"Done. Nothing," Murphy chimed in.

"Then check with the local hospital and medical offices to see if any unreported morphine is missing from their inventory."

He knew it was a weak avenue to investigate. Even if it had happened, no medical office in its right mind would admit such an irresponsible lack of action. But Danny was grabbing at any possibility.

"I'll get right on it."

With nothing more productive to do, Danny hovered as Hawkeye searched online for a list of all the medical offices and hospitals within a five-mile radius of each murder. With only a cursory review, he hit the print button. A thick mass of paper spit into the printer tray.

Murphy gave a condescending nod. "Hawkeye, you're killing trees unnecessarily. Narrow down the search radius and start with the first vic."

Hawkeye's revised search produced only a few pages. He found a slightly dried highlighter in the desk drawer and marked the emergency clinics first.

They listened while the phone rang endlessly. No answer, human or automated. He hung up and dialed the next one. A recording came on: "If this is an emergency, please dial nine-one-one immediately. Otherwise, please leave a message after the tone, and we will get back to you as soon as possible." As the message tone beeped, Hawkeye hung up. He was tapping the highlighter against the top of the desk. When he dialed the next clinic, a human answered.

"This is Officer Lorenzo from the Suffolk County PD. I need to speak with the person in charge of the drug inventory."

"You need to speak with Dr. Jacob," a young, female voice replied.

"Great, put Dr. Jacob on," he said.

"Dr. Jacob won't be in today. Let me check when he's on the schedule next. Hold please."

Without waiting for a response, the woman put him on hold, and the calming music played. Danny paced back and forth in front of the board of victims. Hawkeye tapped the highlighter faster until, after what seemed an eternity, the music stopped.

"He'll return Tuesday morning at ten-thirty. You can reach him then, sir."

"Or you can put a manager on the phone now."

"Sir, there is only one doctor and one nurse, besides myself, on staff today," she said, maintaining her professional manner.

"Then put one of them on the phone."

"I'll get Nurse Lobowski. Hold please."

The music cut off, and an older woman began to speak. She was as professional and as devoid of helpful information as the previous woman. He thanked her and hung up.

"Welcome to detective work," Murphy said.

"We're missing something," Danny said into space, rocking back on the chair.

The police had a dangerous psychopath on their hands. They were tired of cleaning up his messes without any indication of who or where he might strike next. If his intention was to enrage law enforcement, he was succeeding.

"Smith."

Danny's blood pressure rose as he listened to his Captain. He sprang up from the chair and stormed outside.

"Cap, you know what this means?"

"Relax Danny. The FBI isn't stepping in to take over. You'll be hearing from SA Gordon Blainey, and I expect you to cooperate fully."

Danny exhaled loudly. "Yes, of course, sir."

"I've had your back during your whole career, right? Trust me on this. You're a few years from retirement. You want to go out on top. Catch this guy and be the hero."

He had always trusted his captain and followed his advice even before his promotion. Why would this time be different? Danny knew the stakes for himself and for the community. Still, it felt like a betrayal. The next move was to call an old buddy with the FBI. He went back inside and pulled a rolodex from the back of his bottom drawer. He thumbed through the cards, frayed around the edges.

"Hey, Smith. Must be something important for you to call and ask for my help."

"Not help, exactly, Adam, just some information."

"There's a difference?"

"What do you know about one of your agents? Gordon Blainey."

"I don't know him personally, but he's got a good reputation here."

Danny wasn't sure which would be better: a so-so agent that he could use for the FBI resources and still come out as the hero, or a great agent that would streamline the process and try to take the glory along with it. It didn't matter what he wanted. His wasn't the only career on the line, and he knew it. Agent Blainey was about to become part of the team.

"I'm glad you came to me for help. The FBI is always willing to work with PD. You know that. Let me know how it goes," Adam said.

"So you guys always say through your federally-issued smiles."

Now Danny had to play the political game himself and sell this to his team. Catching the killer might be easier.

Raina heard the beat grow stronger as Danny drove closer to Michael's party at his and Sloan's parents' house. The bass vibrated in her chest. She was astonished by the lines of parked cars that spilled from the driveway out to the street like multi-colored octopus tentacles. There was no legal spot for Danny to leave his Denali, so he parked it at the tip of the driveway, blocking in a fleet of expensive cars and a beat up old Honda.

Sloan checked in with Raina. "What time are you getting here?"

"We're parking now. We brought Grandma Ida. Danny was at work because there was another woman killed. They seem to be all linked. You know what that means. We have a serial killer on our hands."

"We? We who? I left that job."

Raina laughed. "You know as well as I do that something triggers a serial killer. I'm trying to figure out what it is. That way maybe Danny can get a step ahead of him, prevent the next victim, and catch him."

Danny cringed. "Must you tell her everything?"

Raina, Danny, and Grandma Ida hiked up the length of the long driveway, through the side gate, and back to the party. Crazy Grandma Ida was Raina's mother's mother. She was seventy-eight years young, spoke her mind, was a party animal, and adored Danny.

Inside the gate, Raina scanned the scene. There had to be two hundred people in the three-acre yard, but she still spotted Michael towering over the girls who hung all around him, wearing barely enough to avoid a summons for indecent exposure. Dance music pulsed from seventeen speakers stacked on top of each other, creating a black wall on either side of the DJ, and the remaining wireless speakers were strategically placed around the party grounds. Underwater lights flashed in the pool and created the illusion that it was dancing while reflections from the lights above bounced off the top of the water.

Everyone was having a good time dancing, drinking, and eating. Then she spotted Harvey heading towards Michael. Raina nudged Danny.

Harvey dressed to show off his lean body and went directly to a woman who had to be fifteen years younger than he. Barely legal, Raina thought. Harvey's target was leaning on the permanent bar and laughed at everything he said. She and Harvey sat down, cozily sharing a lounge chair at the far end of the oblong pool.

"Leave them alone," Danny said.

They maneuvered their way through the crowd to Michael. Raina pushed up on her toes to get her mouth close to his ear. "Great party!"

"Thanks!" Michael said, puffing out his chest. He and Danny exchanged a manly, shoulder-to-shoulder greeting.

"Do you know all these people?" she asked.

"No. Isn't it great?" Michael said.

Sloan negotiated her way through the sea of models to greet them.

"Grandma Ida, nice skirt," Sloan said. It was denim and complimented her white, cotton, buttoned down shirt over a blue tank top fabulously.

"Thank you, dear. I've got on my dancing shoes, too." She turned to Danny, clamped her hand around his wrist, and led him to the dance floor.

Raina called to him, "Careful with Grandma."

"I'm afraid I won't be able to keep up with her," he yelled as they evaporated into the mass of bodies.

Sloan stood with Raina, and they watched Grandma tear up the dance floor.

"Raina Prentiss," a voice yelled from behind her. It was the same voice that bellowed at her daily.

"Harvey. How are you?" Raina asked.

"What?"

"Are you having a good time?" she asked louder.

"What?"

Raina smiled and twisted her hand in a never-mind gesture. The music was rocking, and conversation was not one of the main attractions. Harvey smiled back at her and moved on into the crowd. They did not see him again that night.

Thanks to Grandma Ida, Raina was Danny-less, and Michael moved in. "Wanna dance?" he asked.

Before she answered, his plan was foiled. Someone had cut in on Danny and took over dancing with Grandma Ida, and Danny was making his way back to Raina.

"How about later?" She saw the disappointment in Michael's face.

She took Danny's hand and led him away from the crowd. They sat on a stone wall off to the side of the property where the music was slightly quieter and the nearest people were twenty feet away. Her plan was to try to resurrect *the* conversation.

Say something, speak. Her mouth was as dry as the desert.

Raina took a deep breath in preparation and was filled with the scent from the roses climbing on the trellis behind them. She looked into Danny's eyes. Misguided, he leaned in to kiss her, but before they connected she saw his jaw tighten. She cupped his face in her hands and kissed him softly on the lips.

He pulled back and checked his phone. "I need to get back to the precinct."

She looked over at his screen but saw nothing. "What happened?"

"I've gotta be missing something."

"They'll call if there's anything to tell you." She paused. "I thought we could talk."

"I'll make it up to you."

"How are Grandma and I supposed to get home?"

She threw her arms up and stood alone in the crowd, watching as Danny went off to save the world and left her behind.

CHAPTER 12

Monday morning had arrived with a dreary, sunless sky. Danny and Hawkeye printed the photos from the CSI and waited for the DNA results. Hawkeye pinned them on the wall along with a list of potentially relevant details. Danny paced and twirled his key ring. It had taken three murders for the killer to make a mistake, and he hoped that one misstep would be enough to identify him.

Danny rocked in his chair until his phone rang. "Smith."

It was his captain. Danny put his hand over the side of his face and listened to his boss order him to put all other cases on the back burner. Did he think this wasn't the top priority? The captain reminded Danny how it was the capture of the last serial killer that had made his career, before Danny's time. It was an opportunity for Danny. There was no more room to delay in calling the M.E. He needed an answer now.

"We've got the DNA, but there's no match in CODIS," Garza said.

"Fuck. The body count is piling up." He slammed his fist on the desk beside the phone.

"Find a suspect, and the lab can match his DNA to the evidence," Garza said.

"Yeah," Danny said.

A loud thud drew everyone's attention as the precinct door blasted open and slammed against the wall when Detective John Stone bolted through. "I'm back! Let's hunt down this mother fucker and fry his ass!"

Stone stood inside the entranceway, sleeves rolled up, baseball cap on backwards, and his shoulder holster packed.

Danny greeted his best detective with a smile and a feeling of relief. He knew Stone well enough to know he wasn't going to let a hunt of this caliber pass him by. It was just a matter of time. Danny counted on that.

"I gotta read about this dick in the papers? Take me off vacation. I want a piece of him!"

"You got it. We could use the help. Stone, Hawkeye, Hawkeye, Stone," Danny said. "Hawkeye is on loan to our squad, and he's been a big help so far."

"Really, what've you got…Hawkeye?"

Hawkeye stood silent, and Stone redirected his attention to Danny.

"Tell me everything about the Morphine Murderer," Stone said.

"Shit, I hate that name." Danny cringed and shook his head. After the third victim, the press dubbed the killer the "Morphine Murderer." The name gave the killer power and recognition.

"This is all over the news, we're going to be famous." Stone couldn't contain his excitement.

"*He* will, anyway," Hawkeye said.

Stone focused on Hawkeye's dark eyes but spoke to Danny. "The last serial killer we had on Long Island was in the early nineties, not long before we were on the job. Something Rifkin, right? He killed prostitutes."

"Joel," Murphy said as he clicked the keys with precision speed and searched "Rifkin." Seconds later, Google displayed pages of links. Murphy read off facts. "Joel Rifkin, pulled over in 1993 for a missing license plate. They found a dead body under a tarp."

"What a lottery ticket!" Stone said.

"What?" Hawkeye asked.

"They pull him over for a missing plate, and they apprehend a serial killer. Nice collar!"

An officer pulls over a car for a minor infraction and his captain's a hero. Luck like that wasn't about to happen twice. Danny had to rely on solid police work.

"Let's focus on the Morphine Murderer, now, in current time," Danny said.

Hawkeye whipped his head around to Danny.

"I know. Let's get back to work," Danny said.

From her desk she heard Harvey's morning bellow. "Raina Prentiss!"

She stood un-noticed while Harvey typed on his phone in a frenzy.

"It's easier to do that on the computer with the full size keyboard, Harvey. You're sitting right in front of it."

Harvey chucked some papers across his desk at her.

"What's this?" she asked.

"Application. Complete it."

"Okay, nice talking to you."

As Raina turned to leave, her eye caught the photo on a business card on his desk. Her heart fluttered in her chest and pumped her full of adrenaline. She whisked herself back to her office to pull up a news website, sure that she had seen that face posted as a victim. The photo on the card did match the photo in the news, and it was on Harvey's desk on top of a pile of cards. The article listed the victim's name: Briana Mosley. Raina needed to match the name to the card for positive identification. Her only focus now was to scout out the perfect window of opportunity to get into Harvey's office alone to complete her newly planned *Mission Photo*.

She glanced through the door each time she heard someone move by it and waited for Harvey to leave his office. When he did, she followed him, failing to keep up. He had a stride that seemed to propel him effortlessly down the hall. From a distance, she saw Harvey standing by a loan processor's desk reviewing a loan file. She hoped he would stay there long enough for her to get back into his office and then out without notice. It was a high-risk gamble given his short attention span.

If she walked at her usual pace, no one would notice. Breathe, she told herself.

She checked behind her before she entered. The business card was on the desk exactly where it had been before. It would probably be there for weeks. Only when the mountains of paper started to lean and threaten to topple would he sort through them, usually throwing most of it in the trash. The card read, "Sweet Homes Realty, Briana Mosley, Agent. President's Club," and listed her contact information. Raina struggled to contain her excitement. Without disturbing the potential evidence, she snapped a picture with her phone.

Mission Photo complete. She pressed her lips together to prevent a smile of satisfaction.

Raina realized that it was only circumstantial evidence. The card wasn't proof of anything. She needed to focus. She needed a plan.

Harvey followed her into her office. She panicked. Had he seen her in his office? She waited for him to speak first. He bounced from foot to foot. The anxiety bubbled in her stomach. Did he see her take the picture? Was he intentionally torturing her?

Finally he spoke, "I need Georgia's number."

"I gave you that number three times last week. You said you called her."

"I did call. I called her a dozen times, but she never answered." He fiddled with his device. "It's not here," he said, shaking his cell.

Raina scribbled the requested number on a yellow sticky note. When she was about to hand it to him, he had already disappeared.

"I wonder if he stops long enough to sleep at night," Raina said.

"I wonder if his wife sleeps with him," a co-worker chimed in.

"I wouldn't do him," a deep voice said.

She hadn't realized anyone had heard her mumbled comment, and it had become a three-way conversation. Raina recognized Tyler's voice and spun around in her chair to see him leaning against the doorframe.

"How's Jean?" she asked, deflecting any unwanted thoughts.

"About the same," he said.

"Is she responding to anything yet?" Raina continued.

"She tracks. Her eyes open, and she tracks people as they move around the room."

"That's good, right?" Raina asked.

"Yeah, it means at least that part of her brain is working." Tyler's voice was starting to crack, and his eyes quickly welled up.

She was saddened by his pain and regretfully jealous of Jean because she had someone who cared so deeply for her. Raina was disgusted that such a feeling could exist within her but still wished that Danny could feel about her as Tyler did for his wife. Would Danny ever put her before work and everyone else? Would she ever be the most important thing in his life? That's what she wanted.

Fearful of where that thought process would lead her, Raina tried to lighten the conversation. "So you wouldn't do Harvey?"

He laughed, seemingly accepting her intentional segue. "Nah, I hate hairy legs."

"I better get back to this application before Harvey comes looking for it," Raina said.

"Come by my office before you leave for the day," Tyler said.

Embarrassed by the big smile that spread across her face, she tilted her head down as he walked away. "Okay."

Her brain synapsed with a dozen reasons why Tyler wanted her to stop by his office. While she was overanalyzing his probably meaningless comment, Raina heard the muffled ring of her phone buried in her bag. It was Sloan's brother, Michael, calling.

"Hey, what's up?"

Michael was speaking so erratically that Raina could barely understand him. He sounded like he had run up ten flights of stairs, huffing between words.

"I'll call you right back," he said.

When he did, he explained to Rania that two detectives had just left his house after they interviewed him and Charlie about a murder. The victim, whose name he learned was Michelle Donnelly, had signed with a modeling agency in Manhattan and was found dead in her apartment five miles from the Millers' home. She was last seen leaving his party Saturday night with a tall, thin man. The detectives had separated him and Charlie and interviewed each of them for over an hour. The police wanted to know how he knew the girl, but Michael didn't. She came with some friends, only one of whom he vaguely knew from school. He couldn't provide a list of all the guests like the police requested. He didn't know half the people at his house that night. When the detective asked him about drug use, Michael insisted that he only provided alcohol. If any drugs had been brought in by guests, it had happened without his knowledge. After comparing notes, the detectives concluded that Michael and Charlie were telling the truth. Their answers were the same and seemingly unrehearsed. He wanted her to assure Danny that he had nothing to do with any part of a murder.

"There is one more thing," he said hesitantly. "They showed me a pic of the dead model." He didn't wait for her to respond. "Raina, that model left the party with your boss."

"Harvey?" she whispered. "Did you tell the police?"

"No."

"Why not?"

"I don't know."

"I'll take care of it, Michael." Raina pushed the button and ended the call.

That made four murders. Her investigative wheels were spinning out of control.

She rotated in her chair and pulled up a spreadsheet that continued across both of her side-by-side monitors. The header read: TMM Connections and Possible Triggers. She had abbreviated the Morphine Murderer for time's sake. Raina had pulled the news articles from the day of and the day before each murder to search for a significant event that had occurred each time. She had spent hours listing everything notable from political commentary, various crimes, and obituaries to sports scores, engagements, the gossip columns, and the weather. She reconciled a few possibilities. A major celebrity had died the day before each murder. There was a spree of home invasions. Drug related deaths were reported, and the temperature soared above ninety degrees. Thanks to years of DB Nights, she knew that triggers varied depending on an individual's personal traumas, usually some combination of childhood physical, sexual, or psychological abuse. It could be something as seemingly random as intense heat that triggered a memory because it had been an extremely hot night when their father had come home drunk and molested them.

Raina was focused on her *Mission Trigger* until she heard the material of Harvey's suit shifting as he bounced his weight from side to side at her door.

She stared at him as he fiddled with his phone. No shifty eyes. No unexplained scars or recent bruises. There wasn't a single thing about him that even whispered killer.

"The application?" he asked.

"Working on it," she said.

She clicked to minimize the spreadsheet on the screen, hoping he didn't see it.

CHAPTER 13

At seven, Raina headed to Sloan's for their weekly DB Night with a new level of excitement for the whole process. This time she was working on a live case. They devoured dinner before they headed downstairs to the media room.

"Want to hear my research results on the first vic's husband?" Sloan asked.

Raina choked on the Snapple half way down her throat when she rushed to respond but could only nod.

"Levy owns a small pharmaceutical company. Guess where he travels? Ever heard of *The Golden Triangle*?" Sloan said.

"The what?" Raina asked holding her throat.

"It's a large part of Southeast Asia where most of the world's heroin comes from. His passport is cluttered with customs stamps from there. When his wife was killed, he was in Afghanistan, which is one of the world's biggest drug producing countries."

"So he's cleared from the murder, but he had access to the drugs that killed her. Think he paid someone to do it?"

"Seems to be some connection, but I'm not sure what. I'll keep digging. It gives me something to do while I wait for Jocelyn to be born."

"You named her?"

"I was just trying it out. Like it?"

"Sure."

Raina sank into the leather chair and kept her notebook within close reach. When she saw Sloan struggle to bend close enough to reach the remote, Raina sprang up and helped her.

"It's getting harder," Sloan said.

"Two more months."

"I won't be able to lift my own fork by then."

In the middle of the second show of the evening, Raina shifted her weight in the chair and then back and forth again. She held her pen braced to write, and her notebook rested on her lap opened to a blank page. She grabbed a pillow from the neighboring chair and placed it behind her lower back. Not long after that she flung it away. The constant movement caught Sloan's attention, and she paused the show.

"There's nothing related to our case on these shows," Raina said.

"You were expecting to solve a real case by watching television?"

When Sloan put it that way, Raina had to acknowledge how ridiculous it sounded. Did she really think that? She did. Although she had learned a lot from Sloan and Danny over the years, she learned even more from her DB Night shows. Even if she wasn't about to admit it out loud, Raina knew that she would help solve the case.

"Hit play," Raina said.

Tuesday morning Raina was in her office still obsessed with the details of the TMM case. Most of the details were circumstantial, but she chose to share her suspicions with Danny anyway. With two victims connected to Harvey, he had to be a suspect. Since Sloan's information on Levy didn't provide a clear connection, Raina would hold off on discussing that angle with him. Plus, if he knew Sloan still had her access, he might cut it off. Sloan's help was invaluable.

She left the office suite and the building and called Danny.

"Smith."

"I'm almost far enough away," she said.

"From what?" Danny asked.

"Hang on, one more row of cars, and I'll be at the grassy end of the parking lot."

She shielded her eyes from the sun with one hand and held her phone with the other as she filled Danny in on the information she was pretty sure he didn't already have. At least there was no way he knew about the business card on Harvey's desk.

"How do you know that name?" he asked, referring to Briana Mosley.

"It's all over the Internet."

"Shit." He took a breath. "Just because he has her card doesn't mean he killed her. I'm sure lots of people have her card, and she and Harvey are in the same business."

"Sloan's brother has pictures from his party of Harvey with another victim, and he said Harvey left with that girl."

"Who?"

Silence came from the other end of the phone when she relayed the contents of Michael's call.

"How did this get past me?"

She heard the slight tremble in his voice.

"I'm sure the information is on its way to you. You'll get the report. I'm the prelude to the official messenger."

"It could all be a coincidence, but I'll have Stone follow up. Maybe you found us a lead," Danny said.

Thrilled that he seemed to have lowered his blood pressure a bit, she continued. "Are you going to question him?"

"We have to do a little leg work first, Babe. Go back to work and try to take your mind off this for a while. I'll call you when we have something."

All of a sudden, she froze as if the consequences of being employed by a killer had never occurred to her before that moment. A burst of wind blew a small amount of sand against her leg, and the faint scent of fried grease passed under her nose. Every part of her body was overly sensitized. The phone was still against her ear.

In a faint voice, she said, "He's sitting in the office right next to me."

"He knows you, and he knows me. He's not going to mess with you," he assured her and probably himself.

The sentiment was simple but enough for her to push past her paralyzing fear. She always felt protected with Danny. On the way back inside, she choked down the emotions that had swelled in her throat.

To avoid entering Harvey's line of vision, she took the long way around the office. It was her plan to keep away from him for as long as possible. She stacked the papers spread over her desk into one mountain, leaving the application package Harvey had given her earlier centered on her desk.

Better get it done, don't want to piss him *off.*

The application was seven pages long. In between each page, Raina checked her phone and hoped that Sloan would call so that she could update her on the case. It wouldn't be productive for Raina to stop in the middle of a project and call Sloan. But if her phone rang….

The application took her half an hour to finish. She quickly double-checked it for completeness, tapped the edge of the sheets together on her desk, and set them aside for Harvey to sign prior to the overnight delivery pick-up. Nothing more would stand in her way. She snatched her phone and dialed.

"Do you really think Harvey is the Morphine Murderer?" Sloan asked.

"We've only linked him with two of the four victims. Now we have to see if we can make a connection with the others."

"Do you have a theory on motive? I mean, why would Harvey want to kill these women, or anyone?" Sloan asked.

"We have to figure that out, too."

"Aren't Danny and his team working on this case?" Sloan asked.

"Yeah, but I have access to Harvey that they don't. Without a warrant, that is."

"I'll see what I can find on him."

"That would be great."

Raina pictured Sloan reaching over her belly for the keyboard, laughed to herself, then focused on Harvey and planned her next mission: *Mission Datebook.* Despite his high-tech options, Harvey kept his schedule in a leather-bound book. It was usually on his desk and open to the current day. That mission presented no challenge. Harvey had left the office for a meeting, and Raina photocopied the pages from the past few weeks and three into the future. She stuffed the copies into her handbag to read later, offsite.

Via a series of text messages, Danny had informed her that Harvey had no criminal record. He must have had Murphy on the search before Sloan took it on. Aside from two traffic tickets, a DUI, and a couple of banking department complaints, he was clean. Based on the photo of him with the victim on the night of her murder and that he was the last one to be seen with her alive, Danny would have Harvey questioned.

In the meantime, keep your eyes open, one on Harvey and the other on yourself, Danny texted.

She took that assignment seriously.

Raina sent a text to Sloan: *Live DB Night tonight.*

Sloan's response chimed on Raina's phone: *What does that oxymoron mean?*

Before Raina had time to forward her response, Sloan called.

"We need to follow Harvey," Raina said.

Sloan hesitated a moment, then asked apprehensively, "Shouldn't Danny's guys do that?"

The answer was 'yes,' but Raina had already concocted the plan. "Why are you backing off?"

"Give me the phone," Raina heard Paul say in the distance. Then he was as loud as if he were standing in front of her. "We're on our way to the hospital. Something's wrong with the baby."

"What? I'll meet you at the hospital."

"Don't. We have to keep Sloan as calm as possible. No visitors until we have more information. Please."

Two hours passed, and there was no update call from Sloan or Paul. One minute she was fine, and the next, she was in pain. It wasn't time for the baby yet. Raina's computer screen was filled with possible pregnancy complications, but she had no details. She hadn't had any idea how many things could go wrong. The nurse at the hospital began to recognize her voice from her constant calling. Each time she inquired about Sloan Randall, the nurse told her that she didn't have a room yet, and she couldn't share any medical information.

After another couple of hours without any responses to her many texts to Paul, she bolted from her desk and took off for the hospital. Nothing would keep her from her friend's side. She slowed the car to pull into the lot and rushed through the entrance to the emergency room. She spotted Paul standing in the distance next to Sloan's gurney.

"Paul!"

Raina almost collided with the gurney as she arrived at Sloan's side. Sloan's hand seemed weak and fragile as she reached for Raina's.

"What happened? Are you okay?" Raina asked.

"I had some pain, and Paul rushed me here. My blood pressure was very high, and my sugar level's really low. I tried to explain to them that I hadn't eaten. What did they think? Paul scared the crap out of me. Of course, my pressure was through the roof."

"Do you feel any better now?"

Raina watched Sloan's eyes tear up.

Paul motioned for Raina to leave. Although she didn't want to leave Sloan there, Raina knew she was in the best hands possible with the doctors and Paul taking care of her. Raina would only be in the way. She headed back to her car and realized that she left it angled over the line into the next spot. She burst into tears. The doctors didn't really know what was wrong. Endless scenarios played in her mind. Each one ended with death, disease, or deformities. Fifteen minutes went by before she drove off. Sloan's baby scare was the last straw. Her best friend in the hospital, her boss a killer, a kiss with her co-worker, problems with the boyfriend…what else could happen? Better to focus on the mission. That was the answer. If she focused on the mission, she wouldn't have to think about everything else. Compartmentalization was the only way.

The office was on her way home, so she decided to swing by and see if Harvey was still there. She'd try to complete the mission. It occurred to her as she sped down Route 110 that slowing down would be a good idea. It wouldn't help if she got pulled over by patrol. She could imagine the call to Danny. *Lieutenant Smith, we have your girlfriend here for speeding. She said she was rushing to a stakeout to follow a murder suspect.* A single bolt of laughter relieved some tension, and she let off the gas. The endless rows of single-story shopping centers bordering the four-lane road were less of a blur as she slowed the car. Store after store was set behind lines of parked cars. These were all places that she passed every day and that went unnoticed. Her destination was her only mark.

Her timing was perfect. Harvey was with a coworker in the office parking lot. She killed the headlights and pulled behind the only pair of cars left together. The night was looking better.

By the time Harvey was finished with his conversation, the sky was dark. Raina was starved, but curiosity got the best of her. Harvey was a partier. No way was he headed home this early. She remained in her car and waited for Harvey to reach the stop sign that led to the road. That's when she started the car and followed far behind. He led her to Kelly's. It was nine, and the last time Raina had eaten was at lunchtime. She stayed in the car, shuffled around the contents of her glove compartment, and found a cereal bar flattened within the foil wrapper. She snacked on it and examined the copies from Harvey's datebook. There was nothing suspicious.

A car passed by slowly, so slowly that she turned and caught a glimpse of the driver. His head was turned toward the entrance to the bar, but he didn't stop. Not more than a minute later, the same car rolled by again. By Raina's calculation, that was about how long it would take to circle the block. This time he parked a few cars away from her. The man from the car turned toward Raina before he arrived at the bar entrance. It was too dark to see his face. Through the tall paned window, Raina could see him go half way to the back of the small, narrow interior of the establishment. Then he disappeared into the crowd.

CHAPTER 14

Hawkeye sat at the end of the bar at Kelly's and took notice of the occupants. It was filled to capacity. The noise bounced off the wood paneled walls, increasing the volume. Four guys of various ages seemed to know each other at the far end of the bar. They were wearing business suits, three wore wedding bands, one was loud and obnoxious, and they were all drinking heavily. There was a group of girls in the booth near them and occasionally their conversations joined together. Detective John Stone sat two booths over with a hot, young blonde and a drink on the rocks. Another blonde, strawberry, tall, in her early to mid-twenties, and full of alcohol was hanging all over his target, Harvey. An instant flashback to Hawkeye's single days crossed his mind. Thinking about the good old days made him hungry, that and the overcooked pot-roast his wife had been proud to serve for dinner that night, so he ordered some wings. As his thoughts returned to the present, he saw Stone closing in on him.

"Hey brother, what are you drinking?" he asked.

"I'm working," Hawkeye responded quietly and nodded his head towards the end of the bar. "We got a lead on that guy. Tall, suit, blonde girl attached to his side."

Before they could continue their exchange, Harvey and his companion got up and left. That was their cue to move. Stone motioned to Hawkeye, and they followed Harvey outside. Stone positioned himself against a car with a clear view to Harvey in the parking lot and sent Hawkeye back to the car.

Another blonde stormed through the front door of the bar screaming and waiving her hands after Stone. "Asshole! You left me there! What-the-fuck is that?"

Stone pushed her against the wall, blocking her from Harvey's sight. With his hand over her mouth, he flashed his gold detective shield. She nodded in recognition of the badge. Slowly, he released her with apologies and told her to go back inside. She didn't look any less angry, but she left him there and quietly accepted his direction.

Hawkeye saw the SUV's headlights light up, then drove through the parking lot intentionally blocking Harvey while Stone jumped in the car. Hawkeye backed up the unmarked car and let Harvey drive away.

"Who was that girl?" Hawkeye asked.

"Move over rookie," Stone demanded.

"I'm an excellent driver, highest ranked in my precinct."

"Move, Rainman!"

Hawkeye put the car in 'park,' jumped from the driver's seat, and ran around the front of the car, so Stone wouldn't drive off without him. He was pretty sure he wouldn't run him over. Stone threw himself across the seat to the driver's side and took off as Hawkeye was pulling the door shut. It was dark, but they could see the silver SUV making a right turn ahead.

"That girl was pissed at you," Hawkeye said.

"What can you do?"

"It wasn't really you. It's been a pattern her whole life. Her pain was carved deep into her being. I saw rejection in her face, anger in her eyes, and heard the defensive inflection of her voice. She couldn't have cared that much about a guy she'd just met."

"You saw all that?"

Stone kept the length of a football field between them and Harvey as he glided through red lights without his lights and sirens.

"Let's pull him over. He's DUI, swerving all over the road," Hawkeye said.

"No, we'll follow him and see where he's taking her."

"His MO is to kill them in their own homes, except for one."

"Right, so we follow him."

They drove for less than fifteen minutes to a gated community on the north side of the Long Island Expressway where Harvey stopped the car at a set of iron gates. After he inserted a card into the slot, the gates automatically rolled into the landscaped sides as he drove in. Stone and Hawkeye pulled up. Stone flashed his badge at the guard, and the gates held open. They followed the SUV through a community of condos. Each row of two-story units was indistinguishable from the next. Only the road names and occasional door adornments differentiated one from the others.

Harvey pulled into a driveway and walked with the blonde to the door of the middle unit. They stood next to the door for a while, and the cops observed from the corner.

"That guy is skyscraper tall," Stone said.

"6'5"," Hawkeye said.

Stone turned to Hawkeye.

"I pulled his DMV record."

They waited as Harvey and the girl made-out enthusiastically. She was up on her toes. Her hand rubbed his groin over his pants. He had one hand up her shirt on her breast and the other around her back and down her pants. One side of her blouse slipped off her shoulder and exposed her bra. Harvey took his hand from her breast, moved it to her back, and pulled her hard against him.

"Rainman, ever see live porn? Perk of the job," Stone chuckled.

"We could have arrested him a half a dozen times already tonight." Hawkeye counted off the violations as he held up corresponding fingers, "DUI, moving violation. He sped through two red lights, lewd behavior in public. What did I miss?"

Harvey and the girl broke apart. She had pushed him back. The detectives couldn't hear the words but could tell the situation had turned sour. Harvey adjusted himself and stormed back to his car leaving the blonde alive.

Tailing Harvey had ended for Raina when it led to the gated community. Although she had considered it, she didn't try to charm her way in when she spotted Stone. Instead, she left him responsible for the safety of the woman in Harvey's company.

Now she was enjoying her favorite spot on the couch in Danny's arms. For the last ninety minutes, they had been snuggled together watching a movie. One dim light was on, Codis was close by curled up on the chair, and Danny's phone had been silent. She couldn't remember the last time that happened: spending time without police interruption.

After the movie ended, Raina sat up and asked more about the investigation of Harvey.

"That boss of yours sure leads a wild life."

"I know, but what did they find?" she asked.

"Not much, nothing to help our case. The last vic fought back, and they collected some skin cells from under her nails, so we have his DNA."

"How do you know it was her killer's skin?"

"We don't for sure, but considering her defensive wounds and her murder, it's likely."

Raina's eyes lit up.

"I know that look," Danny said.

"Do you want saliva, hair, skin, blood?"

"No way, Babe."

"Come on, I'm with him all day long. I can get you his DNA to compare."

He shook his head.

"It'll be easy. Don't worry," she said.

Danny contemplated the situation, then reluctantly agreed. "Let's stay away from blood. Get a water bottle. Make sure you see him drink from it first. And be careful."

"I know."

Raina knew she wasn't going to get a good night's sleep. There was too much to plan and plot for her *Mission Bottle*.

Morning didn't come quickly enough for Raina. As soon as the sun began to brighten the sky, she sprang up from her bed, stretched her arms above her head until she heard a crack, and then made a mental list of everything she wanted to accomplish. Codis jumped from his bed as a reaction to her movement and trotted to the back door to go outside. The forecast was for a bright, sunny, beautiful day. It would have been a perfect summer morning for the beach if she hadn't had a case to work on or a job to go to. Raina stepped outside while Codis bounded across the yard after a squirrel that scurried along the fence. The intermittent cool breeze and the heat of the sun alternated on her skin. There was no time to enjoy a leisurely morning. *Mission Bottle* was her top priority, and she wanted to get to it, stat.

"It's the crack of dawn." Danny stood inside the house, squinting out the door.

"Gotta get to work. Things to do, missions to accomplish."

They shared a light breakfast, and Raina practically shoved Danny out of the house.

It seemed an eternity before Sloan answered her phone. "Raina, too much wind."

She leaned to speak closer to the microphone. "Sorry, the top is down. I'm on my way to work, but I wanted to check in with you and make sure everything is okay,"

"The baby's vitals are stable, but they're keeping me here for observation. You know how I hate being trapped."

"Like the summer you had your tonsils out and missed camp. I'd sneak around the back of your house and talk to you through the window. Once I had to convince you not to climb out."

"I don't know why my mother wouldn't let you in. It wasn't like I had something contagious."

"I don't know if I ever tried. It was an adventure to get around the house without her seeing, then back out. Did she ever know I was there?"

There was a series of clinks followed by static.

"A nurse is here, I gotta go. We'll talk later."

The conversation distracted Raina for the ride. She rushed out of the car, banging her head on the frame. At the door to the building, she twisted sideways and lowered her body to position her bag in front of the electronic reader. The magnetic card to unlock the door resided in the outside pocket of her bag. She thought it ironic that the killer was inside the secured building.

There wasn't a real plan until a light bulb flicked on in her head. Actually, a light bulb walked by: Tyler. Tyler was the perfect solution. It took him a few minutes to finish discussing loan details with his processor, and then he was standing in Raina's doorway as though she had summoned him telepathically.

"Morning."

She tried not to notice the charisma oozing from his tanned face. "We have a mission," she said.

"I'm intrigued."

Over the next minute or so, she gave Tyler the Cliffs Notes version of the case.

When she stopped to breathe, he said, "Why are you reporting old news to me?"

"We have reason to believe it might be Harvey and…."

"Our boss, Harvey?"

"Shh-shush, we don't want him to hear us. Yes, our Harvey," she whispered.

"Who exactly is 'we'?"

"Just listen," she said and then she continued to explain *Mission Bottle*.

"The police suspect him?"

"Yes, and you can consider yourself recruited and deputized, so let's plan details."

Tyler had gone to his desk to take care of some business but promised to return to Raina shortly. By then, Harvey would have at least one open bottle on his desk. During the day, Harvey opened many bottles of water, green tea, and various other drinks, which could be found abandoned on desks and cabinets all throughout the five thousand square foot office. She had never seen him return to retrieve one. Raina and Tyler agreed that they had to appropriate one from his desk to be sure it was his unless one of them witnessed him drink from a bottle and then they would take it, bag it, and deliver it to Danny. On second thought, they decided that one of them also had to see him drink from the bottle to be positive it was his. That was the plan until they came up with a better one. They would collect multiple specimens to ensure a usable sample.

After lunch, Tyler went to Harvey's office under the pretense of discussing a loan file, watched Harvey drink from the open bottle of water on his desk, and then reported to Raina. As soon as Raina saw Harvey head elsewhere, she hurried into his office to collect the bottle.

Crap, where's the cap?

What was she going to do with an open, half full bottle of water?

Okay, I'll carry it to the bathroom and dump the water. Wait, will that wash off the DNA? Crap.

An addendum to the plan was added. First step: Take the bottle to her desk and call Danny. Next step: Follow Harvey to the Processing Department to see if he has another bottle with him. She did. He didn't.

No problem, the day is young.

She returned to her desk and concentrated on her paying job for a while.

A bottle was placed on her desk as she typed on the computer. She didn't need to look up to see who was there. Tyler's scent wafted over to her. He was so close she could feel the heat from his body. She gave him the 'is that what I think it is?' look. And he returned the 'yes it is' look. She nodded her head in approval and was relieved to see the cap was screwed on. She placed the bottle in a plastic bag that she had taken from her desk drawer and noted the date and collection location and source on the plastic. Then she placed the evidence bag back in the drawer. Tyler had disappeared before she was done. It was a totally silent transaction.

She returned to her work until she saw Harvey striding around with a bottle of Green Tea. She saw no reason to limit the number of bottles, so she didn't. She stealthily followed Harvey back to the Processing Department and watched from behind a tall, metal file cabinet. He spoke to one of the processors and then turned to leave. Raina opened the file drawer and sifted through it, pretending to look for something. She watched as he spoke to one of the loan officers and then strode back to his office, so she returned to hers. That bottle was off the table, so to speak.

Work should have come first, but Raina was too fired up about her real live case. This time it wasn't she and Sloan taking the clues given on television and trying to solve that case. This was real. Clues weren't handed to her. She had to actively investigate. With *Mission Bottle* in play, she thought about Sloan and called her.

"How are you and the baby doing?"

"I think we're fine. I feel fine," Sloan said.

"What did they say happened?"

"They are running every test under the sun. They've poked and prodded every inch of me. Nothing to do but wait for all the results. Tell me what you've been up to."

Raina wanted to believe that it was nothing. *It's nothing until they find something.*

She shared the adventures of *Mission Bottle*.

"Really? Danny agreed to this?"

"It must be the pressure he's getting, but he did. Sloan, it's so exciting. I wish you were here"

"Let me help."

"You're supposed to be resting. We'll handle it."

"No, I'm fine. I have my laptop, and I'm stir-crazy. Please."

"Okay, if you're sure. Search for anything on morphine. There has to be a specific reason why he uses that as his weapon of choice over another drug or another way to kill altogether. And how does he get it?"

Raina heard the tapping of the keys as Sloan began her search.

"Morphine's a narcotic," Sloan read.

"I knew that."

"Comes in pills or injections."

"The killer's using injections. This guy knows how to use an IV needle and find a vein. I don't think finding a vein is so easy, and there's only one mark on the bodies, not like he poked around to get it right. That means he has some medical knowledge or training, and he has access. One week on DB Night weren't they looking for a medical professional and it turned out to be a veteran from one of the armed forces? He was a medic trained in triage or something. Danny said the victims were sedated first. That's probably a different drug."

Raina made more notes in her book.

"Basically, morphine puts you to sleep," Sloan continued reading, "It slows the heart rate until it stops dead, reduces breathing until you're breathless. Deceased, passed on, departed, finished, gone."

"I get it, dead."

"Lethal dosage is 120mg for an average person." Sloan paused. "That's about it, the rest is pretty redundant. Wait, there's a short bio on a woman convicted of killing her boyfriend with a morphine overdose. She was a nurse and had access. We know any nurses?"

"Aren't you surrounded by them?"

Tyler sauntered into Raina's office and presented her with a partially drunk bottle of Green Tea. "Good job, Prentiss."

"What do you mean?"

"Great plan."

"What plan?"

"You got him out of his office and away from the bottle long enough, so I could slip in and take it unnoticed."

"Hi Tyler," Sloan's voice echoed on speakerphone.

"I've got to get back to the mission. I'll give you a call later. Keep resting and call me if you get any news," Raina said.

Tyler was standing extremely close to her, closer than before. She felt the weight of Danny's gift heavy on her wrist.

"Here." He handed the bottle to her and left.

Another mission accomplished. She carefully placed the bottle in a second plastic bag and called Danny.

"Smith."

"*Mission Bottle* complete, Babe," she said.

CHAPTER 15

Crack. The sound of the aluminum bat hammering against the baseball was music to Michael's ears. He and Charlie were at the batting cages swinging in the seventy-mile-an-hour section. It was a cool afternoon on the South Shore because of the proximity to the ocean, the overcast sky, and the breeze. The establishment was packed. A dozen or so eight-year-olds monopolized the miniature golf course at the other end. The 'Happy Birthday' balloons explained that.

Crack. "Awesome hit, dude," Charlie said.

"Thanks man." Michael adjusted his baseball cap.

Crack. Crack. Crack. "You're on a roll to-day!"

Michael reached his hand into his pocket and came up empty. "Your turn, I'm out of tokens."

Swoosh. Swoosh. Swoosh. Crack. Swoosh. "There's a damn hole in the bat." Charlie threw the bat at the fence, stomped from the cage, tossed Michael his last two tokens, and sat on the bench.

"Don't blame the bat. You suck," Michael said.

Before Michael dropped the token in the box to release the pitches, he heard a voice. "Hey man, awesome party."

Michael turned around to see Harvey behind him sporting a Cheshire cat smile.

He swallowed, hoped his eyes didn't look as bugged-out as they felt, and answered, "Hey."

Charlie chimed in as he got up from the bench. "Dude, that one chick was all over you."

"Yeah, she was hot," Harvey agreed.

"And drunk," Michael added. He lifted his cap, raked his fingers through his hair, and returned the cap to his head.

"Yeah, drunk too," Harvey agreed again.

"Too bad about her," Michael said.

"What about her?"

"It was all over the news." Michael glanced over at Charlie, and they exchanged looks.

"I guess I missed that story."

"She's dead," Michael said.

"Oh shit, really?"

Michael was taken off guard by Harvey's surprise. He had no preconceived notion of what a killer's response should be. When he thought about it though, he thought it should include remorse, regret, or fear. Then again the killer wouldn't want to get caught, so feigned surprise made more sense.

"Really. The cops were at my house. Apparently that was the last place she was seen alive."

"That sucks," Harvey said. He put his bat on his shoulder and jumped into a sixty-mile-per-hour cage, two cages down.

A large screen television hung from the far wall above the ball machine in weather and theft proof casing. The sporting event that played on it was interrupted by a newsbreak. A middle aged man dressed in a conservative business suit stood in front of the government buildings. He was a police department official holding a press conference on the multitude of recently publicized drug overdoses in Suffolk County. An investigator from the federal Drug Enforcement Agency stood beside the official, urging anyone with information to call the number on the screen. The broadcast concluded with replays of the news clips from the preceding weeks.

Most batters around them didn't break their concentration. The ball machine didn't stop. But Michael, Charlie, and Harvey watched intently while the drug overdosed victims' families outwardly mourned and comforted each other.

Harvey packed his gear and stormed out of the cage. Michael and Charlie could smell the rubber burn as Harvey revved the engine and peeled away.

Michael slipped the remaining tokens into Charlie's bag, and they agreed to call it quits for the day. As soon as they got into the car, Michael called Raina to tell her about their interaction with Harvey.

"You two see a lot of each other these days," Raina said.

"What? Do you think he knows we know?"

"Doubt it. He'd be acting weird."

"He didn't seem to be affected by seeing us or the mention of the dead girl," Michael said.

"He wouldn't be. Serial killers have no conscience. They're damaged goods, feel no regret, and are usually highly confident," Raina said.

"Well he was a little weird. He hit a few balls then tore out of here like a bat out of hell."

"Nah, he's ADHD. That's not weird at all."

The afternoon heat forced Raina inside the hospital to wait for Danny. She watched people go in and out, glanced at the guard a few times, then at her watch, and then went outside to use her cell. Danny was standing to the side, staring down at his phone.

"Babe," she said.

"Ah...."

She contorted her face to question him. He took her hand and guided her to the bench where they sat as the sweat moistened the edges of her clothes. Each time the doors glided open, they felt a quick burst of cool air joined by the antiseptic scent.

He spoke in a tone she hadn't heard from him before. It was a quiet, defeated voice.

"Today's the anniversary of the death of one of my men, Jesse. He died here, in this hospital, five years ago."

She laid a comforting hand on his leg. "What happened?"

It took him a few minutes to get started and then he told her how Sergeant Robert Jesse had pulled over a blue van after it made an illegal right turn on red. The driver was polite and cooperative. Jesse followed textbook protocol, but as he was handing back the driver's information another person popped up from behind the seat and aimed a gun at him. It was a young teenager who held the gun with shaky hands and fear in his eyes. He was ranting about not losing his father, that no one was going to take his father from him. One shot to the chest took Jesse down. The driver hit the gas, the van's tires spun, and he sped away, but Jesse had had enough strength to call for help. With a reported officer down, the ambulance arrived to the scene in minutes, but EMS found him unconscious next to the patrol car. Jesse was rushed to the hospital and spent the next fourteen days fighting for his life. On the fifteenth day, he lost the battle. Danny had been by his bedside every day between shifts and had spent many hours consoling the family. Because of his emotional distress, Danny was ordered to join a support group, which he attended for a month before he abandoned it. After a short chase, two patrol cars had stopped the van and arrested the kid and his father. Detective John Stone, then Officer Stone, was one of the arresting officers. The investigation revealed that the teenager was high on drugs and that the man driving the van was not his father. He was a drug dealer with sufficient quantities to put him away for a very long time. The kid was then fourteen years old and was lost somewhere in the juvenile system.

Raina put her arm through his and held him tight. He turned and gave her a kiss, squeezed her, and maintained the embrace. His strong, confident voice had returned, and they ventured inside.

Now it was her turn to have a slight anxiety attack. This would be the first time she, Danny, and Tyler would be together since the kiss. She huffed down two breaths of oxygen and banned the fear from her mind.

"Watch your back," a young man said as he whizzed by with a cart.

Danny simultaneously turned to look, put his hand flat against Raina's back, and guided her out of the way. From the hall outside Jean's room, they watched a young nurse move the patient's leg up and down to bend her knee and straighten it back to its original position. The nurse had a pleasant face and caring touch. Tyler was on the opposite side of the bed mirroring the therapy on her other leg. After a few minutes, they stepped towards the head of the bed and maneuvered Jean's arms in unison. Her eyes were closed, and she had a peaceful expression across her face. Tyler was engrossed in his work and hadn't noticed the company until the nurse greeted them as she exited the room. He walked the few steps towards them. He kissed Raina on the cheek, shook Danny's hand, and then offered them chairs.

"You okay?" she asked.

"Yeah."

"Have the doctors given you any new information?" she asked.

"Not really."

Danny and Raina watched as Tyler held Jean's hand and stroked her hair.

Raina spoke to Jean, trying to be humorous. "You look pretty good. Aren't you ready to go home?"

Jean's eyes flashed open and startled Raina and Danny both.

Tyler held up his hand. "It's only a reflex."

Raina continued to talk to her quietly. "Remember how much fun we all had at your house in the Hamptons last summer? I know you do. That was the summer you decided to learn how to scuba dive, and the whole time we were there you were walking around with pieces of equipment hanging off you, in and out of the pool to practice."

There was no movement beyond Jean's breathing.

"What about the huge party you had in your Hampton house on the beach after Tyler came to work with us? Everyone was there, even my friend Sloan and her husband."

"Stone was there, too. Who could forget that bash?" Danny said.

"Yeah," Tyler said nodding his head. "That was the celebration for my biggest paycheck ever. Still haven't topped that one."

Danny caught Raina's attention, lifted his arm, and tapped the top of his wrist.

"If there is anything you need, anything we can do," Danny started.

"Thanks," Tyler said.

Danny departed and Raina went to find Sloan's room.

"Let me check to see if you are on the list. Name?" a nurse said to Raina when she asked for Sloan's room number.

"Raina Prentiss. Why?"

"Related to Lorraine Prentiss?" She frowned. Sloan had done that on purpose.

"Yeah, that's me."

"ID?"

Raina presented her ID and a guard appeared and escorted her to a private room at the far end of the hospital. She couldn't believe her eyes. She stepped over the threshold into luxury. The wood framed bed, patterned curtains, and area rug all resembled a hotel, not a hospital room.

"Sloan?" she said with the inflection of a question, requesting an explanation.

"What's going on with the case?

"Explain this room first."

"What do you think? It's Paul's doing. His family donates huge sums of money to the hospital. They do whatever he wants. He wanted a private, luxury room, and he got it. He wants them to run more tests, they run more tests. There's nothing wrong. I want to go home."

Raina knew better than to say anything bad about Paul even though Sloan was bringing up the subject. His control issues had come up in the past, and Sloan had always defended him.

"Gotta give him credit, it's a nice room."

Sloan glared at her.

CHAPTER 16

Michael sprang from the lounge chair when he saw an incoming call from Raina. This could be the moment that she had come to her senses, dropped Danny, and realized that he was the one for her. Instead, she gave an account of her day. She had caught up with Harvey by the office an hour after he left the batting cages. He was there for a while, then she followed him home. Raina told Michael that she bet he had fabricated an excuse for his wife about where he was going.

Michael walked around the pool as he half listened while she explained how Harvey had switched gears. She never got around to the dumping Danny part. She said that she had begun to think about Harvey's behavior in another way.

"He was unaccounted for by his wife, the usual alibi. I waited until Harvey reappeared at the door, flipped open the mailbox, and then hopped in his SUV. When he turned down the block, I followed him. When he pulled in front of Delicious Dancing Dolls, that's when I got concerned and called you. I need a favor."

During her brief pause, Michael's thoughts were a jumbled cacophony of fragmented ideas.

"How would you and Charlie like to go to a strip club?" she asked.

A moment of initial excitement, followed by a slightly panicked sensation spread through him. "Why are you inviting me to a strip club?"

"I'm inviting you to tail Harvey while he hunts for his next victim."

"Sounds like a win-win to me."

He charged back to Charlie to relay the request.

"Hell yeah, dude!" Charlie was in.

"Stay sober, so you can drive," Raina said.

She gave him the location and told him that she would watch the door until he and Charlie arrived. It took them half an hour.

Michael and Charlie made their way over to a table on the right side of the stage where they had a clear view of Harvey and the dancers. It was a cozy but mostly empty establishment. The high ceiling and the darkness concealed the exposed pipes and lighting structures. Music played as an exotic dancer who was wearing only a red sequined G-string slid her leg around the stripper pole and rubbed up and down.

After the music changed and the third dancer began her routine, Charlie turned to Michael. "Dude."

Michael ignored him.

"Dude."

"What?" he asked without turning his head from the stage.

"Where did Harvey go?"

"Shit. Weren't you watching him?"

"Weren't you?"

"We agreed to alternate. It was your turn to watch Harvey," Michael said.

"Wrong. You had the last girl with the braids and the skimpy school girl outfit," Charlie said.

"No. You were watching the girl with the braids. I watched the one before with the giant tits."

"So where's Harvey?" Charlie asked.

"Let's look and see if his car is still parked outside," Michael said, wondering when it was that Charlie had become the more responsible of the two.

Charlie gulped down his drink, and they sped to the door. Michael was a few steps ahead of his friend and abruptly slammed into an incoming guy. The man was solid. He shot Michael a dirty look that Michael ignored only because he had to find Harvey, whose car remained parked and unoccupied. Michael and Charlie leaned against another car and debated their next step. Michael didn't want to admit defeat or let Raina down or leave the show. Harvey was already gone, and they had no idea where to look for him. There was no other decision but to go back inside.

Lights flashed and changed color as a redhead, sporting lipstick that matched her hair, danced. The music had a strong bass beat, and the redhead was dry humping the pole. She wore stiletto heeled, tall, black leather boots and a matching black leather corset and thong. Her talent included cracking a long lunge whip as she rode the pole. Michael scanned the place. Customers were spread out away from each other, each one positioned as if the show was intended for him alone. Some seemed timid, shy, and reclusive while the one slightly to the right of Charlie was loud and boisterous and waving dollar bills.

The redheaded dancer turned to face the man with the money. She pumped her hips back and forth in his direction. Her arm straightened, and her elbow locked into position. Her hand remained clamped to the pole as her body got closer to him. She released her grip and did a little twist, lowering herself toward the floor of the stage, curling her finger to encourage him closer. He took the bait and stuffed bills in the front of her thong, reaching in as far as he could until she tilted her hips away.

In a low, sexy voice she said, "Hey, Sweetie, how about some Lincolns?"

As he reached into his jacket pocket for his wallet, she turned around and danced within inches of his face. She smiled as he placed more bills inside the elastic back of her leather thong.

Charlie and Michael's attention was glued to the dancer. They had heard her request and had witnessed the results. Charlie seemed content to have this guy pay for the show upgrade, but Michael's competitive nature overcame him. He reached for his wallet.

"Hey, Baby, what would you do for some Jacksons?"

She gyrated over to him, kneeled down on the stage, and leaned close to him. As she shimmied her shoulders and jiggled her breasts, she cracked her whip and Michael jumped. Charlie broke into a fit of laughter and nearly fell off his chair. He continued to laugh as Michael regained his composure and placed the twenty in her cleavage with his teeth. Charlie joined the fun, pulled his wallet from the back pocket of his jeans, and waved a bunch of mixed bills at her without a word. The redhead slid off the stage and onto his lap. Harvey's whereabouts were the last thing on Michael's mind. In fact, he had forgotten all about Harvey. As Michael grabbed her ass with the hand not stuffing money into her garments, he felt a strong hand jerk his shoulder back and away from the dancer.

"Fuck's your problem?" Michael said to the man.

"She was dancing for me, not you and your fuckin' *compadre* there." The man's hand curled into a fist, white knuckles facing Michael.

Beer balls intact, Charlie said, "Fuck off, dude, she's dancing for me."

The man elbowed Michael in the gut. As he bent over in pain, the man swung his fist into Charlie's jaw. The redhead quickly backed away around the side of the stage by the curtain.

"I paid to get in and see the whole damn show!" a man yelled.

Someone threw a bottle, and all hell broke loose. Charlie appeared by Michael's side and clocked the man on the side of his head. As the man prepared to retaliate, Michael threw a hard kick into his gut, which sent the man backward, and slammed him onto a table. The table broke, and the man crashed to the floor on top of the pieces of wood and glass, screaming about the revengeful wrath that would fall upon them, but his pain rendered him temporarily harmless.

Cops seemed to materialize from nowhere and ended the fight, and the boys leaned on the stage. Charlie held a napkin filled with ice against his bloody jaw. The loudmouths from the other side of the stage had exited the premises in a hurry. When the dance lights stopped and the overhead lights came on, Michael took account of the situation. Harvey was gone, and he dreaded the call to Raina.

The manager was enraged about the damage to his establishment and the interference with his profits for the night. He informed the cop that he and his bouncers could have taken care of the matter without the police and without any monetary loss.

The cop looked him right in the eyes. "My ass."

Raina was in her car, neatly camouflaged between two others, as she watched for Harvey.

The Bluetooth interrupted the radio: *You have an incoming call*

"Babe, I need Harvey's cell number. We lost track of him during a ruckus. I'll tell you all about it later," Danny said.

Raina had witnessed the ruckus from the anonymity of her car. Michael and Charlie were in and out of the bar. Stone had showed up and crashed into Michael on one of his trips out the door. There was a brief exchange of dirty looks. Then she heard the muffled bar fight. Glass breaking, furniture and bodies crashing, and then guys and dancers were flying out the door as though the place was on fire. Maybe it was. When Harvey left, he was accompanied by two dancers still in costume. She guessed there was no time for them to change. She didn't wait around for Michael and Charlie to follow Harvey. Raina took off after him.

She didn't need Danny to tell her about the events, and she gave him Harvey's cell number.

"But," she hesitated for a split second, "Harvey's at Tierney's." She knew Danny was cringing.

CHAPTER 17

Hawkeye was left alone to catch up to Harvey after Stone received a call and bolted. Danny relayed Harvey's whereabouts without a hint of disappointment. Both of their actions were curious to Hawkeye. They had left the lowest ranked of the three to trail a suspected serial killer. Hawkeye pondered what could be more important. Before he had had a chance to come to a conclusion or make a move, Harvey and the two dancers strolled down the street right in front of him. Huge, old tree roots had pushed up sections of the cement sidewalk. Each time Harvey tripped over one, he was steadied by the dancers. One stumble sent them scrambling to the side, trying to catch each other and themselves, legs and arms flailed in every direction. Hawkeye couldn't contain a chuckle. He watched as the brunette dancer returned to the club, and Harvey and the blonde got into his car. The backup lights came on. Harvey swung his SUV around and sped out onto the street. Hawkeye kept up with them, maintaining his distance even though Harvey seemed oblivious to anything outside of his reach. Harvey pulled over five miles down the road right in front of a bar, and Hawkeye found himself back at Kelly's. The same bar he had followed Levy to. He considered all the possible connections between the two men and was still unable to come up with a viable one.

"Smith."

"It's Hawkeye," he said and filled Danny in on the details. Hawkeye had hoped Danny could connect the dots.

"I'll have Stone look into it and let you know if we find anything," Danny said.

As soon as he mentioned Kelly's, Danny's demeanor changed. His response struck Hawkeye as odd. He couldn't see Danny's face, but he read something in his voice, something he couldn't quite put his finger on. Danny was almost dismissive. Why did he want Stone to look into it? Didn't he know?

The silver BMW parked across the street from Kelly's caught Hawkeye's attention, and he fumbled for his pad. He checked his notes and matched the license plate to Levy's. Levy was in the bar again: in the same bar as the suspect, together at the same time. What wasn't Danny telling him?

He entered the bar. Harvey was cuddled up with the dancer in a small booth along the dark paneled wall. They had ordered some appetizers and seemed to be set to stay for a while. Hawkeye took the opportunity to survey the rest of the patrons. It was late, after 2:30 in the morning, and the bar's customers were sparse. Besides his target and his company, there were just two men, each drinking alone. The suited man was nursing a beer, watching the news on the television above the bar, and the other ignored a glass of caramel colored liquor on the counter in front of him. Hawkeye hadn't seen Levy exit. The back room was his only possible location. Hawkeye walked by and swung the door open. Empty.

He sat himself strategically on a backless bar stool, ordered a club soda with lime and loaded potato skins, and watched the news. He kept Harvey in sight. Via a reflection in the mirror, he was able to see Harvey and the door to the back room.

"Those drug addicts deserve what they get," an inebriated man at the end of the bar slurred. His aggression escalated with the crash of his bottle against the screen. Glass sprayed in every direction.

Hawkeye popped off the stool and, without much effort, cuffed the man who was so focused on his televised opponent that he never noticed the cop coming at him. He walked the man through the door, pulling him upwards each time he stumbled, and turned his head to avoid the stench of alcohol. Still loudly slurring his words about something, Hawkeye guided the cuffed man towards the marked car without much force.

Stone pulled up to the front of the bar and headed directly to Hawkeye. "What the hell, Rainman?"

"He needs to go home before he gets in real trouble."

"Our job tonight wasn't cuffing every schmuck who had too much to drink. Where's Harvey?"

The cuffed man had quieted down to watch the cops banter.

Stone continued. "You know we do detective work. That's why they call us detectives. At least that's why they call *me* a detective."

"I've got it covered. A cab will be here shortly, and I can see the door. Keep an eye on Harvey while I stay with this guy," Hawkeye said.

Stone was about to walk away, but Hawkeye stopped him. "Wait. Find his wallet, so I can get his home address from his driver's license."

Stone pursed his lips and shook his head. "You go inside and check on Harvey. I'll wait for the cab."

The cuffed man in the backseat was out cold. The muscles in his neck had relaxed, and his head had dropped forward. Given the man's state of unconsciousness, Hawkeye felt relatively confident that Stone wouldn't let him loose. Hawkeye pushed the front door inwards. Harvey was gone. He checked the back room. No Harvey. He had been right at that small booth with the blonde dancer.

"Smith."

Danny retraced the GPS on Harvey's cell phone and reported the location back to Hawkeye.

"That's where I am, and I don't see him."

"I'm calling the phone," Danny said.

"Shit." Hawkeye picked up the ringing phone from the table in an empty booth.

"You and Stone check Harvey's residence."

"10-4."

Hawkeye busted out the exit. "Harvey's, let's go."

"Rainman, ditch the drunk. We don't have time to wait for a patrol car."

Hawkeye lifted the man's eyelid and got no response. He closed the back door and shrugged.

"Whatever." Stone shook his head, jumped in his car, and took off.

Not more than ten minutes later, Stone had beaten him to Harvey's. He put his palm flat against the top of Harvey's hood and snatched it right back.

"Hey man, what are we doing here?" the cuffed man asked.

Neither responded directly to him.

"Did the bar owner want to press charges?" Stone asked.

"Didn't have a chance to speak to anyone."

"Cut the guy loose already. He's sobering up, and you can't drag him around all night."

"What am I supposed to do now?" the man asked, looking around in the middle of a residential area.

Stone dialed his phone, arranged for a cab to pick the man up, and told the man to walk north a quarter mile to the nearest main road. The man rubbed his wrists together after Hawkeye released them, then the man stormed off. Stone reported into Danny. Their presence was requested back at the precinct.

When they got there, Danny was standing in front of the expanded sea of white boards screwed into the old walls. Additional boards had been set up with a timeline, the photos of the victims and crime scenes, and all known details. Danny stepped backwards and sat on a wheeled desk chair, rocked back and forth, and stared at the layout.

As Danny rocked his chair back again, Hawkeye grabbed one from a nearby desk, slid it over by Danny, and sat.

"We'll get him," Hawkeye said.

"Damn right," Stone said.

Saturday morning was an exceptionally humid, New York summer day, the kind when clothes absorb the moisture right out of the air like a sponge. The ground was wet from an early morning drizzle, but the sun was already burning it off and had created a fog near the ground.

Without much sleep, Hawkeye and Stone arrived on the scene of another murder. The officer that radioed it in was leaning against his vehicle flipping through the newspaper. It was open to a two-page spread of interviews with family and friends of the latest drug related victims.

"Lucky your sergeant isn't here to see that," Stone said as they walked by.

"There was nothing for me to do but wait."

They had been briefed on the way over. Speculation was that it was a possible victim of the Morphine Murderer.

The victim's parents sat at the side of the front steps as the EMTs went through their routine. They watched each time someone went in or out of the house as though it was all a big mistake, and their daughter would come bouncing down the stairs as she had many times. The mother was bent over with her head in her hands. The father had draped a robe carefully over her shoulders, and then sat stoically at her side.

Hawkeye and his wife had discussed kids. They shared the dream of a happy family, having dinner together, going to the park, and sharing experiences. He saw the pain in their faces and imagined the dreadfulness of losing a child.

"Lose the emotion and focus on the job," Stone said

"What?"

"You think you're the only one that can read faces? I see how you're looking at the vic's parents."

Hawkeye tried to shake it off and joined Stone to question them.

Stone spoke first. "We are very sorry for your loss. Is there anything you can tell us about what happened?"

Tears streamed down the mother's face, and the husband responded to the question in his best English. "We do not know what happened to make her dead."

"She is so young. Why does this happen to her?" the mother sobbed.

After a few minutes, Stone thanked them for their help and waved Hawkeye away from them. They had learned that the victim, Alexis Koslov, shared an apartment nearby with two dancers to whom her father referred as "her friends from the club." Her parents only knew the friends' first names. Not much help.

"The father was genuinely sad, but he was also embarrassed when he spoke about his daughter," Hawkeye said to Stone.

"Your woman's intuition?" Stone asked.

As they climbed the stairs, the victim's mother tapped Hawkeye on the leg. "Can you give to me her necklace? Please. It was the necklace of my Grandmother."

"I'll check for you, ma'am," he replied and left her standing outside.

"Have you ever smelled a body in decomp?" Stone asked Hawkeye.

Hawkeye shook his head, and Stone handed him an extra towel that he had pulled from his trunk. Hawkeye followed Stone's lead and put the towel over his nose. Inside, Hawkeye winced from the vapor through the towel. No warning could have prepared him for that.

He saw a petite figure leaning over the victim. She was wearing a standard issue M.E. jacket. The body was in decomp overdrive from the extreme heat. The vic's face was bluish. She was posed like the others.

"Where's Garza?" Stone asked.

The M.E. stood up and turned around. "Off today."

Stone raised his eyebrows and was face-to-face with a beautiful woman.

"When do you think she died?" Hawkeye asked her.

She wiped her arm across her forehead. "With this heat wave, it's hard to tell. The windows are closed, no a/c, it's gotta be over a hundred degrees inside this room. Under these conditions, probably not too long ago."

She turned back to the task at hand, and Stone gazed at her ass as she bent over the body.

"Stone," Hawkeye said.

Stone kept his focus on the M.E.

"That's the dancer we saw leave with Harvey."

"Are you sure?"

Hawkeye nodded when Stone turned around. They informed Danny and were sent to pick up Harvey. If this was another Morphine Murder, it would bring the body count to five.

"Stone," Hawkeye said.

"Stop saying my damn name."

"The mother asked me for a necklace. The vic's not wearing one."

"Shit, get a description of it from the mother before we go."

CHAPTER 18

As they arrived at Harvey's house, he was backing out of the driveway. They watched as he caught a glimpse of them and panicked. Black rubber painted the street as the wheels spun faster than the car moved. Hawkeye welcomed the smell of burning rubber since it overrode the putrid odor lingering in his nose from the decomposing body. Stone wasted no time. He shot out of the residential neighborhood and onto the Northern State Parkway, heading east. Hawkeye hit the sirens and reported the pursuit. Harvey weaved in and around the cars, still picking up speed. At nearly a hundred miles an hour, Stone was chasing him with two hands gripping the steering wheel and a look of excitement plastered on his face. He had found the rush he had cut his vacation short for.

"Buckle up, Rainman," Stone warned needlessly.

Hawkeye's right hand was tight around the door handle and his left hung onto the fastened seatbelt. Within seconds, two highway patrol cars had joined the chase. Harvey seemed to be flying without a plan. At that speed, the parkway would end in minutes, and he would be on Route 454 with slower moving traffic and lights. Aware of this, Hawkeye called ahead for a roadblock.

Harvey cut in between two cars creating a third lane. Before he was safely ahead of them, the passenger side of his car clipped the car on his right. The teenager driving lost control, veered off the road, and hit a tree. One of the Highway Patrol cars followed him off.

As they neared the end of the two-lane parkway, Hawkeye and Stone saw the roadblock. There had been enough time to get three police vehicles, two unmarked cars, and a tow truck into place. The officers were out of their cars with their guns drawn. Stone slowed, but Harvey didn't. Only at the last minute did Harvey hit the brakes. The car slid around ninety degrees. He came at the roadblock passenger side first. The officers withdrew from the center of the road, and Harvey's car crashed into the side of a marked car. The combination of the force and the angle of impact lifted his car up, rolled it over the police car, and landed it on the driver's side.

Stone pulled up, and he and Hawkeye sprinted over to the inverted car. Sirens were off, but lights still whirled on the closed road.

"Who is he, Detective?" one of the officers asked.

"A suspect in a murder case," Stone said.

"He's the Morphine Murderer?"

"Maybe. He alive?" Stone asked.

"He's breathing."

The airbags had deployed and were spattered with blood. Harvey was on his side, unconscious. His seatbelt was secured. His car was totaled.

Two EMTs jogged to the car to assess the situation and determined that they needed the fire department's help. They attached a neck brace as a precautionary measure. In no time, two ambulances and a fire truck joined the rest at the scene. A uniformed officer was redirecting the few cars that had slipped through the detour and were heading to the roadblock. A mile or so back, another officer was reportedly directing traffic off the parkway at the exit ramp.

"Head's up," a firefighter called.

All units stood by while he climbed on top of Harvey's car with the agility of a cat and in through a shattered window. A second firefighter was on top of the car. The one inside carefully cut the seatbelt with a knife and supported the body. The second lowered equipment, which was secured around Harvey and used to lift him out. They guided his body without hitting the window frame and lowered him onto a stretcher. One EMT secured an oxygen mask over his face while the other checked his blood pressure and heart rate and inspected him for injuries sustained from the accident.

This event did not elude the press. They arrived almost as fast as the emergency vehicles. Cameras were recording, and reporters were pushing microphones, trying to get information from anyone willing to share. The word had spread that this could be the Morphine Murderer.

Like the game, Telephone, the details had changed by the time the press reported it.

One aggressive reporter stood in front of her camera and spoke. "I'm reporting to you live from Smithtown. The Morphine Murderer has been apprehended after a high-speed car chase on the Northern State Parkway. He's dead."

Sometime during the commotion, Danny had arrived at the scene and was trying to administer damage control with the press; however, they were ruthless and his attempts failed. He delegated press control to an officer and joined Hawkeye and Stone by the ambulance.

"How is he?" Danny asked.

The paramedic by Harvey's head answered, "He's stable – for now."

"Good. I want him transported directly to the hospital by my precinct," Danny said and gave him specific instructions.

"We have to…," the paramedic tried.

"Not up for debate. He'll ride with you." Danny pointed towards Stone. "And keep the perp secured."

"He's unconscious. I don't think you have to worry about his escape," the paramedic said.

Stone hopped in the ambulance with Harvey and engaged his cuffs. One was secured on Harvey's left wrist and the other to the stretcher. Hawkeye backed away as they closed the ambulance doors and followed in their car, leaving the mess behind.

The EMTs rushed Harvey in through Emergency with Stone and Hawkeye in tow. A medical team immediately swarmed the gurney. The EMT rattled off vitals and brief details of the injuries. One held the oxygen until someone else hooked it to a stand. This all took place in seconds while they rolled the stretcher down a hall. The organized chaos was impressive.

"How long before I can speak to him?" Stone asked.

"No way to tell. I can call you when he regains consciousness," the doctor said. "Leave your card at the desk."

Stone instructed Hawkeye to wait for the officers assigned to watch the suspect, then left to join Danny back at the precinct. Later he would swing back and pick up Hawkeye.

On his way down the hall, Hawkeye crossed paths with the highway patrolman who attended to the driver of the car that was run off the road during the chase.

"How's the driver?"

"Alive with only minor injuries, mostly just shook up. The kid's slow speed, seatbelt, and air bags probably saved his life, but he's here so the doctors can check him out: protocol."

Hawkeye continued to the central floor station to get more information on Harvey's medical situation and interrupted a conversation among three staff members.

"He's being screened to determine if there's any intracranial hemorrhaging."

It was possible that Harvey could suffer from temporary or permanent memory loss and even mild or severe brain damage as a result of the head trauma. The effects of the latter two could only be determined after he regained consciousness. At best, the interrogation was on hold until he was awake. Hawkeye realized that even then he might not be able to tell them anything. Frustrated, Hawkeye waited and digested the reality that he was sitting outside the hospital room of a serial killer.

Who's the smokin' hot M.E. filling in for Garza?" Stone asked.

"Lacey Stanton," Danny answered.

"See her ass?"

"Careful. She's dating a judge," Danny warned. "Any idea why Harvey ran?"

"He's guilty?"

"Did you get a chance to get anything from him before he took off?"

"Nothing. He hightailed it out of there right when we arrived."

"We ran the plates. It's his wife's car, and she's been notified of the accident," Danny said.

Danny's cell rang. He lifted it from the case on his belt. It was the M.E. calling to let him know that she had emailed him a copy of the preliminary autopsy report on the last victim. She would continue to collect trace evidence and would advise him later. Danny thanked her and ended the call. He then relayed the information to Stone. Reading emails on his phone was always a challenge. He could deal with text messages, but he was too clumsy with his fingers to navigate through emails without frustration. He tossed the phone at Stone.

"Find her email. See if there's anything useful."

"Where the hell's Murphy when we need him?"

"Good idea, call him. You're no better than me with that thing."

Over the last week, Danny had received a crash course in serial killers from the FBI. Via phone, he sat through the lecture on nature versus nurture. Were serial killers born with defective DNA or was it a learned reaction? A combination of both was the unanimous and official stance from the FBI. It was time to share.

"Something triggered him. Something happened that escalated him," Danny explained.

"Like what?"

"Like the media monopolizing the airways and the Internet with the details of his kills. He's either agitated by that, or it's feeding his ego."

"The FBI hasn't figured it all out yet?"

"Relax, they're helping."

"They'll take all the credit, you'll see."

"Probably, but if this doesn't end soon we'll take all the blame."

Danny hated when he sounded political. As a rookie, he swore he would never cave. He would find another way. Experience, and his captain, had taught him that politics had a useful place in the system.

Stone waved him off, discounting the FBI's potential value.

"Murphy cross-checked the victims' credit cards, cell and home phones, places of employment, and interviewed families and friends. We found no real links between the victims," Danny said.

Stone shrugged.

"It means that the killer is probably killing the same person over and over again, searching for satisfaction or revenge, maybe closure. In his head, these women are all the same person," Danny said.

"Isn't it always because of the mother?" Stone asked.

Danny picked up a checklist he had prepared a short while earlier and read aloud the tasks for his team. When he was finished, he said, "Guys, this is our number one priority. Report back to me immediately with anything."

Danny called Raina to update her on Harvey.

"Hi Babe. I'm on my way there now to see Jean and Sloan," Raina said.

"Stay away from Harvey's room," Danny said.

Raina's misguided confidence was one of the things Danny was attracted to but also one of the things that made him worry. With officers stationed outside the room and Harvey secured to the bed, even if he became conscious, he couldn't hurt anyone but himself. He would still rather not have to worry about Raina.

"He's in custody, right?"

"Raina."

"I'll be fine."

CHAPTER 19

Raina parked in the appropriate lot at the hospital and made the all-too-familiar march inside. Three elevators came and left before she was able to get on one. Visitors buzzed in and out. Doctors stepped off the elevators, paired in deep discussions. Patients were being wheeled on and off.

First visit was to Jean. When she arrived at the room, Jean was lying in the bed looking peaceful, and someone, she assumed a relative, was sitting on the chair by the bed reading a book. Tyler wasn't there. *A visit to Sloan then*, she thought.

Sloan's eyes widened the moment she saw Raina, and she exploded into a rant, arms flailing. Raina expected a nurse or someone to hear the commotion and come in to calm her. How couldn't they hear her? But no one showed up.

"I'm so glad to see you. They are driving me crazy, keeping me prisoner. I keep telling them there's nothing wrong with me or the baby, but they won't release me. All the test results have come back fine except for one that was inconclusive, so they started doing more tests. Paul thinks I need to be here. He's afraid for me and the baby, but I'm telling you nothing is wrong. I feel it. Please, please do something. I can't stand being stuck here. It's boring. It's lonely. I'm going insane."

"Maybe..."

"No, Raina. I know you think that it's my hormones, but I need to get out of here. I need to get back to my life and my freedom. There nothing wrong except that I don't belong in here."

Raina took two slow steps backwards towards the door to try to get someone's attention without taking her eyes off Sloan, but still no one noticed her or appeared to hear Sloan. She would have to find something to say that would be calming enough for the moment. Nothing came to mind.

"Are you listening to me?" Sloan positioned herself at the edge of the bed ready to lift off it.

"Yeah. Where are you going?"

"Come on, I need to walk."

"You're supposed to be in bed."

"They don't literally mean I can't leave the bed. How do you think I go to the bathroom?"

Raina lifted her eyebrows and shoulders in unison.

No one stopped them, and the stroll around the halls calmed Sloan down.

Sloan leaned against the wall. "Sorry, it probably *is* the hormones, but it doesn't help to be trapped in this place."

"Do you really believe that you're fine?"

"Yeah, but they're waiting for results on more tests."

"Think you can get on an elevator?"

"Are you going to break me out of here?"

"Let's go find Harvey," Raina said then explained.

"Lead on."

It wasn't much of a challenge to locate Harvey's room. The elevator door opened, and they saw two uniformed officers seated on hard plastic chairs not far away. One chair was positioned on either side of the door outside a room. Raina recognized one of the officers and headed straight for him.

"Hey Jimmy," she said.

"Raina. What are you doing here?" he asked.

"I'm visiting a friend down the hall. How's Harvey doing?"

"Harvey?"

She put her hands on her hips and shook her head. "Harvey Shore. The man you're guarding."

"How do you know him?"

"He's my boss. Danny told me he was here and asked me to check on him."

"Somehow I doubt that."

"Okay, well how is he?"

"Don't know, Raina, I'm not the doctor."

"Come on," she pushed.

"Really, I don't know. I didn't even know his name until you told me."

Dissatisfied, Raina thanked him and turned around. Sloan had moved across the way and seated herself on a small sofa in one of the rooms designed for family that spent extensive hours at the hospital.

"You okay?"

"Just tired. You try lugging this thing around all day," she said with her arms cradling her belly.

Raina would have loved to someday soon, but she did not let herself head down that rocky road of thoughts.

"Wait here a minute. I'll be right back."

Raina continued to the nurse's station to find out the latest about Jean. She claimed to be a cousin-in-law, and the nurse told her everything. Raina caught herself before her jaw dropped. Jean had been pregnant, but she had miscarried.

"She developed a urinary tract infection most likely caused by the catheterization. Sometimes UTIs are caused by the pregnancy as well. The cause wasn't clear, but the result was the same," the nurse said.

The woman's sterile manner affected Raina. She imagined that the nurse's detachment was a learned skill used to protect medical professionals from the pain of the horrible things they saw every day, but still, it would have been more comforting if she had faked some compassion. It was a good thing that Sloan wasn't with her. That would have been the last thing she needed to hear about right now.

Raina thought about the repercussions of what she had learned. Jean had lost her baby, and she didn't know, or maybe she did, but couldn't express it consciously. Tyler would have to tell her when she woke. He must be devastated. She wondered if they had planned this baby. He hadn't mentioned it. She knew they were ready and that they would make excellent parents.

Raina walked back down the hall, popped her head in Jean's room, and saw the woman still seated in the chair engrossed in her book. No Tyler. She hurried back to Sloan and got her back to bed.

"Would you get my laptop out from that drawer?" Sloan pointed. "I did some digging like you asked. There's nothing on Harvey but a DUI and some parking tickets."

"That's all Murphy found, too."

"I'll keep searching, but there's not much else I can do."

Sloan closed her laptop and leaned back against the pillow. Raina left as soon as Sloan dozed off. She headed to Jean's room and met Tyler on the way. He greeted her without his usual charming smile.

"The nurse told me. I'm so sorry Tyler." She hugged him.

He held her a little too long, but she couldn't resist. With his body against hers, she felt his muscles and breathed in his scent. Tyler made the effort to pull away first which left Raina embarrassed.

Even with the bright, florescent lights reflecting off the hospital-white walls, busy staff traffic, and Danny's cops around, she felt too comfortable in Tyler's arms.

"Do they have any evidence against Harvey?" he asked, breaking her thoughts.

"Circumstantial."

"Like what?"

"Like he was the last one seen with two of the victims. He has the business card of a third DB on his desk. He ran from the cops which is how he got here."

"He's here?"

"Yeah, Danny sent detectives over to his house to talk to him and he ran. They chased him all the way to Smithtown where he crashed into a police roadblock."

"Holy shit, is he okay?" Tyler asked.

"I can't get any info from the cops by his door, and I already told the nurses…" She trailed off as she realized that she was about to expose herself as an imposter.

"If you need any more help, I'm in," Tyler said.

"Excellent. By the way, who is that in with Jean?"

"That's her Aunt Cynthia. We don't get along well, so I'm avoiding too much time with her. She comes once a week to be with Jean. In the past, Jean kept the conversation going without Cynthia and me having to speak to each other." He paused and didn't go there. "It's a real skill Jean perfected."

Everything she knew about Tyler made it difficult to imagine him not getting along with someone. He never bothered to introduce them or acknowledge the aunt's presence beyond his non-explanation. When Raina left, she intentionally took the long way around to the elevators to pass by Harvey's room again.

"Danny send you again?" Officer Jimmy asked.

"Any changes?"

"Still lying there."

CHAPTER 20

After some convincing on Raina's part, Danny agreed to take a break from his endless hours at work for a game of tennis. A quick hour of exercise, rallying the ball, fresh air and sunshine would be good for both of them. Tennis was one of the few times during which Raina was purely focused on one thing: controlling the yellow fuzzy ball with accuracy and power. It was also a time when she and Danny always connected.

The sun beat down and heat rose up from the court, causing sweat to drip from their bodies before they ever swung their rackets. Danny pulled up the bottom of his shirt to wipe his face, then peeled back the metal seal on a can of balls, producing the distinct pop as the gasses were released from the airtight can.

"Ready?" he asked.

She held the racket in front of her and bounced on her toes. "Fire away."

The ball sailed back and forth over the net as they warmed up their muscles. Soon Danny's swings began to pick up power, and Raina adjusted her game. He abandoned the friendly rally and added killer angles to his shots, running Raina around the court. For a while, she was able to return his shots and even win a few points. The competition stepped up a few levels. Danny got more aggressive. He attacked the ball with all his power. The guaranteed connection Raina expected melted away with each shot. She served him the ball but then didn't bother to move or try to make contact with his returns. Pounding the ball from across the court, Danny was miles away from Raina. She felt alone on the court.

Mid game, she walked off the court with her head down. She sat on the narrow concrete base under the fence and twisted off a plastic bottle cap. When she remained there longer than necessary, Danny motioned for her to get up. She didn't want to play that game anymore. Without words, he lifted his arms in question.

"There's no point if you're going to whale the ball at me like that," she said.

When he didn't respond, she continued. "What's your problem?"

"I could ask you the same question."

Danny downed half a bottle of water and sat too far away from her for her liking. The birds were chirping, a few cars passed by, kids were playing an unorganized game of soccer on the field near the courts, a cool breeze intermittently blew by, but they didn't speak. It was tearing Raina apart inside, but she didn't know what to do. Try to talk to him, leave him alone. Either could ignite a fight, and that was the last thing she wanted.

The standoff ended when Danny scooted next to her. She rubbed his leg and left her hand there, hoping to soothe him or reconnect or at least show she cared. He put his arm round her and pulled her close.

She took a chance and broke the silence. "Is it the case?"

He nodded.

"Can I do anything?"

"I'm sorry for ruining the afternoon, but I have to get back to work."

The brief car ride home was another disappointment to Raina. His job had become more invasive to their relationship, maybe a convenient excuse for Danny to hide behind. Raina refused to give up on him, but words were hard to produce. When her house came into view, she knew it was her last opportunity to pierce the veil Danny had created on the court.

As he pushed the gearshift into park, Raina stalled. "Wait."

Danny made eye contact and remained quiet.

"Talk to me."

"I told you everything about the case."

Raina tilted her head. "I know, but I meant how you're feeling."

"Feeling? Try frustrated and pissed off." He twisted his head away from her.

"But you have Harvey in custody."

"Just because he ran doesn't mean he's the killer. His DNA is being tested now to see if it matches the skin under the Real Estate Agent's nails. Even if it does, that's not enough to convict him. This isn't over. Not even close."

"The press...."

Danny cut her off. "The press? The press reported him dead. Soon as they realize that's not the case, I'm sure they'll try to blame us for misleading them. Either way, it's still our burden to get proof. My captain's all over my ass. So's the chief. The press will join them soon."

She had never seen him so distraught or stressed. Each time she tried to say something soothing it backfired, so she kept quiet.

Danny halfheartedly hugged her and promised to call later. She gave him a kiss and hopped out of the truck. She hadn't made it to the edge of the driveway when Danny's tires spun away.

Wheels rattled against the hospital equipment cart as staff charged by Danny, Stone, and Hawkeye. They paced the hospital corridor after having received the call that Harvey was in and out of consciousness, waiting for the doctors to give them access to their suspect. According to the nurse, he wasn't coherent. Danny was there as the lead, Hawkeye as the human lie detector, and Stone, well, Danny knew there was no way Stone would miss such an opportunity, and Danny could use all the help he could get.

Stone pared off from his team to give a young nurse his attention while Hawkeye maintained his post at Danny's side. When the nurse scooted off, Stone angled himself to watch her from behind. Danny shook his head.

"Anything?" Danny asked an aide exiting Harvey's room.

"Nothing yet," he answered without stopping.

Danny went over to the nurse's station and stood tall and authoritative. "I'm Lieutenant Smith, SCPD working with the FBI. I need to speak to Harvey Shore."

"I understand, but they're trying to stabilize him right now."

He was prepared to debate with the nurse, but before he could respond, a doctor joined him, extended a hand, and introduced himself. Dr. Reed was average height. He had dark skin, dark hair, and made short flickers of eye contact. It was an odd quality, and Danny wondered what Hawkeye would read from that.

"You can go in now for a few minutes, but try not to agitate him. He needs all his strength to heal," the doctor said.

They marched, three cops wide, across the newly buffed floor to Harvey's room. Dr. Reed traveled behind them.

The doctor cut in front and held up his hand. "Only one of you can go in. He's weak," he said.

Stone contorted his face. "There were just three people in there working on him, so please don't give me that crap. We're going in."

"He's my patient, and I'm responsible for him," Dr. Reed protested, but not beyond words.

The cops ignored the warning and entered into the room. Harvey was attached to endless tubes. Machines hummed and were lit up with colored lights, some blinked. The walls were cold white except for the dirt smudges near the light switch. A wall-mounted television hung in the corner. It wasn't a peaceful or relaxing environment for healing, and Danny felt a bit nauseous from it.

"He can't respond verbally with that fat tube in his mouth. We're going to have to ask yes or no questions. He can nod his head or use his fingers to respond," Danny said.

"No problem, this freak can read minds." Stone pointed to Hawkeye.

"Not exactly." Hawkeye had a highly developed skill, but it wasn't mindreading.

"Same shit," Stone said. "I have to say, you've been mark-on so far."

Danny raised his eyebrows in surprise at the rare compliment from Stone.

Harvey's eyes were open and focused beyond the police. One wrist remained cuffed to the bed, which was slightly raised to angle him up. He had a lot of scrapes and bruises, and his scraggly beard had grown in.

Danny began by saying, "Harvey, do you remember running from these guys on my left?" He cocked his head towards them.

Harvey strained to focus on Stone and Hawkeye. Very carefully and slowly, he shook his head.

"Do you remember being in a car accident?"

Again, he gingerly shook his head.

"Do you know where you are?"

This time he nodded his head up and down. Danny turned to Hawkeye for verification. Hawkeye confirmed with a slight tilt of the head downward.

Stone challenged him. "How can you tell with the tape on his face pulling his skin?"

Hawkeye ignored him.

Danny pulled the crime photos of the last victim, Alexis Koslov, from an envelope and showed two to Harvey. "Do you recognize this girl?"

Harvey stared without a response. It was unclear if he had recognized her.

Danny punched the photos closer to Harvey's face. "Do you remember this girl?"

Harvey's eyes rolled up into his head. His body began to thrash and set off an alarm from one of the machines. Two middle-aged nurses barreled in. They nudged the cops out of the way and coldly suggested they exit the room. Dr. Reed dashed down the hall and glared at them as he stormed by.

"We got nothing from that except that he has memory loss," Danny said.

"Or it's an act," Stone said.

"He wasn't lying," Hawkeye said.

"What about when Danny showed him the picture and he went into seizures?"

"I think it was a reaction to his medical situation, not the question."

"But it could have initiated the seizure," Danny said.

"You'd have to ask the doc about that," Hawkeye said.

Danny hovered nearby, and every minute or so, he re-checked the situation. He was right there when Dr. Reed finished with his patient, hoping to be able to continue the line of questioning. Danny wanted, needed, was desperate for some information, evidence, or even better, a confession. Some serial killers wanted to be caught and stopped, he had learned from his recent and abbreviated FBI training. A straightforward confession probably wasn't in the cards, but he would accept anything at that moment. The frequency of calls from his captain had increased. The press was out of control.

Dr. Reed rested his fingers on his face and spoke. "He's stable again. He'll...."

The trio wasted no time and hurried back to the room.

"Wait," Dr. Reed raised his hand to stop them again. "You can't go in there."

"You said he was stable," Danny said.

"He is, but he's not conscious. He needs to rest."

Danny shook his head and mumbled, "Waste of time."

"Not totally." Stone held up a small piece of paper with a phone number on it.

"The nurse's number?" Hawkeye rolled his dark eyes.

CHAPTER 21

Michael and Charlie were seated at the bar at the 56 Fighter Group for happy hour. The place was on the site where the P47 fighter aircraft was built during WWII. Rustic timbered ceilings hung above the cozy dining rooms that overlooked the runway. The walls of photos intrigued Michael with proud looking, uniformed fighter pilots from the past and the memorabilia that was all around.

"What do you think it was like to fly an old propeller plane?" he asked Charlie.

Charlie was more interested in the two girls that were headed their way from across the dining room.

"Hi," one girl said.

She was beyond petite. Her friend would have seemed petite on her own. Next to her friend though, she appeared tall. Michael dwarfed them both.

He quickly assessed the situation and without hesitation invited the girls to join them for dessert. He stood up and slid a chair from under the table for one of them. Charlie jerked his body upwards to do the same. During the conversation, they learned that the girls, Lisa and Robin, shared an apartment with a third. All three roommates were attending SUNY Farmingdale. They were working with small theater groups for almost no money while on summer break.

"Want to come over for drinks?" Robin asked.

"Yeah, Tracy is there with some friends," Lisa said.

Charlie turned to Michael. "Okay with you, dude?"

"Great with me." Charlie's blue eyes lit up with excitement.

Michael took care of the check, and they headed out together to the girls apartment nearby in Farmingdale. When they arrived at the apartment, it was dark and still. It hardly seemed as though anyone was home, never mind a party.

"Maybe they went somewhere else," Lisa said. "I'll call her."

Lisa had already unlocked the door and swung it open.

"Doesn't look like anyone was here," Robin said.

"Come in and have a seat. We'll be right back," Lisa said and pulled Robin by the arm.

The guys sat on the worn sofa and looked over the apartment. It was small and sparsely furnished except for half a dozen racks of clothes crowding the rooms. Many days' worth of dishes were piled in the sink, and no artwork decorated the walls.

An earsplitting scream came from the back of the apartment. Charlie and Michael jumped up from the couch and ran to investigate. It was Lisa. She was still screaming and shaking a girl on the bed, and Robin was dialing 9-1-1 with tears in her eyes. They heard her report that Tracy wasn't breathing and saw her lifeless body. Charlie tried to calm Lisa down by wrapping his arm around her back. She became quiet and went into shock, so he helped her to the sofa and offered her some water. Michael led Robin away from the body and closed the door behind them.

"We'll wait with you until the police come," Michael said. He knew it was the right thing to do but wished they had never followed the girls home.

They all squeezed onto the three-cushion sofa. Robin stared into space with her arms crossed and rocked back and forth. Lisa's tiny hands trembled. It seemed like hours until the police arrived, followed closely by the ambulance. One EMT explained to Michael that they had strict instructions from dispatch to confirm death and not to touch the victim unless the girl was alive. Unfortunately, he confirmed her death.

"Why?" Michael asked.

"SCPD set up a direct line for 9-1-1 operators to call and report any deaths that fit the description of the Morphine Murderer. Everyone knows about him."

Michael slipped out to the building hallway and made a call. "Raina, is Harvey still in the hospital?"

"Yeah, as far as I know. Why?"

"Then he's not the killer."

"How do you know?"

He told her about the latest DB and then Michael abruptly hung up. He suddenly realized that Harvey wasn't the only one connected to two of the dead bodies. So was he. The first girl had attended his party, and now he was standing inside the second one's apartment. Since Harvey was still in custody and under guard, he couldn't have killed the latest victim. Harvey was cleared, and Michael would quickly become the next suspect. He went back inside to sit with Charlie with his hands in his pockets to hide the shaking.

Michael whispered to Charlie, "How long do you think she's been dead?"

"No idea, dude."

Michael knew it wasn't his place to question, but he had to find out. Raina would be impressed, and he might be able to clear himself. "Robin." He pulled her closer inside a one armed hug. "When did you see Tracy last?"

Robin began to sob again, catching the attention of a female officer who came over. Michael backed off.

Two detectives entered, and the four guys exchanged a series of looks of recognition.

"We saved your asses in the club fight. What are you doing here?" he asked and identified himself as Detective Stone and the other as Officer Lorenzo.

"We came with those girls." Michael pointed at Lisa and Robin. "The girl was dead when we got here. If you want to know anything else, you'll have to ask them. We just met tonight."

Stone glanced at Hawkeye who nodded. Michael knew he must have looked guilty because the second detective was staring at him.

"Don't mind him. He's just reading your mind."

Michael didn't know what to make of that, but he wanted to have a moment alone to call Raina.

"Did you touch her?" Stone asked.

"One of the girls shook her after she found her on the bed."

"Shit."

Michael watched for his opportunity while the M.E. examined the body. From her little black dress, heels, and smoky makeup, Michael wasn't the only one whose night had changed direction for the worse.

"You're a much better sight to see than Garza," the detective said.

The M.E. carefully examined the body with her magnifying glass. She told the detective that she had found a small drop of dried blood where the needle had been inserted.

"Calculated by her liver temperature, the girl's been dead about four hours," the M.E. said.

Four hours ago, Harvey was still cuffed to the bed, unconscious in the hospital, guarded 24/7. Harvey would be officially cleared for this murder.

"I'll get her back to the morgue and call Danny with the preliminary results." The M.E. handed a business card to Detective Stone. "My cell is on the back."

"I can see it, you know," Hawkeye said.

"See what?"

"She wants you."

"Yeah, what gave that away? Did you need your woman's intuition tell you that?"

Michael listened to the cops banter until the body was loaded onto the gurney and rolled out to the ambulance. That was his chance to call Raina. He backed himself into a corner behind a rack of clothes and quietly made the call. A lot had happened that night. He had gone from a carefree college student on summer break, about to get lucky, to a potential murder suspect - although he wasn't sure that the cops had made the connection yet.

They were all voluntarily escorted to the precinct for questioning.

CHAPTER 22

Immediately after the end of Michael's call, Raina called Danny.

"It wasn't Harvey!"

It took her under eight seconds to recount the night's events.

"I heard from Stone, and I'm on my way in," Danny said.

"He has to be guilty of something," she said.

"He's guilty of a lot, but that's not my concern right now. I called Blainey, the FBI consultant working with us. With another potential body, he decided to join us in person. He reorganized his priorities and booked the next flight from DC, and he'll be here early in the morning."

Raina heard the car door close and then the precinct door creak open as Danny stormed through it. Then she heard the bustling of the precinct.

"Why are you here?" She heard Danny ask, and then she heard Michael's voice.

"Michael's there?" Raina asked.

Danny didn't respond, but the call remained connected. She heard Michael give him the short version of the evening's events and then receive instructions to stay put. At this point, Raina was sure that Danny had gotten sidetracked and hadn't realized he had never ended the call.

"You know him?" She heard Stone ask.

"One of Raina's friend's brother. You know Sloan?"

"Hot chick. Long, blonde hair?"

"And married and pregnant," Danny said.

"You know him?" She heard a female voice ask.

"Yeah, he's dating my sister's friend."

"Danny," Raina said. There was dead silence on the other end of the phone.

Whether Danny hit the button or the service faded, she wasn't sure. Either way, the call was disconnected, and she had heard enough to know what was going on at the precinct. Last she had spoken to Michael, he was in the dead girl's apartment. He had asked her not to tell Sloan because he didn't want his sister under any more stress than necessary. But now what? She'd have to get more facts. Was he being held or was he just in for questioning?

It was a short drive back to the hospital after she picked up their favorite pasta dinner, but she had to figure out what to do about Michael and what she would reveal to Sloan before she got there.

As the front doors slid open, Raina debated her next move. She slowed her pace, let a couple of not quite filled elevators go, and hoped that Danny would call her with information before she faced Sloan. How could she discuss the case and not mention the last victim? Certainly, Sloan had heard about it by now. Maybe she already knew about Michael, too.

Paul greeted her at the door and relieved Raina of the brown shopping bags that held their dinner. She slid the wheeled table in front of Sloan.

"I'm starved," Sloan said and then tore through the containers, stuffing food into her mouth.

Paul took care of the clean-up from dinner and then left them to make a phone call.

"He's probably off to see if he can convince them to find another test to run on me or Christine."

"You named the baby Christine?"

"I'm trying it out, seeing how it sounds." Sloan adjusted her position and the maternal expression disappeared from her face. "I can't believe Michael was with the DB. That's two now, you know. He's at the precinct. So are Charlie and some girls they were with."

That was relief to Raina's ears, and the rest of her body, mind, and soul.

"How do you know?"

"Some habits die slow. Been hacking around the police network and found a preliminary report."

"There's no written report this quickly. Murphy called you?"

"He owed me one, or ten. Professional courtesy or whatever you want to call it. What have you heard from Danny?"

"Not much, but I'll find out more when he's done there."

"I'm not too worried. I know that Michael's not a killer." Sloan paused, then shifted gears. "More inconclusive news on Levy. Weeks prior to his wife's death, there were a slew of inbound and outbound calls to a disposable cell number."

"Can you narrow down the location of the calls? Does the cell have GPS?"

"There hasn't been any activity in the past week or so. Probably has a new one. I might be able to find out a location from when the calls went through, but Murphy can do it faster."

"Don't get him in trouble with Danny."

"Please. I know Danny's great and all, but you think he monitors Murphy's computer or knows what he's doing half the time? No way. Danny can't even operate his cell to a fraction of its potential. Please, he...."

Raina interrupted her. It sounded like she was about to launch into another rant.

"I thought this case was solved, but since it's not Harvey, there's still a killer out there," Raina said.

"And you have a plan?" Sloan asked.

"*Mission Funeral Part 2.*"

*M*ission *Funeral Part 2* was about to kick into action. All the components of the funeral ensemble were together in the front of the closet. No time was wasted with preparation. Raina arrived at the morning burial for the sixth victim, Tracy Reid, early enough to see who arrived together and who slithered in after it had begun. Probably no one would mysteriously saunter over from within the sea of gravestones, but she was prepared just in case. Since it had served her well previously, she spent time in the car snapping pictures and taking thorough notes before someone else noticed *she* was the uncomfortable loner in the crowd of mourners.

Raina stood among a small group of people that were loosely knit together unlike the ones closest to the ceremony, who she imagined to be close family and dear friends. Two of them were holding onto each other, one woman sobbing. Two others were standing alone but without shifty eyes. Their discomfort seemed to be genuine. Across from them was the only person that seemed out of place: a tall man, dressed in a poorly fitted suit, and wearing dark glasses with light silver rims. The contrast of the metal drew attention to the darkness of the lenses. Raina continued to glance over at him. She couldn't see his eyes. He wasn't shifting in place. He also wasn't connecting with anyone there. No words, no comforting touches, no acknowledgement from others indicating that they knew him. He stood in the second row, stoically.

Raina dropped her head as the man returned her glance. The priest's words began to resonate with her while her sight was on the freshly cut grass beneath her feet. It was dark, lush green. Would she be standing over her parents soon or her Grandma Ida? She hadn't seen her parents in months and resolved to call them that night and make plans for a long weekend to visit them. Raina made more frequent trips to visit her parents in the cooler months because Florida was too hot in the summertime. The summer weeks had passed quickly, and she hadn't thought about when her next visit would be. Tears trickled down her face. She fumbled with objects inside her bag, and the woman next to her handed her a tissue. Raina nodded in gratitude.

The woman leaned on her cane and placed her other hand on Raina's forearm. "She was our grand-niece, a very special young woman."

Raina felt a rush of heat shoot through her body. Her mouth became dry, and she could only think to apologize for their loss. Her mission was falling apart. She had her hands clasped together and looked around for an escape. It came in the form of a heavyset man. He strained as he walked over to the elderly couple, taking an audible breath with every step. Raina saw their connection, and then the woman extended her cane-free arm to him. Beyond him, Raina saw the man in the light rimmed glasses walking diagonally across the way towards the line of cars.

It was time for Raina to go. She rushed back to her car. Speeding by the mourners, she trailed behind the prospective suspect and recorded his license plate number. Her foot had lifted unknowingly from the brake. When she realized her car was moving, she instinctively stomped on the brakes, and the tires squealed to an abrupt stop. The man checked his rearview mirror. Embarrassed, Raina waved at him apologetically and hoped he would drive on. *It was feasible that the driving skills of a distraught mourner would become temporarily impaired,* she thought. She sighed with relief when he drove off, and then she made the first possible turn in order to get away from him. The turn led her through the cemetery before coming back around to the street.

Raina spread her funeral photos across the table and studied them. Everyone was dressed in black. Some had their heads down. Many were holding onto each other. As the pictures progressed, there were people comforting each other, sometimes changing partners as family and friends had moved about. Then she saw him: the guy in the light rimmed glasses. She rearranged the photos in a frenzy. He was alone in each of them, no contact with another person. She shivered as she viewed the last photo. He was glaring right at the camera. His eyes burned through his dark lenses straight to Raina. He had seen her all the way from his position, through the crowd to her car. There was no denying it. He had spotted her.

She wrangled her emotions and refocused on the mission.

"Sloan, what are you doing?"

"Just some work for Paul on the computer. Why?"

"Can you run a license plate?"

Raina could practically hear the big grin through the phone. "I can."

"It's a NY plate. Alpha six two...." She read the rest of the plate number from her notepad. It would take a little while to hack into the DMV, and then Sloan would call her with the information.

The photos from the first funeral were filed away. When she added them to the table, she searched for a common face. It was there. She couldn't imagine how she had missed him the first time. The man with the light rimmed glasses was off to the side. With the twist of her stomach muscles, she knew there was only one logical conclusion. He was the killer, and she had to call Danny.

"Smith."

Raina reported her suspicions in one hurried breath. She shared all the details and emailed him some photos, one that included the suspect's plate number.

"Murphy," he called out. "I'm forwarding you an email. Check it."

She heard Murphy acknowledge Danny.

"We're going to discuss this later. You can't be doing this and... hold on." Danny focused elsewhere. "I've gotta call you back. Please stay out of trouble until I do."

Raina changed out of her funeral outfit and went into work late. She tried to be productive, but her case was foremost on her mind. She sifted through a pile on her desk, straightened the piles on the cabinet, and listened to her voicemails.

The police sirens played from her phone at the edge of her desk. "What did you find out?" she asked.

"Something very interesting," Danny said.

"Tell me, what is it?"

"We got the name from the plate. The car is registered to Lehan's Funeral Parlor. The same funeral parlor that arranged the funeral."

Raina thought about the man's emotionless face.

"Well, did they find anything I sent you useful?"

"Not yet. They were following another lead. We had a plainclothes officer attend as well. You know David Finasky?"

"I don't think so."

"He didn't know you either, but he spotted a suspicious person at two of the burials. A woman. Dressed all in black. Alone. She separated herself from the line of cars and drove the long way through the cemetery."

"Which two?"

"Lucky for you, Finasky managed a discreet but poor quality photo with his phone." He paused. "Not blurry enough that I couldn't identify you."

Raina knew what was coming next.

"First off, you had no business putting yourself in danger. What if that guy hadn't been a funeral home employee and was the killer? Why would you want him knowing you exist? Secondly," he said without a pause, "I don't need you creating problems for me here. How do you think it looks when I have to explain why the time they spent watching you was a waste? And why you were even there? Please, Babe."

Of course she didn't want to make him look bad, but she had no intention of aborting her investigation. "Okay, Danny. I hear you."

A funeral home employee? And how did I miss the cop? Her mind spun out of control reliving every moment of both funeral missions.

Raina had to take on some of Harvey's work while he was in recovery. The typical, high energy in the office was absent, and it continued to disrupt Raina's concentration. Each time she tried to focus, the quiet led her to think about the case, about her and Danny, about the kiss with Tyler, and about Harvey lying in the hospital bed. She had known him for years, and with all his faults, Raina had never imagined he was capable of murder. The evidence had led her to that conclusion, but it had been wrong. She had been wrong. How was he going to treat her when he returned to work from the hospital? Did he know she made the initial connection? Would he blame her for ending up in the hospital? Would he be revengeful? Would she even have a job?

She checked her emails. Five had arrived since she had checked an hour before. Two were second notices of invoices to be paid, one was a request for additional documentation for a warehouse credit application, one was a salesperson who apparently didn't watch the news, complaining that Harvey hadn't returned his calls or emails. The last one was an offer to sell some drug, so she could "please your woman all night long." *Delete, delete, save, delete* and *delete*. Seemingly, the bill for the spam filter hadn't been paid either.

The news! Raina put aside a small pile of papers, opened her Morphine Murderer spreadsheet, which hadn't been updated with the latest murder, and clicked over to the news and triggers section. An interview with two teenagers about the loss of their mother had caught her attention. There had been a surge in drug overdoses in the last few months. Raina pulled all the related articles and looked for a pattern.

"That's it!" she said aloud.

"That's what?" Tyler stepped inside her office.

Raina noticed how the ceiling light highlighted the top of his blonde hair and shadowed his square jaw.

"How do you just happen by at the right times?" Raina asked.

"I was at the hospital. Harvey's conscious, and he says he has no idea what happened."

"Do you believe him?" she asked.

"Hard to tell with him. How often is he telling the truth?"

"Good point."

"Did you ask him why he ran from the police if he wasn't guilty?"

"I did, and he gave a typical Harvey non-answer," Tyler said and then his demeanor changed. "Do you have time to come by the hospital on the way home today?"

"Sure."

He smiled and left her to her spreadsheet.

The sight of Tyler, his scent, his charm, and the heat inside her, which rose each time he was near, had one of two effects: either thoughts of him overtook her completely or she immediately started thinking about Danny. This time the confidence in his stance made her think about Danny. She felt secure in his arms. Partly driven by guilt, partly by desire, she called him, and it went straight to voicemail. She spun her Tiffany bracelet.

The link between the drug-related overdose victims and the timing of the murders resurfaced when she hit a key to halt the screen saver. There had been a highly publicized drug overdose shortly before each murder, and she was on the verge of making that connection the moment before Tyler sent her into an emotional tizzy.

CHAPTER 23

"Lovin' you New Yorkers, mate. Pushed right by me to exit the plane. No apologetic words or friendly faces until I got to the baggage claim where I was swarmed by your car service drivers trying for a fare," Agent Blainey said to Danny.

"I have a unit on the way to pick you up. He's ten minutes out."

"No bother. I accepted a ride from one of these fine gents."

Early the next morning they were finally face-to-face in Danny's office. Special Agent Blainey made Danny's six feet feel short, even as Blainey sat in the lower chair on the other side of Danny's desk. His big features matched his large, square, Frankenstein-like head. Only in Blainey's case, he was missing the screws, and his mustache threw off the whole look. They reviewed the details of each crime scene, each victim and circumstance, the few connections, the suspect gone cold, and then planned their next move. With six murders and no viable connections, Danny welcomed the help.

"We'll get this bloody killer," Blainey said.

"We need to take him down before his next kill," Danny said.

"No worries, mate."

Later that day, Blainey spoke with the detectives on the case separately. He reported back to Danny that in his meeting with Hawkeye, he had learned that Hawkeye had been temporarily appointed detective, his skills were sharpening quickly, and his thoughts were clear and organized. Hawkeye had spoken about the potential lead that he couldn't yet connect: the back room at the bar where he followed the first victim's husband and later Harvey.

"I encouraged him to follow his instinct, and he seemed relieved to hear that. Said that Detective Stone was constantly refocusing him. Speaking of Stone…."

Blainey continued to explain that Stone didn't refrain from showing his true personality right from the start.

"Why did they send you? What's wrong with our Long Island FBI friends?" Stone had asked.

"Since 9-11, the NY office has specialized in terrorism," Blainey explained.

Stone made it clear that he was an action guy. He wanted to aggressively hunt the killer. This was also reflected in Stone's file as Blainey read it, as were his highly rated detective skills and his dedication to the job. Although Stone often ignored procedure, he achieved the desired results just as often. Blainey's interest was piqued when he learned that Stone had returned early from vacation to be part of this case. Danny sat twirling his pen until Blainey was finished wasting Danny's time and decided to let him get back to the work at hand.

Danny had the receiver wedged between his shoulder and head and nodded at Stone as Stone took a seat across from Danny.

"What's up with the suit?" Stone asked. "I mean he's more like MI5 than FBI."

Blainey re-entered. "Hello, mates."

"Hey," Stone said, "what's with the accent?"

"Spent most of my life across the pond," Blainey said.

"Don't you have to be a citizen to be FBI?"

"Born and raised in California until the age of six when my father brought us back to England with dual citizenship. Began my career as an MI-5 Intelligence Officer and worked there until two years ago. I wanted to better utilize my Oxford degree in Psychology rather than working counterterrorism, which is now MI-5's primary focus. Anything else you'd like to know?"

"Nope," Stone said and disappeared out the door. Danny gestured for Blainey to follow and begin the address to the unit.

Agent Blainey educated the police on basic serial killer psychology and then shared the working profile for the Morphine Murderer. Danny stood at his side.

"He's a white male in his late twenties to early thirties, confident around women, and probably attractive. Women either allow or invite him into their homes without fear. He kills within a small radius, which defines his comfort zone. He's escalated as evidenced by the small amount of time between the last two killings. There had to be a stressor that caused the escalation. It could be the media attention. He hasn't yet reached out to contact either the authorities or the media. Expect that he will. Serial killers often like to insert themselves into the investigation. There could be more victims that we haven't connected yet. Keep your eyes open, and let's get him before he kills again."

Everyone received their assignments and dispersed. Blainey motioned to Danny to follow him back into his office.

"I wanted to discuss another possibility with you," Blainey said.

He closed the door after Danny was seated at his desk. Blainey stood towering and twisting his wedding band around his finger.

"What is it?" Danny asked.

"Please, mate, call me Gordon."

"Okay Gordon, what's up?"

"How well do you know Detective Stone?"

"Very well." He maintained constant eye contact. "He's been on the force for fourteen years. He's been a detective for nine of those, the last five under me."

Danny considered the clandestine accusation with disdain. It was Stone that had been the first to the scene when Danny's Officer Jesse was shot, a painful and still present memory. Even though kept his emotional connection to Stone well hidden, it was close to Danny's heart. There was no way that Stone could ever be a suspect.

"He returned early from vacation to work this case. Isn't that curious to you?"

"Not at all," Danny said, "and I'm grateful to have the help."

"He's a white male, average age group and...."

Danny's face reddened, and he stopped Blainey, "As is most of the police force."

"He fits the profile, and he's looking to control the direction of the investigation."

"No. I've controlled this investigation from the start." Danny vigorously tapped his pen on the desk.

"He spent a lot of time on the wrong suspect. It was my impression that he had made that connection."

"He didn't. We had information from…," he hesitated, "a CI."

Until then Danny hadn't held back any information on the case from Blainey. Now that Blainey was thinking that Stone might be the killer, Danny wasn't sure how to proceed. To rationalize, he went over the case in his mind, how they had begun with no suspect and had been led to Harvey. First, Sloan's brother, Michael, recognized a model from his party that Harvey had been nestled with, and the next morning she was dead. Second, the dancer that Michael and Charlie, as well as Stone and Hawkeye, had seen Harvey with at the club also wound up dead. And he hadn't forgotten the other victim's business card that Raina had seen on Harvey's desk. The car chase still had Harvey attached to tubes in the hospital. He ran from the cops. Danny felt reassured that he had sufficient information for Harvey to have been a suspect. When he played it again in his head, he noticed another connection: Michael.

"Think about it, mate, and keep an open mind," Blainey said.

Blainey was still pushing his theory and infuriating Danny. He refused to believe that Stone was anything less than a great cop. He had relied on John Stone for years, and his record spoke for itself as Blainey had seen. Danny trusted him, and he wasn't going to stop now. Plus, he owned a gun or three. Why would he need to use morphine? The conversation was over as far as Danny was concerned. Blainey seemed to accept that for the moment and retreated to an empty desk in the corner where they had set up a central station for the FBI.

Danny checked in with Murphy who was comparing the credit card transactions of the latest victim with the prior victims. With each additional body, he added information to his spreadsheet. He sorted the columns in every way possible but found no significant thread. Some victims had been to the same store or restaurant or gas station as another one or two others but nothing relevant. They already knew the victims lived close to each other, so the fact that there were overlapping locations was not a surprise.

Murphy raised his head from the screen. "Who doesn't go to Starbucks?"

"Understood. Murph, I need you to take a break from that and work on this," Danny said.

He handed Murphy a piece of paper with Michael's name and address and instructed him to do his thing. Murphy minimized Excel and searched through multiple databases for anything on Michael

Miller, starting with his arrest record, school records, his social network pages, and so on. Typically after his universal investigation, Murphy knew more about a person's life than they remembered about themselves. Danny rocked from side to side, standing next to Murphy.

"Nothing relevant popped up, but I'll deepen the search. Give me a few."

The desk Sergeant shouted over to Danny, "Big Boss on line two."

His eyes darted toward Blainey in the corner, then Danny stormed into his office and slammed the door.

"Blainey mentioned his theory on Stone."

"No way," Danny said with a force he had never used with a superior.

"Stand down Lieutenant. I'm with you on this."

CHAPTER 24

The first rays of light streamed through the sheer bedroom curtains while Raina slept.

"Smith," Danny answered in a whisper, trying not to disturb Raina.

He rolled off her bed, gathered his clothes from the floor, and got dressed. When he ran his palm across his jawline, he shrugged off a shave. Harvey Shore was conscious again and sufficiently stable to answer questions, and Danny wanted to be there as soon as he could. He jotted a quick note for Raina: *Babe, Harvey's awake – gone to the hospital – call you later.* On the way, Danny called Stone to update him, and then Hawkeye to have him meet him there. Harvey might not be the Morphine Murderer, but something wasn't right. He had run from the cops so fiercely that he had landed himself in the hospital.

The flashing lights in Danny's rearview and side mirrors and the abrupt siren blips were unmistakable.

He pursed his lips together and shook his head. *Highway patrol.*

He slowed and pulled off to the side of the Northern State Parkway, rolled down the window, and waited. The officer approached Danny's vehicle from behind and reacted when he saw the metal from Danny's badge reflected from inside the truck. Hand on his gun, he ordered Danny out of the car.

Knowing how it felt to be in the officer's place with unpredictable people on the road, he cooperated, slowly exited the car, hands in the air, badge in his hand.

"Lieutenant Daniel Smith, SCPD Homicide," he said to the officer.

When he moved his hand from his gun, Danny knew he recognized the badge.

"Sorry sir, you were speeding."

"I'm on my way to question a suspect."

The officer acknowledged Danny with a salute and returned to his vehicle.

When Danny was back in the truck, a text alert flashed on his phone. It was Raina. *Call me when you can. I missed you when I woke up.* He smiled, but he was still focused on the impending bedside interrogation and didn't return her text right away.

At the hospital, Danny rode the elevator with a nurse. As a chill shook his upper body and the distinctive odor of disinfectant mixed with sickness filled his nose, he recalled his brief counseling sessions. The only thing he had taken away from them was the ability to refocus his attention, specifically toward staff members around him in hospitals. Occasionally it worked. It was easier for him not to deal with the memories. The nurse's extra pounds stressed the material on her white uniform. Her hair was graying and tied in a bun, making her look older than her face alone suggested. The elevator sounded as the door opened onto his floor, setting his thoughts back on his task at hand. He smiled at the nurse, thanking her in his mind for the diversion.

Dr. Reed was standing by the nurse's station when Danny went by. Danny held up a hand to prevent the Doctor's anticipated protest.

"I won't agitate him too much," Danny said.

Dr. Reed nodded and picked up a chart.

Harvey was awake and alert. The tube had been removed from his mouth, and he was feeding himself some brown, not quite solid food from a plastic tray. The television was on mute, and a nurse was checking his vitals. She was so boney thin that Danny imagined the blood pressure pad, turned on her, would squeeze her arm until her humerus cracked.

"Pressure's good, Mr. Shore," the nurse said and left.

"Feeling better?" Danny asked.

"Yeah," Harvey said.

"Good. Wanna tell me why you ran from my detectives?"

"I didn't know they were your detectives."

Hawkeye joined them, and Harvey focused on his face.

"So you remember now?" Danny asked.

"I remember up until the crash. I remember driving, maybe speeding." He tried out a smile which didn't work on Danny, then continued. "Then I remember waking up attached to this bed." Harvey rubbed his wrists where the cuffs had been.

"Who did you think you were running from?"

"The private detective my wife hired. She thinks I'm cheating."

Danny checked with the human lie detector, who nodded affirmatively.

"Why would you think they were P.I.s? They weren't concealing their presence."

"I saw them watching me in the club last night." Harvey watched the constant exchange of looks between Danny and Hawkeye. "Then I saw them at my house."

"First of all, it wasn't last night. You've been here for a week."

"A week!" Harvey's voice was two octaves higher. Looking more confused than before, Harvey crinkled his forehead. "It wasn't one long night: the club, the car chase, and the hospital?"

"Try a week."

Danny detailed the timeline and events that had landed him in the hospital. Harvey's mind seemed to have jumbled some of the facts and certainly time. Still confined to the bed by tubes in his arms, Harvey reached for the call button.

"A roadblock," he said aloud to himself. Harvey's expression changed. "Am I in trouble?"

"A little bit. You ran from the cops. You were clocked at over a hundred miles per hour. You ran a young driver off the road. You totaled a police car. A little bit of trouble."

Harvey thought more. "What about my company?"

"Still operating."

"My wife?"

"Knows what happened."

Danny didn't need Hawkeye to see Harvey's anxiety rising. Harvey stared at the ceiling. The color drained from his face, and sweat beaded on his forehead.

"Why were your detectives following me?" Harvey asked.

"You were a murder suspect."

Harvey's eyes widened, and his jaw dropped, but no words formed.

Danny continued. "You remember the model you were with at Michael Miller's party? You were the last one to see her alive." As Michael's name crossed Danny's mind, he realized he hadn't heard from Murphy yet.

"And the dancer from the club was also last seen alive with you. Not to mention the real estate agent's business card on your desk who was also killed."

Danny immediately regretted revealing the last bit of information. He should have protected Raina from any involvement. Harvey could easily determine the source of that intel if he tried.

Harvey went mute. Danny wondered why, if he was innocent. Innocent was hardly a word to describe Harvey, but on the charge of murder, it seemed right. His wife, on the other hand, was onto him. In one night, his detectives had discovered enough evidence on Harvey's indiscretions to award his wife everything she wanted in a divorce. Surely the P.I. had too, and Danny knew there would be consequences for the car chase. He wasn't worried that Harvey would pay for his actions in many ways.

CHAPTER 25

With the FBI's blessing, Hawkeye sat at the bar in Kelly's partnered with a short glass of tonic water and lime. He ordered several appetizers and waited for something to happen. He still didn't know what it was, but there was a connection between the bar and the murders. That he was sure of. Since there were no other leads for him to follow, Danny had agreed to Hawkeye's request to follow it.

Hawkeye was prepared to take detailed notes on anyone or anything of interest. After hours of nothing, his cell phone rang, and he walked outside to take the call. It was his wife. He strolled over to the parking lot and went around the side of the building. It occurred to him that there had to be a back door. There was. It was closed, windowless, and tightly secured. He leaned against a car while he finished the conversation and watched as several young people went from their cars to the bar entrance around front. Something clicked in his head.

"Kathy, I have to go," he said.

Having spent so many hours in the bar, he knew every inch of it. He started at the front corner of the building and counted fifty-seven paces to the back. The math didn't add up. The bar area was thirty-one. To alleviate boredom, he had counted as patrons walked back and forth. The back room was no more than eight feet deep and that left eighteen paces. The walls might have added up to another foot which still left about seventeen unaccounted for. His calculations revealed that the back room was a gateway to a hidden room.

He tried to contain his excitement and not bolt towards the room. There had been a shift change, and a young female took over the bar duties. Her dark ponytail bounced from side to side as she turned her head. She busily reorganized the glasses and served a handful of drinks. When she was finished, she moved over to Hawkeye.

"What are you drinking?" she asked.

"I'm good, thanks," he said.

"Waiting for a friend?"

"Just drinking."

"Only working cops come in alone and avoid alcohol. Who you looking for?"

He shook his head.

"Yeah, let me know if you need anything."

She returned to her work, and he pushed open the door to the back room. He scanned the walls, but there wasn't another door. This wasn't a movie. Could there really be a camouflaged door to a hidden room?

"Lost?" the bartender asked.

"Head?"

"Next door." She pointed.

As Hawkeye exited the men's room, he spotted Stone and another guy come in together through the front door. They were laughing. Hawkeye slipped into a booth. The second guy, stocky with dark hair and wearing a baseball cap, leaned over the bar and whispered something to the bartender. She made a call and then directed them to the back room.

Hawkeye answered his phone.

"Blainey here. How's the investigation getting on?" he asked.

He reported to Blainey about the hidden room and Stone's arrival a few minutes before.

"Good," Blainey said. "Don't let him out of your sight, and don't bloody spook him. Can you get snaps?"

"Snaps, sir?"

"Photographs, mate."

More curious than why Stone was there was why Blainey wanted pictures of Stone. He could easily accomplish that. This could make his night, he thought. He tossed a few dollars on the table for a tip and went to his car. Intentionally parked away from the streetlights, he waited for Stone and his friend to emerge. His fingers were laced together as he tapped them on the steering wheel. Stone and the man had been in and out in less than ten minutes. Hawkeye couldn't clearly see the capped man's face as they jumped into Stone's car. When they were halfway down the block, Hawkeye started the engine and drove after them. Stone was driving slower than his usual NASCAR speed, stopping at lights, and using his turn signal. Hawkeye had only known him for a few weeks, but he knew enough to register the change in behavior. He followed a distance behind for about twenty minutes. Hawkeye mentally logged the route. The car was stopped, pulled by the curb, and Stone and the capped man exited the car. Hawkeye cut the engine and headlights and quietly coasted to the curb across the street. The only sound he heard was of the tires rolling on the pavement.

They climbed the stairs to the front porch of a house, knocked, and a light flashed on inside. A woman wearing a dark green robe and matching slippers opened the door. Then she closed it. Stone and Capper stood on the porch, more lights flicked on, and then a man opened the door. His angle to the door prevented a clear view. The man shut the door after a minute, and Stone and Capper headed back to the car. Hawkeye didn't see anything but a verbal exchange among the three. He could read expressions, but not lips, and it was too dark to take pictures without a flash.

The trail continued. They pulled into a shopping center a few miles down the road. Stone slowed the car. Capper leaped out, didn't look back, and sped away. The brakes screeched before Stone bolted from the car, drew his gun, and ran after Capper.

"Damn it," he heard Stone mumble.

Capper picked up speed then took refuge behind a parked car. Instinctively, Hawkeye jumped out of his car and ran around the side. He had the advantage. No one knew he was there. Capper popped up, moved away from Stone, and took cover behind another car.

Stone followed him deeper into the lot. "You can't escape. Let's do this the easy way."

"Stone, I've got your back," Hawkeye said.

"Rainman?" Stone said. He kept his eyes on Capper. "Good, cover me."

Hawkeye pulled his gun from the holster, released the safety, and aimed it at Capper. Stone dashed after him. Capper thrust himself at a fence. As Capper leaped, Stone caught his leg, tackled him to the ground, twisted his arm behind his back, and cuffed him. Hawkeye ran up behind him and caught a small package Stone had tossed his way.

"Evidence," Stone said to Hawkeye. "You have the right to remain silent."

"I know my rights, asshole," Capper said.

Stone shoved Capper in the back of the car after he properly Mirandized him, and then he drove and deposited him at the precinct.

Capper sat in a holding cell while his paperwork was processed. The expired New Jersey driver's license Stone pulled from Capper's pocket was in the name of Marshall Guy, twenty-seven years old, brown hair, brown eyes. Stone compared the picture to Capper.

"Hey, Marshall."

Capper jerked his head towards Stone.

"Looks like him," Stone said to the officer. "See if he's got a record."

"What's the story?" Hawkeye asked Stone.

"It was a case."

"Assigned by who?"

"Since when do I report to you, Rainman?" Stone asked.

"Sorry, I wanted to …."

"Sit down."

Stone deposited a bill into the vending machine, hit a button, and reached down to retrieve a can. He popped opened a Coke, took a swig, and began. "It was a case I was working on before my vacation. Steve, or Marshall," he focused in the direction of the holding cell and continued, "had tried to sell me drugs, but instead of prosecuting him, we made a deal. He was going to introduce me to his supplier."

"Since when does Homicide investigate drug crimes?" Hawkeye asked.

"I was on a homicide case that led me to him," Stone snapped back. "He contacted me tonight and said he'd hold up his end of the bargain if I could meet him outside that bar."

"You trusted him to keep his word?"

"I'd have caught up to him again."

"Shouldn't you turn him over to drug enforcement?"

"We're working together."

"Why didn't you tell me about that bar when we were there last week?" Hawkeye asked, watching Stone's face intently for any signs of deception.

"I didn't know about the bar then. Stop asking questions, and let me tell the story." Stone paused for a moment. "So I met him, and we went to the bar. Marshall gave the bartender a code. She called back, and they let us in. There's another room behind the room you see."

Hawkeye cracked an almost undetectable smile, the kind only people like himself had the skill to see, and gave himself a mental pat on the back.

"They sent us to another guy, so I followed his directions, and when we got to the parking lot, he wanted to make contact first. I knew he was going to run, but it was easier to arrest him outside of the car. I had it covered, but I appreciate the backup."

"Wait, why did you stop at the house?" Hawkeye asked.

"Why, exactly, were you following me?"

Hawkeye caught himself before he revealed that Blainey wanted Stone followed. "Blainey got me clearance to follow the bar lead."

"That's no lead."

"The husband of the first vic went there. His wife died from a drug overdose. I thought there could be a connection, and Blainey agreed."

"You're working for the FBI now?" Stone shook his head and walked off.

Hawkeye followed him into the interrogation room. Capper, aka Marshall, sat at the metal table with his head down on top of his folded arms. He wasn't giving the cops a bit of satisfaction, but that didn't seem to bother Stone. With his fingers splayed, Stone slammed his hand on the table. That got Capper to raise his head, suck his bottom lip, and stare into Stone's eyes.

"If you want any leniency, you'll give me your contact now," Stone said.

"Look man, the guy calls me from a private number and tells me when to meet him at Kelly's."

Mr. Levy had to be buying drugs, Hawkeye thought. That's why he was in the back room at the bar.

"Give me my cell, and when he calls, I'll let you know."

"Right," Stone said. "Why don't we set you up with a room at The Plaza while you wait? Order up room service, rent movies, invade the mini-bar. Hell, take a stroll down Fifth Avenue and shop. All on Suffolk County."

Capper shook his head. "Look asshole, it's how he contacts me. Take it or leave it."

Hawkeye had read Capper the whole time. He wasn't lying.

Stone told Hawkeye to stay with Capper, and he slammed the door as he exited.

"You've met him before. Describe him," Hawkeye said.

"Man, I don't know. Medium height, thinning hair, glasses. Usually wears a suit."

"What else?"

Capper shrugged.

Stone swung the door open and threw something on the table. The door hit the wall, and it boomeranged itself back to the closed position.

"Put this in your pocket. If for one second we don't hear you, the officers will arrest you. No more chances."

"Seriously, a bug? You want to hear when I hit the head, too?"

"We'll hear you, and we'll know where you are. I'm not kidding, Ste- Marshall. Last chance." Stone handed over Caper's cell and set him free. "And check in with me every four hours. You have my number."

CHAPTER 26

The sudden absence of chirping crickets unsettled Raina. Until then, she had been relaxed on her lounge chair with Codis by her side, enjoying the warm evening, missing Danny, and craving ice cream. She checked the time. Danny was overdue by his typical thirty minutes.

When she heard tires turn on the stray pebbles at the end of the driveway, Raina was up and through the front door. She opened the truck door and hopped in.

"Ice cream! Stat!"

Danny accepted her direction and shifted into reverse. A left, a right, and then another left, and in minutes, they were in the shopping center outside the nearest Häagen-Dazs. As they approached the door, they took note of the horde of teenagers inside and dreaded the auditory assault that awaited them. Raina tilted her head, raised her eyebrows, and smiled in question. Danny rolled his eyes and reached for the door. They agreed to share the ice cream in the tranquility of his truck.

Halfway through her cone, Raina glanced back and saw the case files nestled against a pile of sweatshirts and a baseball mitt in the back seat.

"Bodies piled up so quick. I was going to re-read them tonight," Danny said.

"So what do you think about my possible trigger?"

He scooped the last spoonful into his mouth and nodded.

"Yes what? I was right?"

Danny sucked a drip off his bottom lip. "It's a definite possibility. Murphy did some research and found that the ODs that occurred right before the kills were specifically women with young children left without a parent to care for them. The FBI added it to their profile, but besides a guy without his mother, we still don't know who we're looking for."

"But now you know when he'll kill again, right? So as soon as there's another OD, you'll be prepared."

"It's too short a window, and we can't have cops watching every blonde in Suffolk County. It's not that easy," Danny said. "Buckle up. We're going home."

The day's newspaper rested on top of a pile on Raina's coffee table. The front page headline read, "Gun sales rise as the Morphine Murderer remains at large." The caption below it read, "Blondes aren't having more fun." Danny lifted his knee to deflect Codis' jump to greet him and protected the case files against his chest. He balanced the files on top of the newspaper, intentionally covering it from their view.

"Call Grandma Ida," he said.

"It's late, Danny. She's probably asleep."

"I want her take on this case."

"Why Grandma?"

"She's got a unique sense of things."

"Kooky is more like it."

"Sometimes her kooky ideas are the ones I need. Call her, please." Danny used unfair tactics to get his way. He made puppy dog eyes, smiled a hopeful smile, and finished with the head tilt, but it was always his dimples that made Raina cave. She dialed.

"Hi, dear. I have company, can I call you back?" Grandma Ida asked.

"Company? Who?"

"A man, dear."

"A man?" Raina screeched. She turned to Danny. "Grandma has a man over!"

Danny smirked and reached for the phone.

"Hi Grandma, it's Danny."

"Oh Daniel. Are you protecting Raina?"

"Always. What do you think about this Morphine Murderer?"

"Well, dear, I hope he's available when it's my time to go," she answered.

"What? Why?"

"They should call him the Angel of Death. I heard those people were suffering from painful and incurable diseases, and he sent them to rest in peace."

"Who calls him that?" Danny asked.

"The people at the senior center. They think he's a hero."

Danny cringed.

"Okay Grandma, thank you. Don't overdo it with your man tonight," he said.

Grandma laughed. "Don't you worry. We'll be fine, dear."

"Give me two more minutes," he said to Raina.

Danny didn't seem to go for Grandma's explanation, but he wouldn't totally discard it without having it checked on first. He asked Stone to check with the M.E.'s office on the health of the victims prior to their murders and to get back to him as soon as possible. Afterwards, he systematically checked in with Hawkeye and then Agent Blainey.

Keeping Danny within earshot, Raina gathered the case files from the table and scooted into her office. Page by page, she guided them through the printer to make copies, tapping her hand against the papers as if that would quicken the process. When it sounded like he was about to end the call, she returned the files and was back in the kitchen clanging dishes and pots. It wasn't enough time to copy everything on her personal printer.

"I don't think these are mercy killings," Raina spoke to him from the other room. "Can you put this bowl up on the top shelf for me?"

Danny appeared by her, leaned over, and scooped her up as he kicked the dishwasher door closed. Her hair spilled over his arm as he carried her towards the bedroom.

"I'm all yours," he said.

For the first time since before Raina could remember, they shared the whole night and the next morning, all without police interruption. She submerged herself in a fantasy that it would last, and someday soon it would become their life. Every morning they would wake up together and enjoy breakfast as the early morning rays brightened the room. He would read the paper with his old man reading glasses that she hated, and she would sip her coffee. They would go off to work knowing that they would end the day together as well. As she was daydreaming and clearing the table, her harsh reality rang back to her.

"Smith."

He strolled out to the deck beyond earshot. It didn't matter what he said, she knew what it meant. Any moment he'd be gone. *If he's going to work on the TMM case, so am I.* By the time Danny walked back inside, Raina was dressed. Her bags were by the door, and Codis was hovering close by. Danny didn't seem to notice.

The familiar hospital building came into view as Raina rounded the corner. Each time she saw the expansive brick building her stomach flipped. Lately, she had found herself passing through those doors too often. The guard smiled at her as if he recognized her. Upstairs, she swung her bags onto the visitor's chair in Sloan's room. Sloan wasn't there.

She peered down the hallway and saw Sloan moving slowly, arm hooked onto Paul. It took a while for them to get back to the room and settle Sloan in the bed. Paul set her pillows with confidence and brushed her hair to the side as though he had done so a dozen times before. Sloan readjusted the pillows and put one under her arm.

"If you were lying down and your face was turned, you'd look like one of the TMM's victims."

Paul whipped his head around. "The what?"

"The Morphine Murderer."

"Do you think about anything else?" He kissed Sloan on the forehead. "Raina, call me when you leave. I need to go make a few calls." And he was gone.

"How are you feeling? You look good."

"They're keeping me and won't say for how long." Her voice began to tremble, and Raina laid a comforting hand across hers. "I'm scared."

"You have the best care. Everything will work out fine. Stay positive and think all good thoughts. And if you need anything, I'm here."

Raina hoped her words offered some comfort, but she was worried, too. How long would they keep her there on Paul's money alone? Didn't they have to think something was wrong?"

Sloan dried the tears from her face with a tissue. "Tell me what's new on the case."

Raina extracted six photos from her bag and placed them across Sloan's bed.

"You're crazy," Sloan said.

"Thorough."

"Where did you get those photos?"

"One guess."

"Should have known. Haven't the police been all over that?"

"Yes, but I come at it from a different perspective. I'm not trained in protocol, and I don't have any bias from previous cases. I see the facts and make observations without preconceived notions."

"So?"

"Danny made me call my grandmother who, by the way, had a man over late at night, because he wanted a view outside law enforcement."

"Well, your Grandmother does have a different viewpoint, a wacky one." Sloan paused in thought. "What do you mean, a man?"

"She rushed us off the phone. I should call and check on her."

Sloan laughed. "Maybe a young stud she met at Michael's party." She glanced at the sobering photos on her lap. "Is the FBI still working with Danny's team?"

"Not with his blessing, but yeah, and so far they have very little," Raina said.

"Well, the victims all live in a small radius within the county."

"Right. So the killer probably lives or works around here, and the DBs were in the wrong place at the wrong time. Victims of opportunity," Raina surmised. "The motive?"

Sloan worked on that aloud. "They must remind him of someone young and blonde. Maybe a wife, ex-wife, dead wife, or he was jilted before a real relationship formed. Or he was teased as a teenager by a blonde or abused by his mother or family or a close family friend. It has to be a young, blonde woman that did something bad to him. It might have only been in his mind, but it was real to him. It's like he's repeatedly killing in his mind."

Raina continued from where Sloan left off adding that the killer could be a woman, maybe a nurse.

"The method is painless, the killer makes them comfortable on the bed, and women are usually more compassionate and concerned with appearances than men."

She acknowledged that statistically serial killers were usually men, white, and in their mid-twenties to early thirties but reminded herself that they were trying to solve this mystery outside of the box.

"A nurse!" Sloan said.

With the intensity of Sloan's voice, Raina wasn't sure if she needed a nurse, saw a nurse, or agreed it could be a nurse.

Sloan's voice became a whisper. "I almost forgot to tell you. I've been doing some research during my walks. Come with me."

Sloan pushed herself off the bed.

"Should you be getting up again so soon?"

"It's fine. Come on."

Raina scooped the photos back into her bag. It wasn't difficult to catch up to Sloan as she shuffled down the hall in her socks.

"Yesterday I noticed the door to the pharmaceutical supply room was unlocked."

"I can totally see you trying every door handle as you make your way down the hall."

"I wasn't *that* bored. Actually, I lost my balance and grabbed it to steady myself. It prevented a fall, but I twisted my wrist."

"Are you okay?"

"Yeah. Anyway, I had to investigate. I knew that wasn't right. It turns out that there's a Nurse Snow, and when she's on duty, she leaves the door unlocked, so she can send someone else to do her work."

"Which one is she?" Raina asked.

Sloan pointed to the overweight woman behind the nurse's station. She was sitting at a narrow desk facing a computer monitor with her back to the hall.

Raina made a mental note. "Anyone can get access if they choose the right time?"

"Pretty much," Sloan said. "But they would find the discrepancy during inventory control, and Nurse Snow would be held accountable."

"Nothing has been reported missing. Danny checked."

"Give me a few more hours, and I'll find out when inventory is done."

"You're awesome. Now take care of my niece in there," she said as she held her hand against Sloan's belly, "and get some rest. I'll let Paul know I'm going."

"Yes, Aunt Lorraine."

No way was Sloan going to get her with that. Raina almost flew through the hospital to Jean's room in search of Tyler with her new information. It was Sunday morning. Tyler would surely be there. She slowed her pace before she hit the corridor with Jean's room, slowed her breathing too, and entered casually. The sun's rays were strong, bouncing off the metal edge of the table, and brightening the room almost cheerfully. Nothing was cheerful about the machines attached to Jean and keeping her alive nor was anything cheerful about the TMM and his victims. Why was she so excited to be standing there?

"Jean, I don't know if you can hear me, but we all miss you," she said.

"I miss you most of all, honey."

Raina spun around. "You keep appearing out of nowhere. It's getting creepy."

Her description words in her head. There was nothing creepy about Tyler.

"I just saw Sloan. She said you'd probably be here."

"She did? Did she tell you about the break in our case?"

He shook his head, and Raina filled him in. He gave her that half smile that disturbed her, and he didn't say anything for an awkward moment. When he perked back up, they discussed work. It was something she preferred not to do on the weekend, but for him, in his emotional state, she was happy to do anything that made him feel better.

As she exited the hospital, the humidity hit her like a hot, wet wall. It wasn't a hard decision to go back inside the cool lobby to call Grandma Ida to check in.

"He's there again, Grandma?"

"It's fine. We're having a good time. Give Daniel a big hug for me," Grandma said.

She would call her parents and see if they knew that Grandma was spending so much time with a new man. Not being able to keep a close eye on Grandma had been the hardest part of moving for her mother. She counted on Raina to keep her informed.

As she passed the guard this time, he gave her an uneasy look. He probably wondered why she was there so often. It barely fazed Raina. She was on a mission. On the way back to Sloan, she took the long way past Jean's room. As she approached it, staff moved in and out with machines on carts. Her heart skipped a beat, and she wondered what was going on. The closer she got, the more chaotic it appeared. Tyler was at his post by Jean's side, overseeing her care.

A man with thick, dark glasses and a matching goatee was backing out of the room. "Twice a day. Remember to work her muscles twice a day in addition to our sessions," he said.

"I'll be back to wash her hair this evening, probably after dinner," said a woman wearing a pink uniform.

Raina was relieved when she learned that Jean's condition hadn't taken a turn for the worse. On the contrary, the bustle around Jean was because the staff was taking special care of her. She elected to pass by without stopping back in and headed to Sloan.

"Excuse me. ID please."

Raina huffed and presented her driver's license for the second time.

"Do you ever rest?" she asked Sloan who had her laptop open.

"You wanted information? I hacked in. There hasn't been an inventory check recorded since before the killings started."

CHAPTER 27

Despite the fact that the morning arrived with misting rain, Raina woke early, highly motivated to continue her investigation.

"Is this what Danny does?" she asked herself as she studied her case wall, a close approximation of the one at the precinct. She sat for a long while searching for new information, a clue that they had missed. Nothing. Like writer's block, she was experiencing investigator's block, and Raina didn't know how to proceed.

"Do you wanna go for a walk?"

Codis twisted his head, jumped up, and bounded to his leash by the front door. He trotted back and forth while Raina put on her sneakers, a light jacket, and a baseball cap. It was an unusually peaceful, Sunday morning. Very few cars were on the road. People were inside because of the weather. Lawnmowers, garden-edgers, hedge-trimmers, pool vacuums, and the like were all benched because of the rain.

They traveled to the edge of the neighborhood. Codis sniffed every bush along the way, marking those he deemed necessary. Raina considered the wet landscapes. The rain had weighed down flowers and delicate ornamental grasses, and she knew the tallest ones would need support to regain their vertical state. Her thoughts drifted back to the case. There had to be a connection right in front of her, and she needed to figure out what it was.

A car headed towards her from the far end of the road, very slowly. Too slowly. The driver was a man wearing a baseball cap and dark sunglasses, but the bill of the cap obscured his face. She twisted both ways to check the street. No one else was around. Her body tensed. All of a sudden her arm was jerked forward, almost out of its socket. Codis had lunged for a squirrel. She held on, but her sneaker slid on the wet street, and she lost her balance. Her torso turned sideways, her leg jolted forward, and she landed on her hip, scrambling to keep her focus on the car. The tires rolled by at such an ambling pace that she could practically see the tread. She scooted back onto the grass next to a dense tree trunk and watched the car continue by. The brake lights went off, and the car sped around the corner.

She tried to brush off the dirt but only smeared the mud into her jeans. Codis had run to her side and growled at the car until it was out of sight. The leather leash was soaked and dirty, but she didn't care. She wanted to get home fast. They picked up speed and jogged the whole way. When she was inside the house, she slammed the door, bolted it, and armed the security system. She struggled to catch her breath. What if she had just seen the TMM? What if he was scoping out his next victim? Her hair was up in a cap. Had he mistakenly thought it was blonde? Did he know where she lived?

She remained on the floor next to Codis until her hands stopped shaking, then she grabbed the landline.

"Can you describe the car? Did you get his plate number?" Sloan asked.

No, she hadn't gotten his license number. As she thought about it, she had no idea what color the car was. How could that be?

"Dark," she said.

"That's it? Dark?" Sloan asked. She was quiet for a moment. They both were. "You're scared. I've never known anything to affect your skills of observation."

Fear was dominating her thoughts, and she had to get control of the situation.

"Is your laptop booted up?"

For the first time, everything became real. There was a killer in her neighborhood. She leaned her back against the base of the couch while Sloan searched for serial killers.

"Oh, you're not going to like this. One quick search, and I found a grand handful. Most recent and closest to home was Joel Rifkin." Sloan read off the information on him.

"A landscaper!" His victims were prostitutes. Not so on *her* case. "Go on."

"Richard Angelo worked at Good Samaritan Hospital and injected poison through IVs. The TMM's injecting into IVs as well. He had an uncontrollable need to be the hero. He poisoned dozens of patients with the intent to then save their lives and gain recognition as a hero. The plan reportedly failed more times than it worked."

Raina thought about it. The TMM showed no desire for recognition. He hadn't contacted the press, the FBI, the police, or the victims' families. He hadn't offered any taunts or clues to follow, superior ego, or any form of communication.

"He's killing for revenge," Raina said.

"David Berkowitz killed couples. Not the TMM's MO. Edward Leonski, born in New York, joined the army in his early twenties, wound up in Melbourne, and killed various people there, male and female."

This wasn't productive. She already knew most serial killers were white males in their twenties and early thirties. She checked that off her list as she rubbed the bruise darkening on her hip from her earlier fall.

She and Codis both heard a noise.

"Hang on, there's a car out there."

She groaned as she pushed off the floor. Codis had beaten her to the window and was wagging his cropped tail. She pushed the curtain back a few inches and saw the Denali. With the sight of Danny came a sigh of relief.

"I'll call you later. Rest," Raina said to Sloan.

She disarmed the security system and opened the door. Codis slipped by her to greet Danny on the front steps. After the dog backed off, she flung her arms around Danny. He was only two feet inside the house when she blurted out what had happened on the walk. He didn't seem very concerned. Why not?

Now that some time had passed, it hardly seemed like an incident at all. So a car drove by. Maybe he was reading the house numbers and didn't even see her.

"Sit down. Wait here. I'll be right back." She pushed him into the living room.

When she returned, he was on the recliner, and she saw his big smile disappear.

"I thought you were coming back in something sexy," he said.

"I've been working on the TMM case," she said.

"What case?"

"TMM," she repeated, and then explained.

"Uh, Babe, that's my job."

"Yeah, well, you need my help. Did you know that we've had serial killers in New York, in Long Island? One poisoned hospital patients with injections in their IVs?"

He was bobbing his head up and down. "I wish I didn't, but I do."

"Well, did you know that the hospital in town leaves their drugs unattended and accessible when a certain nurse is on duty?"

"What do you mean?"

Raina couldn't speak fast enough. "I mean, there's a fat, lazy nurse named Snow, and she leaves the door to the medications unlocked, so she doesn't have to get up. She sends one of her underlings to retrieve the drugs when she's the one with the proper authorization."

"Why doesn't she give them the key?"

"I can only figure that it's easier to say 'oops! I forgot to lock the door' than to explain how someone else got your key. The point is that there's access for anyone who knows about it."

"And how do you come to have this knowledge?"

"Results from my investigation. Why don't you seem interested?"

"I'm interested, watch." He made a call and told someone to check on her information.

"One last thing, if you find out..." she began.

"I'll call the hospital administrator and check the inventory schedule and report the fat, lazy nurse, okay?"

She laughed. "How did you know what I was going to say?"

He rose from the chair and scooped her up. "The same way I know you're about to get lucky."

Overall it was an exciting weekend, but Monday arrived with all the work she hadn't completed during the prior week. She remained focused for hours until she heard the familiar police sirens from her phone. That always brought a warm feeling inside and a smile to her face. It meant that Danny was thinking about her.

"Tell Sloan that her detective work was a success. As promised, I called the administrator, who happens to be young, blonde, and fearful of the TMM. She initiated an emergency inventory count, and they found half a dozen vials of morphine missing. 200mgs."

For the briefest moment, she reveled in the fact that not only had he called her, but he had used her acronym.

"And they fired Snow?"

"She was escorted to the administrator's office and broke when they presented the facts. She 'fessed up to leaving the door unlocked, but she stuck to her claim of innocence on the issue of theft. Her defense was staff shortage after recent budget cuts. The hospital agreed not to press charges if she provided a written statement and resigned. Murphy's looking into her life."

I bet Sloan is too.

Danny spoke as though he was speaking to himself. "That's not enough to kill more than one or maybe two small people."

"Yeah, but…"

The call ended.

Raina rocketed out of her office to share the news with Tyler. He looked over at her with that smile, the one that seduced her every time, and listened while she reported the latest. When she mentioned the part about Nurse Snow, his expression shifted. Meant as a gesture of comfort, Raina touched his shoulder. A tingle shot through her chest, and she yanked her hand back. Without a word, she returned to her desk and reviewed the layers of embarrassment she just created. She should have considered that Tyler might be upset that Snow was fired.

Maybe she took care of Jean. Maybe she was an otherwise good nurse.

Her move to touch his shoulder was an instinctive reaction to his disappointment. That might not have been so bad if she hadn't snatched it away with such haste and then run away from the whole situation. After too much consideration, she decided that she would head back to him a while later and try again, even though she knew it best to leave it alone.

Raina continued her work on a spreadsheet until Tyler came by to let her know he was headed to the hospital for a while. His dedication to his wife was enviable and made Raina consider her own relationship again. If she were in a coma, would Danny take the time and care the way Tyler did with Jean? Would Tyler visit her? Similar questions circled around Raina's head for the remainder of the afternoon. She was emotionally drained.

Raina had driven home without conscious effort, without any recollection of making turns or stopping at lights, the way they warn you about in defensive driving courses.

She plopped herself on the couch and reached for the remote. It was a rare Monday night that Raina wasn't at Sloan's for DB Night.

Raina had thought about dragging over the uncomfortable visitor chair and watching television with Sloan, but she had called, and Paul was already in that chair while Sloan slept. Paul mentioned that there was a Post-it note on Sloan's laptop for her. "Nothing on Snow," it said.

"Are you planning a ski trip?" Paul asked.

Later, Raina realized that she had dozed off when she was awakened by the phone.

"Babe, the hospital administrator called back after a full investigation was completed. Apparently prior reports had been falsified for months, ever since Snow was in charge. Mega doses of morphine were stolen along with various amounts of Vicadin, OxyContin, Fentanyl, and other drugs."

"They think she stole the drugs? Would that make her the TMM?"

"Probably not. Murphy found nothing on her, not even large cash deposits in her bank statements or expensive purchases. Whoever did take them knew about the unlocked room."

"So we've narrowed down the source of the drugs. The killer has to have some association with the hospital."

"You got it. You know, Hawkeye is going to be upset. He spent hours on the phone with medical centers and doctors' offices to find one with missing inventory."

Raina smiled to herself.

"Babe, maybe SCPD should give you a detective shield."

CHAPTER 28

Mug Shots was a local bar, small, dark, and unimpressive but always packed with patrons. Location was its main attraction. The back opened out onto a bulkhead thirty feet deep and twenty feet wide. On a warm summer night, every Long Islander found a place to be outside. If it was on the water, even better, and if there was a breeze to keep the mosquitoes away, then perfect. This night Danny and Stone chose Mug Shots to have a drink and catch up. They had been too busy to do so ever since Stone returned from his vacation to work on the TMM case.

"Where's Blainey been?" Stone asked.

"The FBI pulled him. He said he would be back after this weekend."

"Something bigger than our serial killer?"

"I don't know," Danny said. "You know the FBI. We have to share everything with them, and they don't tell us shit."

"Who needs 'em?" Stone raised his glass, and Danny raised his to meet it.

"Yeah."

Inside, the bar was landscaped with bodies fitted together like a puzzle. Most of the women were young. The men were a mix of ages, mostly older than the women.

Stone's phone chimed. "Marshall checking in, right on time."

"How's things with the hot M.E.?" Danny asked.

"I'm supposed to meet her later. She's sexy and smart, too."

"She done dating the judge?"

"Yeah, she said it was one date, but you know how fast information like that gets exaggerated. Glad she's on to me."

Stone raised his glass again. Danny met it, then put his back down on the table without a taste to reach for his vibrating phone.

"Hang on, Sergeant. I can't hear you in here." Danny strolled outside along the weathered dock, but his signal got worse until he lost the call. He rejoined Stone.

"Come on, something's going on," he said.

They made their way through the tight crowd, through the inside bar, and to the street, but he still had no signal. When they hit the parking lot, Danny was finally able to reach the precinct.

"Another body. Follow me," Danny said to Stone.

With that, they each jumped into their cars, and Stone followed Danny to the scene fifteen minutes south from the bar.

As they walked to the door, M.E. Garza exited having already released the scene for further investigation.

Danny stopped him. "What do you think? Is this our guy again?"

"Doubtful. I couldn't detect any needle marks in her arm, but you know I can't say for sure until I get the body on the table."

"Why was the body moved before I saw it? Who took photos? I need to see the positioning!"

"I'm no detective, but this woman is older than the others. Her hair only has blonde highlights, and she was on the floor next to the bed," Garza said.

"You shouldn't have released the scene until I got here."

"That's not how it works, Lieutenant. Relax. I'll run a tox screen on her as soon as I get back."

"Call me as soon as you know anything."

Garza saluted him.

"Hey," Stone said, following behind Garza.

"I already spoke to your superior. Get lost," Garza said.

"Your substitute was a lot nicer than you. Hotter too," Stone said.

"So?" Garza asked, as he continued to walk. "What? You want to bang her? Too late. She's seeing someone."

Stone stopped in his tracks. He pulled his phone from a pocket, gripping it with a white knuckled fist. Danny knew that look.

"Hey Stone."

"Did they find anything?" Stone asked.

"Nothing yet. Get out of here and go meet your M.E. I'll call you if there's anything," Danny said.

Stone didn't wait around. As he turned to leave, he was assaulted by a disorienting pattern of flashes. It was the press and their cameras joined by the onset of questions. Three reporters had pushed microphones to his face and wanted details about the safety of the residents. They had already concluded it was the TMM and wanted to know what the police were doing and when they supposed they were going to stop him. Stone motioned to Danny, and Danny called for backup units.

Danny stood in the middle of the crime scene, less the body. This one would bring the count up to seven. The press army had grown in strength and numbers, so Danny contacted his captain and suggested a press conference. Within five minutes, he received the okay to notify the press that the chief would make a statement the following morning at eleven. He went outside to rescue Stone. Danny held up his hand to draw the reporters' attention, stated his name and rank, and announced the scheduled press conference. Instead of being satisfied, the press unleashed another barrage of questions.

"Do you have any leads?"

"Are you close to arresting anyone?"

"When will we be safe again?"

"Who is the Morphine Murderer?"

Danny repeated the scheduled time of the statement and headed to the street with Stone.

"Enjoy the M.E.," Danny said.

"I plan to."

He was tired, but it wasn't too late to spend some time with Raina, and the thought of relaxing on her couch after the hard day was very appealing. Besides, there was no plan of action until he heard from Garza.

When Danny arrived at Raina's, Codis gave him the usual enthusiastic greeting and then sat for his treat. Raina gave Danny a kiss.

"Hard day at the office, hun?" she asked.

"Yeah, another murder."

"That makes seven! You'd think people would be extra careful knowing he's out there."

"I'm well aware of the count. He's getting nationwide attention now. You should have seen the press from everywhere. I think there was even one British news team there today."

"Think that FBI agent alerted them?" Raina walked to the kitchen, "Are you hungry? I can put something on the grill for you."

"Please. I'm starved, haven't eaten since this morning." He blew her a kiss, plopped down on the recliner end of the couch, and put his feet up.

She took two pre-formed burgers from the freezer and fired up the BBQ. In the interest of time, she put frozen fries on some foil and popped them on the grill as well. When she brought dinner to Danny, she found Codis with him on the couch, Codis' head on Danny's lap. In unison, they watched her come closer with the food. As she handed the plate to Danny, Codis' eyes opened wide. He rested his head back down but never took his eyes off the plate.

While Danny inhaled his food, Raina asked him if he had heard about the salons overbooked with appointments for hair coloring. Blondes, real or enhanced, were flocking to their hairdressers to darken their hair. Store managers reported a big rush on brown and red hair dye. Some couldn't keep the shelves stocked fast enough, and others were totally sold out.

"Did you see the drug store on Route 110 and Jericho? It has a sign on the front door: No dark hair dye."

"Everyone is panicking," he said. "You know how each time they predict a snowstorm, everyone rushes to the supermarkets, and the milk racks are emptied, and the store looks like the entire NFL came through, ravenous, after a game? Then it snows an inch."

She laughed at his description. "I can imagine dozens of muscle-heads pillaging the supermarket, grabbing items, knocking over displays and little old ladies as they grunt." She pushed Codis over, so she could sit on the couch next to Danny, then her tone became sullen. "But it's not like that at all. It's not a false alarm. Women are dead."

He nodded.

"And that's not all they were talking about."

"What else?" he asked through a mouthful of burger.

"They also said that the self-defense schools are packed with new students. Everyone is afraid, Danny."

"It'll be alright."

"They're blaming the police, saying that you're doing nothing about it. I hate when they do that," she said.

He cringed. "We hate it too, believe me. If this guy's made any mistakes, we haven't found them. He's obviously someone these women feel comfortable around."

"What about the skin under the real estate agent's nails?"

"Yeah, but it doesn't match anyone in the system."

"You think each victim knew him?" she asked.

"Maybe, but we haven't found any connection to indicate that. We will." He shoveled in a handful of fries. "In fact, I'm waiting for Garza to call on this last victim."

As if on cue, his cell rang. He fumbled with the phone to answer it on speaker.

"Garza's running the tox."

"Thanks Hawk. Keep me posted."

Raina took his empty plate to the kitchen and returned with a blanket from another room. When she returned, Codis had taken her spot.

"Move," she said to Codis.

He got up and moved to the love seat. She snapped open the blanket and curled up under it next to Danny.

While Danny was on the phone, she had gone through a mental list of all the blondes she knew. Sloan was protected in the hospital under constant watch. The women at work and her friends had all changed their hair color. *Zoe!* Raina remembered that Danny's niece was blonde. She had only met Zoe a couple of times because she attended college in Boston, but now she was home for the summer.

"What about Zoe? Isn't your sister worried about her? Aren't you?" Raina asked.

"She's taken care of. As soon as the blonde connection was made, I told her to send Zoe back to school early. She's outside his territory there."

There was nothing more Raina could accomplish that night. She was too tired. She pulled the blanket tighter and pressed the remote.

"Want to watch *Criminal Minds?* Maybe this episode will shine some light on our serial killer," she said.

"No. Don't you ever get tired of that show?"

"No. *CSI? NCIS? Law and Order? Criminal Minds?*"

"Isn't there a game on?" he asked.

"*Criminal Minds* it is."

Most of the night had passed when Raina was awakened by a vibration on her arm. She was still on the couch pressed against Danny's phone, which was clipped to his belt. Her legs were pinned under the blanket since Codis had rejoined them.

Danny swallowed and spoke. "Hawk, don't you ever go home?"

"I was waiting on the blood results."

"And?"

"Blood thinner was the only drug they found in her system. Garza's declaring the COD as a heart attack."

"Okay, thanks."

As he ended the call, she heard his text alert chime. He moved the screen so she could read it. *COD - Cardiac Arrest - natural causes - Garza*

"I've got to get to work. You can go to bed for another hour or so. Come on."

She wanted to close her eyes and fall back asleep with him next to her, but he was wide awake and determined to get back to work.

"You have to get up and lock the door."

She sat up, pushed herself up off the couch, and tried to find the strength to drag herself to bed. The night sky was giving in to the sun. It wasn't totally dark, but it wasn't light either. Still time to be in bed as far as Raina was concerned. The thirty-second warning tone from the alarm sounded as Danny hit the button to arm it and left. The sound jump-started Raina's brain. She sprang up from the couch wide awake and called Danny before he had left her driveway.

"Or... the TMM could have set the alarm on the way out like you just did, but that wouldn't help us with a suspect! There's only one viable reason why he might have done that: to make it appear that there wasn't any foul play." The words flew out of her mouth so fast that there seemed to be a delay in Danny's comprehension.

"I'll keep all that in mind."

Raina tossed and turned under her covers as a million thoughts about the TMM case rolled around in her head.

CHAPTER 29

The first rays of sun glittered over the horizon as Danny pulled into the precinct lot. He found Special Agent Gordon Blainey, joined by a second agent, waiting in his office. Not what he wanted to deal with so early in the morning.

"Welcome back," Danny said.

"Morning, Lieutenant. This is Agent Judith Bryant. She'll deliver the statement to the press at eleven today, as promised," SA Blainey said.

Danny extended his hand. "Thanks for coming. We welcome any help on this one."

She shook his hand. "I'd like to read all the police files and then sit with you before the release."

"Anything you need," Danny said. "We're working on a few small details this morning."

He led her to an unassigned desk where the files were already stacked, instructed an officer to check with her every so often to see if she needed anything, and returned to his desk. He contacted the captain's office.

"Is this call really necessary, Smith?"

"Come on, Cap. Why did the FBI take over the news conference? It's only been a few hours. How do they even know?"

"They'll be handling the release of all information going forward. Politics is part of the job. Deal with it." The captain didn't wait around for a response.

Danny handed the alarm company contact to an officer with instructions to call and have the report faxed.

"They doubled," Stone said.

"The FBI will do that. You have a good night?" Danny asked.

"Great."

Hawkeye reacted to that statement with a doubtful look.

"What's your problem?" Stone asked.

"Nothing," Hawkeye said.

"Say it. What? You think I'm lying?"

"Forget it. Let's discuss the case, okay?"

Stone glared at Hawkeye.

An officer gave a light knock on the door, pushed only his head and arm through the doorway, and handed a report to Stone who relayed it to Danny. He studied it.

"The report shows that Marlo Levy, vic 1, used her remote to arm the system at 11:17AM on the day of the murder," Danny said. "The report also indicates that it hasn't been used since that time."

"So she was alive after the killer left?" Hawkeye asked. "Or she may have tried to hit the panic button and turned it on instead."

"Time of death is close," Stone said.

"Double check the evidence inventory, but I don't remember a remote listed," Danny said to Hawkeye.

Hawkeye was up and back in a flash. "No boss, it wasn't recorded as evidence."

Stone was tasked with contacting the husband to ask about the remote's location. After a few calls, he learned that Mr. Levy was out of town again. The next instruction he received was to get a warrant and a team to the house to search for the remote.

There were two hours left before the press conference, enough time for Danny to meet Stone and Hawkeye at the house and be back before the conference began.

Warrant in hand, Hawkeye rang the bell.

"Why are you doing that? The husband's away," Stone said.

"You never know. Someone might be in there."

"Open the door like you did last time."

He bent his arm and smashed the window with the back of his elbow. The alarm sounded

"Ow!" The glass sliced through his shirt. A circle of blood expanded on the material.

"What the hell, Rainman?" Stone said, then addressed an officer by the street. "Get the first aid kit over here and help him."

Danny pointed at two officers. "With me, inside. Check the bedroom first: under the furniture, between the sheets, everywhere."

"Stone…"

"On it."

It was hard to think with the siren blaring, but Stone handled it quickly. The house had been perfectly neat until the cops searched through it. Window glass was on the floor, drawers weren't properly closed, things were moved, and their contents emptied. They had checked every crevice of the house. No remote.

Hawkeye came through on the radio. "Press is here."

They crowded towards the police.

"Why are you back at the victim's house?" one reported asked.

"Do you think the husband did it?" another called from the back of the pack.

"Are you any closer to an arrest?"

Stone forced a camera away from his face and told the reporter to shove off. Danny presented them with the appropriate political-babble. The conference was set to begin in less than twenty minutes. Why wasn't the press at the precinct, preparing? He hoped to have the remote in hand by then, something to show the FBI and the people that they were making progress. The fact that the remote was used after the murder and was missing meant that it was likely that the killer had possession of it. It was something.

With five minutes remaining, Danny bolted into the precinct and approached the agents.

Bryant stopped typing on her laptop and explained more about the unidentified subject, or the 'unsub' as they called him.

"He's going to get a lot of media attention in the next twenty-four hours. The attention often prompts the unsub to contact us. It could also trigger him to kill. We have to be prepared for either."

"What do you need from us?" Danny asked.

"Usual procedures if we get him on the phone. Keep him on, so we can trace the call, and try not to agitate him. Any detail about him could be helpful," she advised. "We're ready. Let's go."

The press conference was held in front of the precinct to allow unlimited attendance. Reporters crowded close with their camera people and equipment. Creative parking left one open lane on the two-lane street, backing up traffic for a mile.

"There's gotta be over a hundred people here," Murphy said.

"How many guys do we have weaved into the crowd?" Stone asked.

"A dozen," Danny said. "The killer could be here. Blainey said that it happens a lot. Gives him a sense of control and power."

"I bet it feeds the sick bastard's ego too," Stone said.

While the press recorded the speakers, Murphy was video and sound recording the crowd. He was in the second row behind the FBI, next to Danny and Stone.

Stone nudged Danny with his elbow and lifted his head to direct Danny's gaze. He expected to see a young, white, male fitting the FBI's profile, but there was no one he could distinguish as a killer.

"Two o'clock," Stone said.

Bryant turned her head, pursed her lips together, and shushed them.

Danny turned his head two inches to the right and identified Stone's subject. He shook his head and showed a hint of a smile.

That's my girl. Raina wouldn't miss a chance like this, he thought.

It took a while for the area to be cleared after the press conference.

"Stone, in my office," he heard Danny call from his desk.

Everyone within earshot turned his head with curiosity to see Stone's reaction. He rose from his desk with confidence, peppered with arrogance, unaffected. He strutted into Danny's office, closed the door, leaned against a two drawer high file cabinet topped with photos, and crossed his arms. Not sure why he had been ordered in, he waited for Danny to begin.

"What's going on?" Danny asked.

"What do you mean?"

"What's going on with you? I could tell by Hawkeye's reaction earlier that he detected something. Trouble?"

"That guy's a freak show you know," Stone said.

"A useful one. Spill."

"Eh, it's over," Stone said.

"Look," Danny said. "I can't have your mind elsewhere during this case. It's too big, too important."

"It's not, don't worry. I messed up with Lacey. It's over," he said.

The night before, Stone had confronted Lacey and accused her of cheating based on Garza's comment. That had ignited a fight, which had ended badly.

"I overreacted to something stupid," Stone said with his head angled towards the floor.

"That shit with the ex two years ago?" Danny asked in a tone that sounded more like a statement than a question.

"I guess."

"This isn't the ex. Apologize and tell her you're an asshole."

Stone nodded in acknowledgement but said nothing.

"I need you focused, Detective."

"I get it, Lieutenant."

The office door opened without warning as the FBI agents came through. Stone wasn't disappointed that the subject was about to change although the Feds weren't his choice distraction. The press conference had ended more than six hours ago, and there had been no contact from the unidentified subject. All available hands were answering phones. Hundreds of people called the tip line with potential information, lots of questions, and concerns. The most interesting callers offered strategic plans and psychological profiles. Detailed notes were taken on each caller for review since occasionally unidentified subjects were known to call in anonymously and offer clues.

"Bryant and I are reviewing the notes hourly," Blainey said.

"Maybe he didn't see the press conference. Maybe he's busy killing his next victim," Stone said.

"Let's hope not," Bryant said.

The phone buzzed at Danny's side. He let Stone see that Raina was the caller.

"Give me one sec," he said to the agents.

He answered Raina's call, briefly explained, and promised to call her back later.

Stone sat at his desk and answered calls from the tip line, distracted, restless, and edgy. He knew that Danny was right. He had been an asshole. This time he didn't want to just move on to the next girl. Thoughts of Lacey's soft kisses and silly laugh made him smile. He was determined to fix things, and he wanted to do it as soon as possible. Resolved to get her back, he asked Danny for an hour of lost time. Danny raised his brow, Stone nodded, and Danny waved him approval.

As Stone drove off, he turned on the radio and headed toward the flower shop. Mid-trip he decided to axe the flower idea, too cliché, and turned the car in the direction of the bakery where they had stopped one night and overindulged themselves on delicious, flaky pastries. He hoped the thoughtfulness would gain her forgiveness. Next stop: the morgue.

Stone entered the building and asked for her at the desk.

"In her office," the receptionist said.

As he walked down the corridor, he saw the door to her office open and heard two voices. He slowed his stride, deciding what to do next. Should he wait until the other person left? How long could he stand in the hall listening before someone came by and he looked like an idiot? He stood against the wall, a car length from her office, and debated with himself. It became apparent from the conversation that it was about to end, so he took a controlled breath and walked the rest of the way. Lacey hit the speaker button on the desk phone. She was aware of him but said nothing.

"I'm sorry for the other night. I've missed you." Although completely sincere, he still had to force the words.

Lacey looked through him.

Unsure of her feelings, he extended his hand. "I brought this for you."

The name on the bakery box caught her attention, and her eyes welled up. The chair rolled back from the force of her legs as she rose up to move around the desk to hug him. The chair hit the file cabinet with a bang causing them both to laugh, breaking the tension. Stone stayed only long enough to apologize again and win her back.

"Can I take you to dinner tonight?" he asked.

"I'd love that." She smiled.

He returned to the precinct with a clear head.

CHAPTER 30

Sunlight filtered into Raina's bedroom and woke her. She blinked to adjust to the brightness then focused. Ecstatic that the sun was shining bright, she jumped out of bed and went to the back door with Codis right behind her. On the deck, she extended her arms towards the cloudless sky, palms and face up, soaking up the rays. It was Raina's version of yoga sun salutations. Codis ran around her, lifted his leg on the nearest tree, and flew back into the house for breakfast.

She followed him inside, fed him, then took a shower.

As she stepped out of the bathroom, she heard someone at the door. Codis wasn't barking. It was Danny holding up a bag for her. "I brought breakfast," he said.

She secured the deadbolt and followed him to the table. He laid out everything: food, drinks, plates, and all.

"Let's eat," he said, pointing at the bagels with a knife.

Raina sat preoccupied by her thoughts. She smeared some vegetable cream cheese on her bagel, took a bite, and decided she would try to bring up their relationship again. It was as good or bad a time as any. Her face became rigid. Her hands were shaking, so she moved them to her lap beneath the table for cover.

She forced her lips to move and began in a quiet voice. She knew her body language revealed her tension. The only time she was like this around him was when she wanted to talk about *them*. He drew a breath and waited.

She fiddled with the bagel, stopped breathing, then blurted out, "Danny, I want more from you, from us, for us. I think we should live together."

"Babe, you know I'm in a middle of the biggest case of my career right now."

"You're always in the middle of a case. So what does that have to do with us?" Her breathing became uneven and forced.

"Everything is good."

"I'm not good. I want more, and I want you to want more. If we lived together at least I'd see more of you even if it was while we were asleep."

"I can't focus on that. You know as well as I do that we have to get the TMM off the street," Danny said.

"You have to have a life too," Raina insisted.

"I'm here now. I thought of you. I picked up breakfast and came over to see you."

"I know, but that's not enough."

"Why are you starting with me? I came to have a nice breakfast with you." He put down the bagel and looked at Raina in a challenging way.

"Starting with you? Since when is a discussion 'starting with you'?"

"I don't want to have this conversation now," he said.

"Well I do. We keep putting it off for a better time. There's never a better time than now," she said.

"I can't do this now and lose focus on the case. I'm gonna go," he said. He threw Codis a piece of bagel, got up, and left without another word.

Raina sat at the table no longer hungry or intoxicated by the sun. Her blood boiled as she held back the tears. The sound of his tires peeling out of her driveway upset her further. Maybe he was gone forever. His actions along with his words made it clear. This was as far as he wanted their relationship to go, and it wasn't up for discussion. She knew that they had reached an impasse and that she wanted more, but she wasn't ready to let him go either. *Maybe I should.* Elbows on the table and head in her hands, she remained there listless.

By the time she got to the office, it was late morning. It was quiet at Shore Mortgage Funding for most of the day. At a few minutes to four, there was a commotion in the reception area. Then loud voices and laughter filled the office. Harvey had returned. Raina's heartbeat sped up. Guilt, embarrassment, and fear heated her body. She hadn't seen Harvey since before the car wreck. Flashbacks played in her head of her and Tyler following him around the office and collecting his bottles, of Michael, Charlie, and her following him around town, and of Danny questioning him after the car chase. The guilt of the car chase plagued her most of all. It was his fault for running, she tried to rationalize. It was she who told Danny about the victim's business card on his desk, the photos of him at the party with another victim, his time with the dancer, who was killed too, and all this led to the car chase which landed him in the hospital. He could trace most of that information back to her especially since it had been Danny questioning Harvey. If he blamed her for everything that had happened to him, she was afraid to think what he might do or say. Since he wasn't a killer, unemployment was her biggest fear.

"Raina Prentiss!" The familiar call came from Harvey's office.

She pushed her chair back from the desk and moved quickly to see what he was bellowing about. Hopefully it was business as usual.

"Did you see this? We have only two lawsuits that we're supposed to pay monthly installments on, and this one wasn't paid. Why not?"

"You think only two?" She was relieved to see that he had returned to his normal abnormal self.

"Two, four whatever, what difference does it make? Why didn't this one get paid? Why's it in collection?" He was holding a letter in his hand, shaking it at her.

Raina moved around like a bobble head doll trying to follow his hand, attempting unsuccessfully to read the letter. "Can I see it, please?" she asked.

He threw it down on his desk, and she picked it up.

"This is from WB Mason," she said.

"I know. Mason is the borrower, one of the plaintiffs. Why isn't it paid? I want these paid on time."

"Harvey, this is WB Mason, the office supply company. It's simply a past due invoice, one you said not to pay. You shouldn't be so stressed. You're still healing from your head injury."

A wide grin sprawled across his face. He snatched the paper from her hand, crumpled it, and threw it in the trash. Then he scissored his long legs down the hall, and he was gone.

Raina raised her voice before he was fully out of sight. "Welcome back!"

Everything was back to normal in the office. Harvey was as unfocused as ever. If he knew that she had led the cops to him, he wasn't acting like it.

Raina noticed a shadow fall across her desk and stopped typing. Tyler's broad frame pressed against her doorway, filling it.

"Hey, you're blocking the view," she said.

"Of what?"

"How do I know? You're blocking it."

He moved inside and sat on the edge of Raina's desk. She looked at him with a questioning face.

"I need you to go with me to a broker's office. Harvey already agreed," he said.

"Why?" she asked.

Focus on Danny.

"You're the expert on the new licensing requirements, and they need help."

"When because..."

"Now," Tyler said.

"Give me five," she said, and Tyler disappeared.

Raina dialed Danny, but her call went to voicemail. Not exactly how she wanted to hear his voice. Instead she sorted through the papers and folders on her desk, grabbing the ones she needed to take. On the road, she realized that she was spending more time with Tyler than with Danny. To avoid thinking about either of them, she focused on the lines on the road, and when they were on the parkway she tracked the pattern of the mowed grass on the side. It was cut unevenly in wavy tracks, and some areas had been missed altogether. After that stopped distracting her, she decided to retrieve her make-up bag and check her face. Her mascara needed some attention, so she unscrewed the top and slid out the brush. Just then the car rolled over a series of small bumps, and the applicator fell in between the seats. Tyler cringed.

"Don't worry, black on black," she said with a worried smile.

As she reached two fingers between the seat and the center console, she inadvertently pushed the applicator beyond her reach. With MacGyver in mind, she raked a comb against the applicator and pushed it onto the floor behind the seat. Tyler glanced over a few times.

"Leave it and I'll get it later," he said.

"By then, it will dry and be useless, and I need it now."

He exhaled loudly enough for her to hear while she depressed the seatbelt release and turned on her knees to face the back. The side of her face was pushed up against the seat as she stretched her arm to feel around. Something was there, and she pulled it up. It wasn't her applicator though. It was a set of keys.

"The suspense is killing me. Did you reach it, or is my car soiled with your make-up?"

"No, but you've probably been looking for these."

She tossed the keys to the front of the car and stretched for the applicator until it hurt. It was too far.

"I'll have to get it when we get there," she said and reseated herself.

They arrived at the offices of Broad, Stern & Lavin Mortgage Brokers a few minutes late, so she left the applicator retrieval mission until after the appointment. The office was a typical storefront office in Syosset with five desks topped with computer monitors and piles of legal sized manila folders, ringing phones, and expensively suited, young guys pacing around while they talked on their wireless headsets.

They were kept waiting for over half an hour which didn't endear them to Raina. She knew that Tyler was counting the potential dollars in his head and dealt with it. She fiddled with her phone.

"No word from him?" Tyler asked.

Raina diverted her eye contact and shook her head.

"Can I do anything to help? I feel like you've really been there for me lately, and I can't help you."

"I don't know what to do for myself. Thanks though."

"He'll come through, you'll see. He loves you. You know that."

When the meeting finally occurred, Raina smiled, forced a few compliments, asked a few questions, and gave her presentation. After she answered their questions, she left Tyler to cement the relationship. Her interest was elsewhere.

She strolled to Tyler's car and was peering through the window for her makeup wand when something caught her eye under the driver's seat. The doors unlocked, and she turned around.

"Raina, what are you doing? Get in. Let's go." She felt his strength as he guided her to the passenger side door and opened it for her.

He spoke, but her focus lingered on his touch.

She watched him drive. The top of his hair was blowing from the wind coming in through the sunroof, his eyes squinted from the sunlight, and his lips were pressed together. She turned her head to watch out the side window and, with guilt, thought about Danny.

CHAPTER 31

The warmth from Codis penetrated the side of Raina's leg as he curled up next to her on the couch. The television was on, but she realized that she wasn't paying attention to it and had almost dozed off when the phone rang.

"It's DB Night. Where are you? Paul is at his weekly card game, and I'm at the hospital alone, bored out of my mind," Sloan said.

"I'm leaving shortly. Just going to take Codis for a quick walk."

Raina had to walk the dog and check in with Grandma again, and she still hadn't booked a trip to see her parents. How could she when there was a big case to be solved? Sloan was waiting for her to arrive, and she'd probably see Tyler at the hospital as well. And Danny... no wonder she was exhausted.

She checked her cell and home phone in case she had missed a call. There were none. No sign of Danny electronically or otherwise. She stood at the bathroom sink and stared into the mirror. *He'll call.*

"Wanna go for a walk?" she said to Codis. In response, he raised his head and focused his eyes and ears on her.

Codis burst with energy when he heard her open the front closet and touch his leash. She clipped it to his collar, and he bolted through the front door. Raina stretched on her front steps for about thirty seconds, during twenty-nine of which Codis had the leash pulled taut, and then they were off. Codis trotted next to Raina as she rushed along and occasionally stopped to lift his leg on some unsuspecting bush.

The car ride to the hospital was uneventful. At two different stop signs, she checked her cell in case the rumbling of the car engine had drowned out the sound of an alert. Still no texts or missed calls. The guard waved as she carried the DB Night dinner past him. She returned the wave. As she rode the elevator to the maternity floor, she wondered if Tyler was nearby with his wife.

Raina was quiet while she ate her pizza. Her hair was pulled back in a ponytail as she hunched over the top of the pizza box on her lap, catching pieces of eggplant as they were squeezed from the folded slice.

"Good to see you have an appetite," Sloan said.

Raina wasn't good company but lacked the strength to make an effort. She knew that Sloan wished there was something she could say or do to comfort her friend, but it was Sloan that needed the comfort. She was the one in the hospital. Even though the doctors predicted a healthy baby, Raina knew she was worried. How could she not be? They were keeping her there.

"I almost forgot. Madison left a small envelope for you at the house: tickets to a fashion show, I think."

"When was Madison home?" Sloan said.

"She must have stopped by today. The tickets were on the table when I got home from work."

She pushed aside a few papers to find the envelope from Madison in the bottom of her large, leather bag. It had wedged in the metal key ring circles on her keychain. She held it and mindlessly slid the envelope from the ring, handed it to Sloan, and dropped the keys back in. A delayed vision flashed in her head. She crinkled her brow and reached back in. These weren't her keys. A key ring with a remote rested in her open hand. All of a sudden, her heart began to beat faster, and a lump grew in her throat. Her bottom jaw dropped. She looked over at Sloan.

"What's wrong?" Sloan asked.

Raina froze in place.

"What is it?"

Raina pressed her lips together and extended her hand out further to show it to Sloan. "This is for the Levy's alarm."

"What? How do you know? Why do you have it?"

Raina moved slowly to the chair and sat. She swallowed, stared at the little black rectangle, and then spoke. "The police are searching for this. I'm not sure how it got in my bag, but I found it in the back of Tyler's car."

"What were you doing in the back of Tyler's car?"

Raina knew that Sloan's imagination would run rampant as soon as those words left her mouth. "You missed the point."

"You and Tyler were in the backseat, and that's not the point? You weren't planning on telling me about this?"

"*We* weren't in the back seat." Raina explained about her mascara wand.

"How do you know it belongs to the victim? That would make Tyler...." Her words trailed off. What she was about to say scared them both.

Raina got control of her thoughts and shifted into detective mode. "I just have a feeling, but we need to find out for sure. Prepare for *Mission Remote Verification*. Call Michael."

"Okay." Sloan dialed her brother.

"Wait," Raina said. "I don't want to put any more prints on the evidence."

"Of course you don't."

Raina used a plastic bag from Sloan's drawer to secure the evidence.

When Michael answered his phone, Sloan tossed it to Raina. She filled him in on the plan and told him that she was in possession of the remote. They would take two cars. Michael would scope out the house on foot to make sure no one was home. After confirmation, he would stand by the front door to listen for the tone as Raina pressed the button to disarm the system. It was dark, he would be quiet, and no one would notice him on the property.

"Ah, one question," Michael said and continued without waiting for a response. "How do you know where the house is?"

Raina opened her mouth to speak, but he cut her off.

"Never mind; Danny," he said dragging his words.

"You don't mind if I take off for *Mission Remote*, do you?" she said to Sloan.

"That's more exciting than sitting in here. Wish I could go with you."

"Remember, we're the only two who know about this. We have to be sure before we tell anyone, okay?"

Clouds blocked the stars and muted the moonlight, both of which gave even better cover for *Mission Remote*. The humidity and heat of the evening went unnoticed. Raina drove with the device inside the evidence bag on the seat next to her.

She parked across from the house and prepared for her part of the plan. Two dim lights were on inside on the main level. The neighborhood was quiet, and no one was on the street. Michael and Charlie pulled in behind Raina and waited for the signal to go.

From the car, Raina saw Michael's head drop and then saw his face illuminated. She knew he was reading her text with instructions to go. They opened the car doors and closed them so slowly that Charlie had to hip-check the passenger side to catch the latch. Although the Jaguar wasn't exactly a fade into the background kind of car, it also wasn't out of place in the neighborhood. They quickly strode across the street and onto the property. As they hit the front walkway, each veered off to opposite sides. They walked around the house, peering into each window as they passed, until they vanished from sight. After less than a minute, Charlie was on the side of the house, and Michael was by the front entrance.

Charlie gave him the thumbs up, and they took their assigned positions. The bushes rustled as Michael pushed in behind them. It was a tight fit. The bushes had grown quite close to the house. Raina received his text: *We're in place. Hit it!*

The plastic bag crinkled as Raina held it up and aimed the remote at the house. A small amount of sweat glistened on her forehead. She wiped her arm across it, then pressed the button. Everything was quiet. She held her breath.

Adrenalin shot through her chest when Michael held up his hand, which was the 'affirmative' signal that they had devised earlier.

Oh my God. Raina's heart beat faster. Her mind raced from thought to thought. She hit the button again to leave the alarm in the same position as she found it. Michael's hand shot up again. He pumped it as though his team had made a score. Touchdown for *Mission Remote*. Michael pushed out of the bushes and went around the side of the house to Charlie. There were high fives and chest knockings exchanged. Raina was more somber. She had proven her theory, but she wasn't so sure she was glad. Tyler was a friend, and he was going through enough without her accusations. She had already caused enough damage when she believed that Harvey was the TMM.

Raina called Sloan to report.

"You should call Danny."

"No. Not yet. We have to make sure this time before we involve the police."

"I've been hacking," Sloan said, "searching for history on Tyler since you left. Nothing yet, but I'll have something soon. Are you coming back here?"

"I have to go see Tyler."

"For God's sake, why?"

"I can get his DNA."

"This is how he attracts women," Sloan said.

"I'll be fine. I'm a brunette," Raina said, then returned to her original thought. "And he had access to the drugs. And his wife –"

"And his wife is young and blonde," Sloan cut her off to say.

"And the murders all take place within a small radius of his house."

"So why don't you want to call Danny?"

"We had plenty of reasons to believe that Harvey was the killer: the girl at the party, the girl at the club, and the card from the RE Agent. If I can get Tyler's DNA, they can match it to the samples. Plus…"

"Plus what?"

"Danny isn't taking my calls. I tried a bunch of times today, and I haven't heard from him at all." Raina felt sick to her stomach.

CHAPTER 32

Unable to relax, Raina paced around inside her house. The bag she saw under Tyler's seat monopolized her thoughts. It all made sense to her now: how agitated he had been when she was searching under the seats for her make-up wand and again when she returned to the car alone. He must have rushed out of the broker's office to prevent her from seeing the contents of that bag. Now that was all she could think about. What was he hiding? It had to be evidence. Why would he leave it in plain sight? She needed to get to him, to the bag. It was too late to invite him to dinner, also too late to call to discuss work. She collapsed on to the couch and hit the remote buttons, flipping channels so quickly that no show registered with her. She slumped further down into the seat with her notepad while the television made noise in the background. Left with no alternative, she would take the night to come up with her course of action for the following day.

I will get to Tyler's car.

She scribbled notes as thoughts came to her and then crossed them out. In between one desperate idea after the next, she thought about Danny. He still hadn't responded to her calls, texts, or emails. It was getting more painful wondering where he was, what he was doing, and if he missed her or if he still loved her. When would he call? She was beginning to wonder *if* he would call. She longed to be in his arms.

The tone from her cell phone startled her. She assumed it was Sloan calling to check on her. Maybe she had found something on Tyler. She was wrong. The screen read *Tyler*. Her heart skipped a beat, and her hands began to tremble. *I'm not prepared. How can I sound normal? Deep breath.*

One big inhale followed by an exhale, then she pressed the button. "Is everything okay?"

She thought she heard him sigh. "Yeah," he said. It was a long moment before he continued, but she kept quiet. "This whole thing with Jean is getting to me tonight. I could use your company," he said with the inflection of a question.

Raina was thrilled by the opportunity that had just dropped into her lap, but she took a deep breath to conceal her excitement. "I'm sorry you have to go through this. Where are you?"

"At the hospital, where else?"

"I'll meet you there, and we can get a cup of coffee. Have you eaten?"

"Not really," he said.

"I'll see you in fifteen minutes and do my best to cheer you up. I'll tell you Harvey stories." She got a halfhearted laugh out of him.

Raina didn't wait for him to respond. She ended the call and jumped off the couch. Codis bounded behind as she ran to her bedroom to throw on her sneakers and release her hair from the clip, raking her fingers through it.

"Be a good boy. I'll be home as soon as I can." She blew a kiss to Codis who knew he was being left behind and was not happy about it.

Backing out of the driveway, she called Sloan.

Before Sloan could speak, Raina had already started. "Tyler called, and I'm going to meet him at the hospital and find a way into his car. Don't worry, I'll be careful."

"Info on Tyler is trickling in. He's a native Long Islander. I'll check the national database. You wouldn't happen to know where he went to school, would you?"

Raina thought for a moment. "His diploma from Penn State is hanging in his office."

"Great. Oh, there's a nurse here - again."

The call ended. Raina worried for a moment why the nurse might be in Sloan's room, but the mission monopolized her focus. Sloan had sounded fine. She drove as fast as she thought she could without getting pulled over. That certainly wasn't how she wanted her next communication with Danny to come about although it would force contact between them. As the light turned yellow, she punched the gas and made it through. A couple of times the light was already red, and she sailed across the intersection focused only on her goal: to check the bag under the driver's seat in Tyler's car.

It seemed like forever, but she was finally pulling into the visitor's parking area. Again she focused to control her breathing. That was becoming a regular exercise. As she turned off the ignition, it occurred to her that Tyler had sounded quiet and sullen on the phone, maybe he was trying to trick her. Reality caught up with her, and she began to worry about his intentions.

What did he want? He said 'company.' He sounded sad. Did he want my company emotional or physically? Or does he know I have the remote?

Tyler was waiting for her outside when she arrived. She spotted him immediately, sitting on the back of a bench with his feet on the seat. The breeze was moving his hair the tiniest bit. He was wearing a dark, long sleeved T-shirt. She couldn't quite see the color of it in the night, maybe blue or black. It didn't matter. He looked good, and a hint of his muscles showed through as the material pressed against them. Raina's emotions were all over the place. She was having trouble focusing on the mission.

The car, the bag, DNA, focus, she ordered herself.

"Sometimes I need fresh air," he said as she got closer.

She greeted him with a big smile and climbed up next to him on the back of the bench. He leaned over and gave her a kiss on the cheek. Her heart raced, and she was sure he could hear it echoing as it pounded against her chest.

"Thank you for meeting me," he said.

"Anytime."

Tyler rested his hand on her knee as he updated her on Jean's medical situation. Raina heard nothing. She only felt his hand on her. She watched his lips as they moved, remembering how soft his kiss was. His eyes never left hers as he spoke, and she felt the electricity go right through her. Fully aware of how wrong it was, she placed her hand on top of his. His hand felt strong and warm. He could have been confessing to the murders, but she wasn't listening. Although emotionally confused, she felt safer in her belief that he was looking for comfort, not the remote, or worse. That thought immediately jerked her back to reality.

"Do you want to get something to eat?" she asked.

"I do, but do you mind taking a ride with me? I need to get something from home."

Of course. She wanted the opportunity to get in his car. Beyond that, she didn't have a plan.

Her car remained in the hospital lot, and he drove. She fidgeted in the passenger seat, anxious for her chance to look in the bag.

"Come inside," he said.

This time she stopped to consider if that was a good idea. She wanted to check the bag, and if he was really the killer, maybe she should stay where someone could see her. "Um...."

The car door was opened from the outside, and Tyler stood there offering his hand to her. Unable to resist, she took hold of it and joined him inside.

"Sit and relax. I'll be right back," he said.

Without lifting the television remote from the end table next to her, she pressed the power button. A news show flashed on, and she stared through it as her thoughts scurried from her mission, to Danny, to Tyler, and back to her mission.

Glasses clinked as Tyler grabbed two from the kitchen along with a bottle of wine. The pop of the cork unnerved her. He still hadn't turned on a light. After he poured the wine, he leaned over her and switched on a lamp. She could feel the heat from his body. His chest barely brushed against hers sending her heartbeat into overdrive. His scent lingered. The mission was getting lost and her thoughts even more scrambled.

They sat sipping wine. Raina was uncomfortable. Tyler had to notice her squirming.

"Aren't you hungry?" she asked.

This was becoming her standard defense when her attraction to Tyler overwhelmed her, and she needed to distance herself.

"Yeah," he agreed while in motion.

He was slowly moving closer to her on the couch, and she was quickly becoming a wreck. The debate in her head was causing a headache.

Okay, she said to steady herself, *what do I do now? Nothing? What about Danny? What about him? I haven't heard from Danny since he walked out on me. Tyler is right here, and he's going to kiss me. I love Danny. I shouldn't do it. Could this distract Tyler, so I can find the bag? Would Danny understand it was for the mission? Should I....*

Her deliberation ended when he pressed his lips against hers. She didn't protest. Instead she kissed him back, passionately. His arms encased her and pulled her in tighter. She could feel his heart pounding.

She pulled back, but this time Tyler guided her back into his arms. He gathered her hair behind her head holding it in his fist as he kissed her again. Raina pushed aside all conflicting thoughts and submitted to her desires. As she relaxed, she felt his hand squeeze her slightly above the knee and then run all the way up her side, landing on her breast. She arched her back. He moved his lips from hers, kissing a path from her neck to meet his hand on her breast. Once she reached for the button on his pants, her intentions were clear, and he adjusted his position to give her full access. She reached in, made an open fist around him, and felt how hard he was. Tyler stood up from the couch and dropped his pants to the floor. He stepped out of them and reached for hers. It wasn't long before they were naked. He moved back on top of her. She wrapped one leg around him, pushing against him. As he slid his hand between her legs, her muscles contracted with anticipation. She felt his finger push inside. He had taken her so far she didn't want to stop. He didn't. Tyler brought her to climax, then slid himself inside her, back out, and deeper inside only for a minute until he exploded. They relaxed in each other's arms, wrapped up in their own cocooned world.

"I'm afraid of my feelings for you," Tyler said.

His words, between his soft kisses and caresses, lured Raina into a place of comfort. But then she watched his face contort into a pained expression and felt his body tense. He sat up.

"What's wrong?" she asked, terrified of his answer. Fearful that his moral compass had kicked in, she began to feel ashamed and embarrassed.

"You're right."

"About what?"

He backed away without another word. He took the wine bottle and glasses back to the kitchen where he placed the corked bottle in the fridge and the glasses in the sink. Raina dressed, fixed her hair with her fingers, and followed him. She sat at the island while he washed and dried the glasses with the news still humming in the background. She looked around and noticed that nothing was out of place, which she thought was unusual for a man who worked all day and sat in the hospital all night, and also maybe found time to slip away and kill women. She was refocused on *Mission Bag*. Since the kitchen light had been turned on in addition to the one in the living room, she spun around on the stool to take in the rest of the area from her vantage point. The dining room chairs were perfectly aligned with the table. The table was topped with tall, crystal candlesticks and a short, round bouquet of flowers. That perplexed her, too. Who would worry about fresh flowers when his wife was in a coma?

It didn't make sense. She moved towards the table to touch the flowers and confirm their authenticity. As she leaned over to touch them, she was distracted by something on the floor in the corner, the only thing out of place.

She closed her mouth to suppress a gasp, but the words escaped. "The bag."

As she heard the words hit the air, she was filled with fear and regret. Still determined to find out the truth, she kneeled down in front of the bag. As she unzipped it, Tyler was close behind her. Something inside reflected the light, but before she could focus on the contents, Tyler had her in a headlock. She struggled to breathe. Raina couldn't help but feel his strength as she reached up with both arms in a futile attempt to disengage his arm from her throat. She couldn't accept that he would hurt her.

"I wish you hadn't done that," he said.

Tyler moved his arm from her neck and covered her mouth. Her eyes widened. She watched as he reached for the bag and put it on the table. The sound of thin glass against thin glass clinked when the bag dropped. As a result of the twist Tyler performed to reach inside the bag, Raina was faced away from the table. The next and last thing she remembered was a tiny prick in her neck.

CHAPTER 33

"No one is home," Michael said, and they looked at each other with smiles, still on the Levys' property.

"Pick a chaise," Charlie said presenting the line of four chairs by the pool with a hand motion.

They still had another hour to kill before some party started and another hour for it to get into full force. That's when they would make their grand entrance.

"I was hoping for an adrenaline rush, dude," Charlie said.

Michael was shaking his head in agreement. "At least we have a good story to go with all these scratches from the bushes." Michael's arms and legs below his shorts sported long, red abrasions.

They sat by the Levys' pool planning the rest of their night during which time a bet was made to see who could get the most phone numbers at the party.

Sirens broke through the quiet of the night. The volume increased and then the lights were shooting across the side of the house.

"Shit, the neighbors must have called the police," Michael said.

They jumped from the lounge chairs and sprinted toward the back of the property. With his feet on the fence, Michael reached over and grabbed the other side, performing a gymnastic flip into the neighbor's yard. He hurried along the side of the house while a dog ran diagonally across the yard after him, barking insistently. Without a downshift in speed, he dropped his glance down and saw a small, white dog. He classified it as a low level threat. He reached the gate with the dog in tow and was able to escape just as the lights inside the house flicked on.

"Holy shit, man," he said, but there was no reply.

Charlie was not with him, and Michael realized that his friend was most likely in the custody of the police.

Feeling as though he had escaped for the time being, Michael reduced his speed to an inconspicuous walk. He had won a small battle. There was no doubt that the cops would figure out that Charlie hadn't been alone or that his friend would crack under pressure and give him up. The war wasn't over. He reached for his phone to call Sloan and found an empty pocket. He patted the others but no phone. Charlie and his phone were at the Levy house. He was as good as convicted.

It took another ten minutes at a quickened pace until he made it to Round Swamp Road, a dark, winding road where he searched for a pay phone. He spotted one up the ramp to the Northern State Parkway on a dimly lit median. He sprinted up the hill until he was close enough to see that only the thick metal shell that had previously housed the phone was still there. Without access to a phone, he decided to go back for his car. The police should be gone by now, he thought. He patted his pocket again. Not only was his phone at the Levy house but so were the keys to his father's car, both left on the table in the yard and perhaps collected as evidence. He couldn't call Sloan or drive himself anywhere. He was running out of ideas except for a very long walk to Sloan's house, where, he hoped, Paul would be there to help him. It was late enough. He should be home from the hospital. With no alternative, he resigned himself to that plan. A few miles later, he slowed as the adrenaline rush wore off.

When Michael crossed over the train tracks, he knew it was only a few more miles north to Sloan's house, mostly downhill. He might even find a cab in town. A sense of relief spread through him until he saw a police car off the main road. It was hidden out of plain sight on a side street. His heart raced, and he wanted to run. Unsure if that officer was assigned to look for him or wait for late night speeders, he tried to maintain a relaxed gait and an expressionless face and prayed for the latter. No matter what he did, he stood out. There were no sidewalks and no pedestrians. His best bet was not to be seen at all, but there was no other way around. He walked right in front of the police car and glanced at the officer in the driver's seat. The cop was looking down at papers, or a book, or maybe, Michael feared, a police issued photo of him for the search. It was probably too soon for that.

It took all his mental strength not to run and alert the cop to his presence. His breathing was uneven, but with each yard away from the car, he regained some composure. Finally, he was a quarter mile down the road. Now convinced that the cop wasn't hunting for him, he relaxed a bit and moved on.

Headlights raced towards him from a distance. He turned to change direction, and the flashing lights were coming from the other direction as well. It all happened so fast that Michael froze. Before he could think, four cops were out of their cars, shining lights on him and yelling. After they confirmed his identity, which Michael did not try to conceal, one cop moved close to him and cuffed his hands behind his back. The cop physically directed him towards the car, catching the tip of his shoulder as they put him in. He pushed his hips forward in the seat to avoid pressure on his wrists. The cuffs were secured tight enough to make his ride to the precinct additionally unpleasant.

The holding cell door slammed shut behind Michael.

"How did you get caught? I thought you were long gone," Charlie said, seated on a bench.

"How did they know about me?"

Michael's face showed his true question. "No way, dude. I didn't say a thing."

Michael examined Charlie's reaction. "Then how did they know?"

Charlie shook his head. "It wasn't me. That cop with the dark eyes was trying to break me, but I lawyered up. I heard him tell the other cop that the remote was tagged to alert them if it was used, so the minute Raina hit that button, they knew."

"Where's your lawyer?" Michael asked.

"Don't have one. I was going to call you."

"I'll call the family attorney when they let me near a phone."

Danny had been alerted when the alarm was activated with the missing remote, and the police had apprehended a suspect on the property. Despite the one suspect's request for a lawyer, he was on his way to speak to them. When Danny pulled into the precinct lot, it was quiet. The night air was cool, and to Danny's surprise, the press wasn't there. Danny entered through the back door, closer to the holding cells. He accelerated down the hall, stopped, and peered into the cell.

Michael immediately recognized Danny. He stood up and came close to the door.

"Aren't you Sloan's brother?" Danny knew who they were.

"Michael Miller."

Danny walked away without a word and returned later with Hawkeye and the officer in possession of the keys. Against standard protocol, he led Michael and Charlie together to an interrogation room.

"Have a seat," Danny said.

Hawkeye positioned himself in the corner of the room. To put them on edge, Danny said nothing for a few minutes, just observed. After he saw that sweat had beaded on Michael's forehead and Charlie had turned pale, Danny pulled out the remaining chair. Its metal legs screeched against the floor. The suspects cringed. Instinctively, Danny spun the chair around, leaned the back against the table, and put one foot on the seat. Training taught them never to trap themselves, always create the escape. If a situation occurred, it was easier to push back off the chair to move away or move towards the suspect without the chair back blocking their reach.

"Why are you guys back in my house?" Danny asked.

They looked at each other and said nothing.

"I'll ask a different question. Why were you trespassing?"

Still no audible response. Michael pulled the bottom of his shirt up to wipe the perspiration off his face.

"Where did you get the remote?"

Finally Michael spoke up. "Can I talk off the record?"

"No." Danny nodded in the direction of the two-way mirror.

"Shouldn't we wait for our attorney?" Charlie asked.

There was enough visible reaction for Danny to see that the guys were nervous, Charlie more than Michael. Later, Hawkeye would fill him in on the rest.

Danny ignored Charlie's question and pushed forward. "Where is the remote now?"

Michael's confidence was thinning. "I don't want to implicate others in our stupidity," Michael began.

"Others?" Danny asked.

Michael clasped his hands together. Staring at the wall right past Danny, he seemed to be holding out for an attorney whom he hadn't yet had the opportunity to call.

Danny was used to this kind of resistance, but he was growing impatient. It was late. This was his most important case ever. Any minute his boss would be on the phone, and the press would be out front, both hounding him for information about the guys in custody. Right in front of him, he had two people who could give him something, he could feel it. If he could ask the right question and kickstart Charlie's motor mouth, he knew they would have information to share.

"I'm sure there's a reasonable explanation, and you two aren't a team of serial killers," Danny said.

Charlie gasped, and Michael grabbed the table.

"What? No!" Charlie yelled.

"Wait," Michael said in a panic. "You have it all wrong."

"Then tell me," Danny said stoically.

"Okay," Michael paused.

Danny settled in the chair. Hawkeye was on edge. Charlie was turning green.

He began, "Sloan and Raina –"

Danny leaned over the table and stared down Michael. "Sloan and Raina?"

He hadn't spoken to Raina in days. Her name conjured up the torment he was bringing on himself and the pain he knew he was causing Raina. He loved her and couldn't understand why he kept hitting a wall in the relationship. The idea that he could take this time to figure it out and then go to Raina with some kind of explanation now seemed weak. Would she take him back like she had done once before? The thought that Raina was somehow involved began to cloud his focus.

"Raina recruited us for her mission to see if the remote was the remote for the Levy house. It is. Far as I knew, she was coming to you with it."

"How did she get it?" Potential answers to that question unnerved Danny.

"We don't know." Michael turned to Charlie for confirmation, and he agreed. "We don't question her on these missions. We just do our part."

Danny glanced towards Hawkeye for his evaluation. Hawkeye nodded his head.

Without his calm manner entirely intact, Danny spoke quickly. "Just tell me everything you know."

For the next quarter of an hour, Michael and Charlie told their story together, continually clarifying that neither they nor Raina and Sloan should be implicated in a crime. They also asked if their assistance with the case would get the charges dropped. Danny knew they also hoped their connection to Raina would do something to ease the situation. Each time Danny checked with Hawkeye for confirmation, he silently affirmed.

Danny tried Raina's home phone. It rang until her outgoing message came on. It was almost a relief. Then he tried her cell, but it went straight to voicemail. He turned to Michael. "Where's Raina now?"

Michael shrugged. "Call Sloan, she usually knows."

Danny had the officer escort the boys back to the holding cell and scrolled through his phone for Sloan's number. He woke her. She was oblivious to the fact that Michael and Charlie had been arrested. Because of her fragile state, Danny broke the news to her as gently as he could.

"I tried to reach her for an hour before I fell asleep. I don't know where she is."

"When did you see her last?"

"She dropped by before *Mission Remote*, but she called afterward. I haven't heard from her since."

"What did she say?"

"She was going to continue with the case, I think..."

Danny hung up before Sloan could finish, waved to Stone to join him, and handed a small piece of paper to Hawkeye with instructions for him to find the cell's location. Raina's cell number was written on the paper.

CHAPTER 34

Danny tore out of the lot towards Raina's. From the passenger seat, Stone hit the police lights but left the sirens off. Danny pressed the speed dial on his phone for Raina. Still no answer. He stomped on the gas pedal until the car skidded off the main road and into her neighborhood where he slowed to 50mph. The house lights were on, and Codis was in the window. Stone lurched forward as the car slammed to a stop. He jumped out, jogged up the walkway with his hand on his gun, and got to the door first. He pressed the handle, and the door opened.

"Not locked," he mouthed to Danny as he pointed to the door ajar.

Danny signaled him to go inside. With his hand on the release for his gun, Stone stepped through the front entrance. Danny was five steps behind him hitting the speed dial for Raina again. Codis spotted Danny as he was about to lunge at Stone and switched gears from guard duty to tail-wagging happy.

Stone hesitated. "Good boy."

They cleared the house, including the garage. No sign of her absentee roommate either. No sign of any disturbance. Danny rewound his thoughts back to the serial killer, the TMM. There weren't signs of forced entry, defensive action, or robbery. With a sinking feeling in his stomach, he tried Raina's phone yet again, and again he got her voicemail.

"Let's go." Codis leaped out the door and galloped to the car.

He dialed Sloan this time.

Without a greeting, she said, "She went to meet Tyler, and I'm worried. She's not answering her cell, and she always answers her cell. You have to find her."

He ended the call again and drove east to the hospital. On the way, Stone's cell rang.

"Yeah. Okay. Thanks." He wrote something down and hung up. "Here's the address where her cell signal is."

"Tell Hawkeye to meet us there," Danny said as he veered west turning away from the direction of the hospital.

The severity of the potential situation flooded his mind.

Danny's arms stiffened, and his hands gripped the steering wheel tighter.

"What are you thinking?" Stone asked.

Danny jerked the steering wheel, and the tires squealed against the road as the car slid out from the turn. He punched the gas for the straightaway. He sped down the center of the double yellow-line and continued to do so even after a car had turned right off a side road and was heading straight at them. The on-coming driver flashed his lights frantically and pounded the horn. Stone flipped on the sirens giving the driver just enough time to swerve and avoid a head-on collision. As he continued west toward Raina, Danny didn't notice the marked police car until it was close behind him, lights and siren on. Danny had the radio off. When a second marked car was on their tail, Danny knew the officer had radioed for backup when he couldn't contact them.

"Hey," Stone said, trying to penetrate Danny's concentration.

"Sloan said Raina went to see Tyler at the hospital."

"So?"

"So when does Raina go out this late without me? And she would never leave her door unlocked or the security system unarmed."

"I have no idea. When does Raina go out this late without you or leave her door unlocked?"

"This isn't a joke. Do you remember Tyler? You met him and his wife last summer at one of Raina's BBQs."

Stone shrugged his shoulders. "Maybe."

"He's tall, got the sales personality, outgoing, complementary, good-looking. You know the type."

"You think she's cheating on you? Is this some kind of mission to catch her in the act? You remember you requested backup to meet us there, right?"

"No, asshole. Think about it. He attracts women easily. He's the right age. And my girlfriend's with him."

Stone waited for Danny to continue his theory.

"Did you know his wife is hospitalized in a coma and she miscarried from her condition?" He paused, waiting for some acknowledgment from Stone, but got nothing. His voice rose. "A trigger or two?" Danny continued with the information Michael had supplied him.

It finally seemed to hit Stone like a pile of bricks. "Holy shit! You think he's the Morphine Murderer! She's not blonde."

"No, but he must know she's figured it out and needs to do something about it. Radio dispatch, and have them send someone to the hospital to find out when he was last there. Also check his phone. See who he's called and texted."

"10-4."

As Danny turned into the neighborhood, he realized it was Tyler's. His face heated as they pulled up to Tyler's house. The two police cars that had jumped on the convoy pulled in behind him, and within seconds, Hawkeye pulled over to the sidewalk, facing the vehicle in the wrong direction. Danny called out orders for the officers to go around back, for Hawkeye to watch the house, and for Stone to back him up at the front door. Following Danny's lead, all the cops had their weapons in hand, safeties off, and were prepared to fire. The house was dark except for the outside lights and one small light glowing in the front room. Danny didn't wait for a search warrant or an invitation to go inside.

He turned to Stone. "On the count of three."

On three, they kicked the door with full force. It flung open and slammed against the wall, came off the hinges, and crashed to the floor.

That energized Stone and was a release for Danny. Everything was in perfect order except for the front door lying on now cracked tile. They split up and searched the house. No one was there, not Tyler and not Raina. He radioed to Hawkeye to have them check the cell signal again then he dialed her cell phone. He heard the sound of faint police sirens from the living room.

"Fuck," he said and grabbed Raina's phone off the couch.

He ordered everyone inside to search the house for anything that could help them. Her blue screen glowed in his hand. He checked her messages, calls, and texts for clues about where she might be. Everything was cleared. The phone rang in his hand, and a picture materialized on the small screen.

"Sloan," Danny said.

"Did you find Raina?" she asked.

"No, but we found her phone abandoned at Tyler's house. Did you know she was here?"

"She said she was going to the hospital to meet him." He heard the hesitation in her voice. "Danny, I think she's in danger."

"What aren't you telling me?"

She began with the events from earlier in the evening and recounted the story of the remote he had already heard from Michael.

"How did she get it?" he asked.

Sloan hesitated again.

"Sloan!"

"She found it in Tyler's car."

"When was she in his car?"

"The other day."

"So he knows she has it?"

"I don't think so. She found it in his car, and he said it wasn't his."

"That's good. He might not realize that she knows its significance. We need to find her."

Sloan sounded nervous. "Um –"

"What now?" Danny asked, gritting his teeth.

"Uh, she saw a bag in the car when she was in the car, and she wasn't able to see its contents so after *Mission Remote*, she concocted *Mission Bag*."

"What the hell does that mean? We're wasting time."

"Raina thinks he has the morphine and needles in the bag, and she went to find out."

Danny groaned. "She knew he could be a killer, and she went to him anyway, and she didn't call me?"

"I'm sorry, Danny. I should have tried harder to stop her. I didn't really think Tyler could hurt anyone, especially her."

"Why didn't she call me?"

"Raina wanted to tell you, but since she had already wrongfully suspected Harvey, she wanted to get all the facts before she made more trouble," Sloan explained.

"That's fuckin' stupid."

Sloan remained quiet on the other end of the phone. She started then stopped, "And-"

"And what now?" Danny asked.

"She hasn't heard from you. She said she called you and left you messages but never heard from you."

Danny felt sharp pains in his chest like razors to his heart. "Do you know the FBI is involved in this case?"

Of course Sloan knew. Raina would have had told her.

"The FBI and the SCPD are trained and armed and...." He stopped in the middle of his rant, realizing he was losing precious time.

He ended the call without a parting farewell, so he could think and figure out the next step. The pressure from the press, his boss, and the civilians seemed to pale in importance now that Raina was in the TMM's hands. His career and ego had to be shelved. Special Agent Gordon Blainey was the only answer.

"Lieutenant, whatever you need," Blainey said.

"We've had a break in the TMM case."

Danny fed Blainey the facts. He refrained from including the alarm remote in his initial report. Technically the police hadn't found it, and there was no proof where it came from, only that it belonged to the Levy house. Not to mention that the police weren't in possession of it. The fact that Tyler's wife was in a coma, had lost a pregnancy, and fit the description of all the victims added to the psychological credibility of the suspect. He was using the FBI's profile.

"I didn't hear you say the suspect was in custody," Blainey said.

"That's why I'm calling." Danny struggled to ask for help given Blainey' dance around the subject of Stone as a suspect, but he couldn't deny the fact that he needed it. "He has a hostage."

"You've had contact?" Blainey asked.

"Not exactly."

Danny explained, withholding any information that didn't fall under the category of *need to know*. He did, however, include the fact that Raina was his girlfriend, a fact that he was no longer sure was true. His repressed sadness was surfacing, and he wondered if she had finally given up on him. There was no time to dwell on feelings. His thoughts fast forwarded to the present situation. He didn't know if she was still alive, or if she was, did she really know Tyler was a killer? Was he holding her against her will? Had he hurt her? Was she scared? Would he use her as leverage or just make her his next victim? It was a terrible way to think, but he was a cop. Civilians, he used to tell Raina, don't know the horrors that go on while they sleep at night, work during the day, and live their normal lives.

"We're in. Let me make a few calls. No worries," Blainey said.

Danny thanked Blainey and contacted Murphy with instructions to research Tyler Jenkins as far back as he could.

"Right away," Murphy replied.

CHAPTER 35

Raina woke up feeling groggy, lying on her side. Her head hurt, and the recent events were a blur. As the disorientation dissolved, she felt her hands bound together in front of her and her feet as well. Her ankles hurt as the bones pressed against each other. Something was wrapped around her head as a blindfold, and her neck was sore.

What happened? Think, Raina, think. Don't panic, think. Where am I?

It took only seconds for her to realize that she was in a car. The seats smelled like leather. She concentrated on sounds. The windows were closed. The radio was off. The engine was running, and she could feel the car moving.

With her two hands together, she struggled to get the blindfold off. It was tight around her head. The knot was at the back, out of reach, so she used the heels of her hands to push against the material and move it upwards. She moved slowly and was as quiet as possible. The stiff fabric was abrasive against her skin as she pushed it above her eyes. She opened them, and her sight adjusted to the slight change in brightness. Her head was behind the driver's seat. The interior was black leather. She saw the duct tape wrapped around her wrists and ankles, and she knew with some effort that she would be able to free herself. She snaked her body, inch by inch, until she was doubled over against the passenger side door and recognized Tyler. He was watching the road, and the ends of his hair were sticking out of his cap. She wished it had all been a dream, but Tyler had bound and kidnapped her.

It was mostly dark, but a hint of deep orange and pink sky poked through the early morning sky. They were on a highway heading into the rising sun, which meant they were heading east. She had no idea if she had been unconscious for a few minutes, a few hours, or a few days. It was reasonable to think it had been a shorter rather than longer time because she was hungry but not starving even though her bladder was about to explode if she didn't get to a bathroom soon.

To fight her fear, she chose to concentrate on freeing herself. She bent her knees closer to her body to reach her feet and picked away at the tape. It was relatively easy to scratch off the end with her nails, but un-wrapping it was tedious as she struggled to keep quiet. She could see the back of Tyler's head in the space between the back of the seat and the headrest. The two steel posts were fully extended for his height. She pulled the tape an inch at a time. Finally her feet were free. It seemed unlikely that he hadn't noticed her moving, but his focus was inside his head or outside the car, not on her. She had to liberate her hands. This had a higher difficulty rating. First she tried to twist her wrists to make an x, like a half inverted shadow bird position, hoping she could bend her fingers to reach the tape. Next she moved her head to meet her wrists and ripped a small piece of the tape with her teeth. She used it as a tab to peel the rest. As she clenched the tape in her teeth, she pulled until her head snapped back and the tape ripped. All she had to do was pull the rest of the tape from around her skin. She began slowly, cringing silently as the tiny hairs were pulled with it. Tyler turned around. The rip of the tape and her head hitting the back of the seat was enough noise to disrupt his concentration and alert him. She twisted her right arm free from the tape and used her hand to pull it off her left. She was free, except for being trapped in a moving car with a killer. Tyler slammed on the brakes and steered off to the side of the road.

"Tyler, you don't have to do this," Raina said in her best comforting manner, considering the predicament she was in.

Tyler didn't respond. Instead, he sat facing forward and remained calm. His silence was unnerving. The Tyler she knew would never hurt her. He would help her in any way, always did. But this wasn't the Tyler she knew. She was his hostage. He was a killer.

She yanked at the door handles, but they wouldn't release.

"Stone, scroll through the contact list and get Tyler's cell number," Danny said.

He initiated the call and handed it off to Danny.

Tyler answered reflexively, "Yeah."

"Tyler, it's Danny. I'd like to talk to you."

Without responding, Tyler hung up. Danny had to move forward. He called in to track the cell, and a few minutes later, he had the location.

"Let's go. They're on the LIE heading east near exit sixty-nine. That's the Manorville exit, so they have at least a thirty mile head start on us," Danny said.

Tyler was a few exits away from the east end of the Long Island Expressway. After that, they were on their way to the Hamptons.

"You think he has Raina with him?" Stone asked.

"Let's hope so."

Stone stared through the passenger window as the cars, trees, and exit signs zoomed by. Speeding along at close to a hundred miles an hour, lights on, sirens off, Stone belted in, and Codis leaning against the back, his legs braced. At this speed, they would be there in no time.

Stone's phone buzzed. "Yeah… Shit…. Thanks." He clipped the phone back on his belt. "Tyler turned south on Wading River Road, and then the signal was lost. They'll keep trying to track it."

Danny floored it. Stone's head whipped back, and Codis stumbled then regained his stance. The number of cars on the road dwindled the further east they travelled.

With little else to do, Stone contacted the precinct again to check on the trace. Still nothing.

Near the Pine Barren region of Long Island, a long stretch of low pine trees in a preserved area, Danny slowed the car to what felt like a creep at eighty-five miles per hour. Surprisingly, they hadn't attracted any other police cars.

Thanks to Sloan's insistence, Paul had posted bail for Michael and Charlie, releasing them from custody but not freeing them from Paul's lecture. Michael was thrilled to be out of jail and to have his phone back, which had been scooped up by the cops when they caught Charlie. The audible alerts from Michael's phone chimed endlessly, and he fought the urge to check. He was grateful for bail and the ride and didn't want to upset Paul further.

Once Paul dropped them off and backed out of the driveway, Michael retrieved his messages. Sloan had been desperate to reach him, and she had singlehandedly filled his voicemail. He returned her calls.

"Paul went to pick you up hours ago. Where have you been?" she huffed.

"I'm sorry. We...."

"Never mind. I need you to get over to Tyler's house and see what's going on. I sent the address to your phone. Go now, and call me when you're there."

"Okay, but –"

"Go now. It's up to you to execute *Mission Find Raina.*"

After the last mission, Michael should have been hesitant, but another chance to see Raina blinded his judgment. He had received instructions to drive to Tyler's and call Sloan. Nothing outside of the law there, he thought. He and Charlie took off in his jeep while Sloan barked orders in his Bluetooth earpiece. They had already turned the corner on to Tyler's street when they saw a cluster of official vehicles on the left. The property was taped off. He parked behind the last police car.

"Go find out what they know," Sloan said.

The last thing Michael wanted to do was go towards the police. He had just left them. Charlie refused to leave the car, but Michael got out and headed for the house.

"Do you live on this block?"

Michael turned to see a female officer coming directly at him. Her gun was the only thing that made her intimidating as it protruded from her pencil thin body.

"No, I'm looking for Detective Stone. Is he here?" Michael asked.

"You are?" the officer asked.

"Tell her!" Sloan said.

He pressed two fingered against his earpiece. "Shhhhh."

The officer shot him a dirty look.

"I'm a friend of Lieutenant Smith and Detective Stone."

The officer made no reply. She stood, eyebrows raised, waiting for Michael to continue.

He couldn't imagine that this officer didn't know Danny, so he continued. "The girl that they're trying to find. She's with Tyler, this house's owner. He's the Morphine Murderer."

Still the officer was stone-faced and said nothing.

Michael tried to clarify. "Danny, Lieutenant Daniel Smith?" The officer's silence frustrated him. "The Morphine Murderer?"

A light bulb flicked on in Michael's head as he saw the surprise in the officer's face. "You don't know what you're doing here, do you?"

Finally the officer spoke, "Police business. Detective Stone went with Lieutenant Smith. I can't tell you more than that."

He thanked the officer and proceeded right beyond her towards the house anyway.

Michael walked off with Sloan still rambling on in his ear.

"I know Tyler's not there. I tracked his cell. He's heading out to the Hamptons. I need to tell Danny and he won't take my call," Sloan said.

"Hey!" the officer shouted at Michael as he headed to the house. "You can't go there."

Hawkeye emerged from the front door.

"Jeez, you can't stay out of trouble. What's going on?" Hawkeye asked.

Michael relayed Sloan's message frantically.

"Assure Sloan that I'll get the message to Danny." Hawkeye handed him his card. "Tell Sloan she can call me directly if she wants to. I've heard a lot about her."

"What? What has he heard about me? From who? Who was that? What does his card say?"

Michael thanked him and returned to the car, passing the unhelpful, female officer who glared at him.

"God Sloan, relax. It was the cop with the black eyes. Every time I see him, I feel like he's staring into my soul. Do you know him?"

"Heard about him," she said, sounding uninterested. "Hurry here."

They drove to the hospital. When they arrived at her room, Sloan waddled out from the bathroom and picked up her phone from her bed.

"Missed calls. I didn't even hear them," she said.

Before Michael could give her a hug or ask how she was feeling, she was listening to her voicemail.

"Damn, Murphy finally calls back, and I'm in the bathroom without my phone," Sloan said.

She continued to listen, then the color drained from her face.

"There's a message from Tyler. He said Raina's with him, and she's fine. We have to tell Danny." She sat down on the bed. "I'm tired and frustrated. I'm trying to help, and Danny ignores me. He won't take my calls, and I don't know if he's listened to my messages or read my texts. He relied on me when I was on the force, and now...now."

"You better take it easy. No added stress, remember?" Michael said. "Where would Tyler take her?"

Charlie chimed in. "Why is a better question. Do you think he's going to kill her? I mean, dude, she's with a killer."

No one wanted to think about the answer to that question.

The silence was broken by Sloan's phone. "It's Raina's brother calling on the other line. What do I tell him?"

"Just answer," Michael said.

"Hey Shane," she said. "Don't worry. She left her phone at someone's house, and Danny's taking it to her. I'll make sure she calls you."

She ended the call rather hastily. "He's worried because he hasn't been able to get in touch with her."

Michael moved the laptop, so Sloan could stretch out on the bed. "We'll get to Danny."

"What are you doing?" she went on without a breath. "No! Give me the laptop! I can't just lay here when my best friend is in the hands of a killer. Danny needs to take my calls. We need to get to her before something really bad happens. Michael, you're not listening to me. Move the laptop back here. I need it now!"

"Here. Relax."

She clicked frantically. When a tone sounded, she took a breath. "He's almost to the Hamptons. If you leave now, you're only forty-five minutes behind him. I'll direct you when you get to the end of the LIE. Go!" Sloan said.

Michael gave her a kiss on her forehead. "Try your replacement again. I'm sure he can get to Danny."

A plastic pitcher flew by his head and bounced off the wall as he left.

On the way out of the building, they stopped in the cafeteria and grabbed some snacks and all the bottles of water they could carry.

"Dude, what's up with your sister?"

Michael pointed to his stomach.

CHAPTER 36

Heading south on Wading River Road, Stone was asking the same question Michael had. "Where do you think he'd take her?"

Danny had a long while to think about the answer to that question before Stone asked. He angled the sun visor to the driver's side window to block the sun that was rising quickly and heating up the left side of his face.

"We spent a weekend at his house in the Hamptons once."

"Which Hampton?"

"I'm trying to remember. I think I can find it by sight."

"Some info would be helpful."

"The house was on the water."

"Yeah, that helps on Long Island."

He poked at the computer trying to locate a residence in Tyler's name. He searched throughout Suffolk County, but the only hit for a deed in Tyler Jenkins' name was the one they had left a half hour ago.

"What's his wife's name?" Stone asked.

"Joan."

Using two fingers, Stone typed in 'Joan Jenkins.'

"No, Jane."

Stone made the change and the hourglass rotated on the screen.

"It's Jean. Her name is Jean."

"Are you sure? How do I cancel the search?"

"If you can't figure it out, call Murphy. And before we get there, call for back up. Check with Hawkeye and see if they found anything new at the house. Also, see if they can find a bill or something to give us the Hampton address."

Stone's phone chimed. He snatched it up and showed the screen to Danny. Capper had checked in, again on time. He called Hawkeye on speaker. Without anything new to report, Stone relayed Danny's instructions.

"Oh," Hawkeye said. "Tell Danny Michael Miller showed up looking for him. He said that Sloan really wants to talk to Danny."

"Got it," Danny said.

"He's got it. Look for the address."

"10-4."

Danny's phone rang. He didn't bother to slow the car before answering it, "Smith."

"Boss, it's Murph. I found something. I pulled up Tyler Jenkins' birth certificate. He was born on Long Island to a Samantha Jenkins. No father listed."

Danny put him on speaker, so Stone could hear as well.

"There was an article in the Smithtown paper about a young boy, six, who found his mother dead, an OD. They don't mention the boy's name, but the woman was Samantha Jenkins, and the timing would make him about thirty years old now. Does that sound about right?"

"Yeah, what happened to the boy?" Danny asked.

"I'm pulling the file. I'll get back to you on that," Murphy said. "By the way, nothing on that Michael Miller except the usual social network crap. He's a rich, party boy. Nothing criminal until we picked him up at the 7-11 recently, then again last night."

Daylight was in full force. The sky was clear of clouds except the one that hung over Danny like a threat. They turned off Wading River Road and headed east on Route 27, a two-lane road that led to and through the Hamptons. In prime season, the road was a traffic nightmare, jammed with weekenders coming and going. Luckily this weekday morning heading east allowed for some speed.

It wasn't long before Murphy called back with more relevant details. "I got hold of the file. Drug addict mother, in and out of rehab. The grandparents came from Pennsylvania and stepped in when she was away."

Murphy continued to share the contents of the sealed juvenile file. His mother had been blonde, and she had suffered from drug addiction even before her pregnancy with Tyler.

"Despite the drugs, the kid formed a tight bond with his mother. She kept him close, using him as a shield, believing that having him with her would shield her from the dealers, the law, and her family. There were lots of petitions from her parents to obtain custody of Tyler, but all of them were denied. The details weren't clear. A report from Tyler's grandparents said that he often had to take care of his mother when she was unable to take care of herself. He was her caretaker. A six year old! Tyler was found days after his mother's overdose, sitting on the floor rocking in place. He refused to speak to anyone." Murphy stopped for a beat. "Stone, you hearing me?"

"Yeah."

"I'm sending you a photo from the crime scene. Check the position of the body." They heard the clicking of the keyboard through the phone as he paused to send the photo. "I'm on the verge of access to another file. That's all in this one," Murphy said.

During Murphy's silence, Danny heard a commotion in the background.

"What's going on there, Murph?"

"Ah, pulling a pair of officers from another assignment for a fresh OD. A woman's body found in Melville. There's an officer there now with the M.E."

The lump in Danny's throat almost prevented him from breathing. "Details on the body?"

"Pretty beat up with needle marks. Her teenage son called it in. What do you want to know?" Murphy asked.

"Did it hit the news yet?"

"Yeah, not too long ago."

"10-4," Danny said and hung up.

As he watched the road, Danny could only think about the overdose trigger connection theory that Raina had discovered. He gripped the wheel tighter as he thought about her.

"We need to get to her," he said.

"You think he's already heard about the latest OD?" Stone asked.

"It's possible, and I don't want Raina to be the collateral damage of his next psychotic reaction to it."

Stone hit the keys frantically trying to locate the address on the computer. Danny could tell that Stone was worried and assured him he was fine. He was thinking straight even though he would be ripped off the case as soon as his boss got wind that Raina was in the killer's possession.

"I got something," Stone said. "Does Southampton sound right?"

"Maybe."

"A Jean Jenkins owns a house in Southampton on Little Plains Road. I'll put it in the GPS."

"Calculating route," the GPS sounded.

"It's about twenty-five miles from here."

Danny punched the gas, and the speedometer needle pinned to the right.

CHAPTER 37

Danny's service faded in and out as he drove off the main road and headed south towards the Atlantic shore. Speeding became more difficult as they got closer. Toylsome Lane was a narrow, residential road. He noticed the message light on his phone and listened on speakerphone. All, but one, were from Sloan.

"It's Sloan. Call me."

"It's Sloan again. Please call me."

"Danny, it's Sloan, please, it's about Raina."

"He's taking her to the Hamptons. You've been there. Call me."

"Maybe you should be taking her calls. She and Raina seem to be right behind us on this case." Stone paused for a moment. "Shit, maybe ahead of us." He chuckled.

The humor was lost on Danny as he handed off the phone. "Her number is in there. Call her."

"Toylesome Lane in South Hampton," Sloan answered.

"We're on our way there now. Has he called you again?"

"No. I tried him a few times but nothing. I sent Michael to track him."

"Call off your dog. We've got it, and he'll just be in the way. And, you don't want him to get hurt." He ended the call.

Danny struggled with the ego issues involved with Raina keeping pace with the Detective Squad. That was as honest as he could be with himself for the time being. Sloan had been trained during her years on the force, but the fact that Raina had suspected Tyler before him was yet another issue. He had already rationalized that one away many miles ago. Raina had simply had information as a friend of the suspect that he didn't, he couldn't. His conflicted emotions between Raina's bravery and her stupidity for risking her life stirred in his head. Although he tried to push off all emotion while he maneuvered to save her life, Danny loved her and was desperate to find her after the next turn onto Little Plains Road – alive.

"We should have kept Sloan's brother in custody until this was over," Danny said as he reached for his phone. "Smith."

"It's Murph. Got some more info on the kid."

"Go ahead."

"A case worker pulled him from the grandparents' home and placed him in foster care after a neighbor called the police for suspected abuse. This kid never got a break." Murphy took a breath. "Listen to this. It turned out the foster mother was being abused by her husband. She was blonde too, by the way. After the kid met with a state child psychologist they learned that he had grown close to the woman and was trying to protect her by not leaving her alone."

"Poor kid," Danny said disconnecting the kid from the target.

"Seems she was only abused when the kids were away from the house."

"And they sent the kid back there?" Danny asked.

"It was supposed to be a short term solution while the department made other arrangements."

Murphy conveyed the remainder of the report to Danny. The school had reached out to the foster parents unsuccessfully when Tyler's grades had dramatically dropped due to poor attendance. Finally, one day a truant officer went to the farmhouse and escorted Tyler to school. When he returned that afternoon, he found his foster mother dead. The COD was blunt force trauma to the head. Her autopsy reported recent and previous injuries typical of spousal abuse. Tyler blamed himself for his foster mother's murder because he left her alone with her husband, and he wouldn't have been there in the first place if he had kept his birth mother alive. He bounced around the Pennsylvania state foster care system until he turned eighteen and received a special state grant for college.

"A lot of guilt for a kid to handle," Murphy said.

"God, that might be the saddest shit I've heard on the job. Not one, but two dead mothers," Danny said.

"How do you know the kid blamed himself?" Stone asked.

"Psychological evaluations say so."

"Sealed minor files, you mean," Stone said.

Murphy ignored Stone's accusation and continued. "According to his records, he came back to New York after he graduated. Maybe to make the most of his marketing degree or maybe to return to his original home."

"Maybe to avenge his mother's death," Danny said.

"Maybe to punish his mother for hurting him. I'm telling you, it's always the mother's fault," Stone said.

As Danny came around the last turn onto Little Plains Road, the house came into view. It was still a distance down the private road. Maybe it was the driveway. The six thousand square foot brick home stood at the end, built the long way against the ocean for maximum water views. The front entrance was grand and the landscaping professional. He sped up, then slammed on the brakes when he was in the enormous circular driveway leaving two black curls of rubber on the pavers. The smell of the ocean beaches, the sound of the crashing waves, and the cool of the sea air all escaped their notice as they hit the ground running. Rescuing Raina was the only thing on Danny's mind.

There were no cars in sight. Stone checked the garage. He nodded to Danny to indicate that there were no cars in the there either. Danny moved towards the front door, whispering into his radio with Codis at his side. He called to check on the backup and gave the idea of waiting for it about two seconds before he kicked in the front door. No alarm sounded. They split up to search the house, guns drawn and safeties released.

Danny sent Stone westbound, and he turned to the east end of the home, carefully moving from room to room. If she was there, he wanted to locate her as quickly as possible in case she needed medical attention, and if Tyler was there, he wanted to apprehend him without gunfire. He stepped swiftly. Every room was spacious with high ceilings and extensive woodwork. Each had elaborate furniture and drapery.

As he scanned to the left, Danny saw a small, red dot of light shining on the wall, scattering about as though it was aimed by a shaky hand. The beam of light hung in the air close to his face. He reacted instinctively. Fully expecting it to be the red dot sight from the scope of a rifle, he ducked and turned, simultaneously aiming his gun in defense. He looked beyond the window for the source but only saw the ocean. There was no cliff, no nearby house, no boat close by. He moved carefully, closer to the window, used furniture as a shield, and checked both sides. There was no surface for a gunman to stand at the right angle. He backed away for a broad view of the room. That's when he saw the string of crystals hanging on fishing line from the window frame, catching the sun. He exhaled a puff through his nose and then sucked in a breath, almost choking from the jaggedness of it.

"Where's Raina?" Danny asked Codis.

He wasn't a trained rescue dog, but he *was* attached to his owner. It was worth a try.

Codis took a straight path up the stairs to the second level, four steps at a time, with Danny right behind him. Codis turned into the first bedroom. Inside were two beds pushed against opposite, pale blue walls, and the window had a very shear white curtain drawn. No sign of Raina. Codis sniffed around each bed, moving the blanket with his snout. He froze. His ears perked up, and then he shot out of the room. The halls were narrow, each turn was sharp. Danny struggled to keep close behind him, holding his gun at his side, pointed down but ready. Codis' back left leg slid out from under him as he turned sharply into a room at the end of the hall. It was an office with a large mahogany desk that held a computer and three screens mounted on a monitor bracket. One side of the bay window was slightly open allowing the sea air to scent the room. Codis bounded through and whimpered as he sniffed the air from underneath a door at the far west end of the room. Danny had painful visions of Raina tied up in the closet, gagged and weary. Perhaps beaten, tortured, or worse. Dead was not an option he allowed himself to consider. Danny pushed Codis back, raised his gun, and gently turned the doorknob. As the door opened, he expected a dark closet on the other side but instead found himself looking down a narrow hallway lined with book cases. Together he and Codis trotted down the hall to the next door. Danny turned the knob, but the door was locked. Without any thought he kicked it in. He brought his forearm across the top of his eyes. The sun beamed through the window, and he saw Raina lying on the bed. The bed shook as Codis jumped onto it and licked her face. Danny felt for a pulse. Her neck was warm and blood was pumping, but she wasn't conscious even after the long, wet tongue wiped across her cheek.

CHAPTER 38

"I got her!"

When Stone didn't respond, Danny called for an ambulance then Stone's cell.

"How is she?" Stone asked.

"Drugged, but alive. Find any sign of Tyler?" he asked.

"Nothing. I'll be right there."

Danny kneeled and stroked Raina's cheek. He fought back the emotion that gathered in his throat, pushed her hair back, and sat eye to eye with Codis who had settled on the bed next to Raina.

"Good boy. Every time you hunt a rat at the beach or an opossum in the yard, I'll remember how you took me straight to Raina. Extra bagels for you."

"Where the hell are you?" Stone had called Danny's phone. "I secured the whole second floor, checked every room."

It was easier for Danny to walk out of the hidden bedroom, back through the hall, back through the office and get him, than to try to direct him. Stone followed him back, saw Raina, and checked with Hawkeye.

"I'm about ten minutes out," Hawkeye said.

Danny held Raina, relieved that she was safe and in his arms. Anger seeped in and took over. He was angry with himself for letting this happen to her and furious with Tyler. His blood boiled, heating his face. He felt it throughout his whole body. Visuals of revenge flashed before his eyes as he stared out the window at the waves crashing against the shore. When he got his hands on Tyler he would ... He controlled his urge towards violence. He'd let Stone arrest Tyler.

Codis stuck his Doberman snout under Raina's hand and flipped it onto his head. The motion brought Danny's gaze back to Raina. He spoke softly to her, hoping she would awaken. As if he had special powers, she opened her mouth and struggled to speak. Danny placed two fingers over her lips. His stomach muscles began to relax, and he squeezed her hand. The expression on her face was all he needed. It wasn't fear, it wasn't anger. Danny knew that she was okay. He felt it. The deep connection to her was unfamiliar to him; it was on a level way beyond chemistry. It was pure and clear.

Stone bolted to a north-facing window when they heard the sound of rubber against the concrete outside. They expected Hawkeye and the ambulance but hoped it was Tyler.

"God damn it," Stone said.

"What is it?" Danny stayed by Raina's side.

"It's the jail birds."

"Go down there and keep them out of trouble," Danny said.

"10-4." As Stone exited the room he added, "Not an easy task this summer."

There was a loud debate before Stone led them into the bedroom where Raina was sitting up on the bed. Michael zoomed right past Danny to Raina's side. Danny gave them a short moment, then reasserted his position. Respectfully, Michael stepped back next to Charlie by the dresser until his phone rang.

"How is she? I want to talk to her." Sloan's voice resonated from the device.

Michael raised his eyebrows at Danny.

"Sloan," Danny began, "she can hear you, but keep it short."

They could all hear the tears in Sloan's voice. "I'd be there if I could. I'm so happy you're okay, and I'll see you soon."

Raina tried to lift her hand for the phone. She tried to get up, but Danny told her not to move until she was checked by EMS. She still hadn't formed words, which indicated to Danny that she wasn't completely fine.

Another car arrived at the house. This time it was Hawkeye. Stone sent Charlie down to show him upstairs, and he joined them in the bedroom.

A loud voice bellowed from down the hall, "Let me through."

Everyone turned towards the door with recognition and surprise.

"Garza, there must be some mistake, no body," Stone said.

"Thank God," they heard Sloan from the speaker.

Garza frowned towards the phone, then spoke to his trainee. "What the hell? You dragged me here and there's no body?"

"Sorry, I heard it was Danny's girl on the radio, and I thought they should have the best," his assistant, Tony, said.

It was a rare moment. Garza was speechless. "Well," he paused and searched for words, "everybody move and let me see her."

He pushed his way up to the bed and pointed. "Move the damn dog."

Codis snarled and kept his position next to Raina. When Danny made it clear to Codis that it was okay, he moved his lips back over his teeth without ever taking his eyes off Garza. The doctor moved closer to Raina cautiously, returning the dog's stare. Her eyes were clear, her gums were pink, and her pulse was normal.

Garza barked at Tony. "Get me the blood pressure machine."

"We don't…." Tony started to say.

"Yeah right, we don't. Because our patients don't have blood pressure, do they? No pumping heart, medicine 101," he said as he inspected her arms with his magnifying glass.

Danny stood back as patient as he could be as Garza examined Raina.

Stone left the politics at the door. "Stop being a dick, and tell us something."

Garza looked past Stone and at Danny. "She looks fine, maybe dehydrated. Get her some water."

Michael jumped up. "I have bottles in the car, I'll be right back," he said as he negotiated his way out of the crowded room.

Garza continued. "She was probably drugged. No needle mark in her arm, but I'll take blood and send it to the lab, a rush of course. Make sure she drinks lots of water to flush out the remaining drugs." He got up and leaned closer to Danny's ear. "She'll be fine. Get her home and let her rest."

Danny acknowledged Garza's advice and extended his hand.

The CSI team followed Michael back into the room.

"Holy shit," a balding investigator said as he gazed around at the dozen people in the room sitting on the furniture, stepping all over the floor, touching everything, *and* a dog on the bed. "Haven't you guys ever heard of not contaminating the crime scene?" He shook his head and placed his kit on the floor.

His female counter-part spoke robotically. "Please clear the room."

Danny checked with Garza for permission to move Raina. He nodded affirmatively. Then one by one they filed out of the room through the hallway of bookcases. Danny lifted Raina from the bed and carried her to his car with Codis at his side. He put Raina on her feet while supporting her weight and helped her into the back seat before opening the front passenger door for Codis. Danny and Stone remained outside the car.

"Why would Tyler leave her?" Stone asked.

"Well, he wasn't worried about it because she wasn't restrained in any way."

"Except for the drugs. Maybe he thought he had given her enough to keep her sedated until he returned," Stone suggested.

"Maybe he left the house with the intention of returning, but when he tried to come back, he saw all the vehicles in the driveway and took off."

"But he had to know that Raina would regain consciousness and tell us what happened."

There were other questions that weren't answered. If Tyler was the TMM, why wouldn't he have killed Raina as a loose end? And how could they place him at the scenes?

He instructed Hawkeye to have the CSI obtain a DNA sample from Tyler. "Find a toothbrush or something," he said.

"Yes, sir," Hawkeye said. Before he went back into the house, Hawkeye pulled an evidence bag from his pocket and showed it to Danny. Inside was a short chain with a cross on it. "Just like the victim's mother described. Found it at Tyler Jenkins' other house."

"Good. Get it back to the lab and have the mother give a positive ID. Let her know we'll get it back to her as soon as we can, but it's evidence for now." Danny gave Hawkeye a hardy pat and returned to Raina's side.

"Shit," Stone said.

He ran back to the house and returned minutes later, winded. In his hand was an old, framed photo. One corner of the photo had been previously bent and had formed a triangle. Black spots stained the background. A young woman was crouched down to her son's height for the picture. A strikingly similar cross dangled from her neck, partially blocked by her long, blonde hair.

"Very observant," Danny said.

"It was the odd contortion of her body that drew me to the picture in the first place."

"Or maybe that she's busting out of that shirt, and the cross was hanging in her cleavage."

"Just a highly skilled detective."

"Right." Danny got back to Stone's earlier question. "So maybe he's leaving the state or the country."

Stone contacted the precinct to have Tyler's passport monitored as well as all last minute flight reservations. "And of course let us know if his cell hits the screen again."

Raina was barely conscious. Her eyelids hung heavily. Even her mouth seemed to droop at the edges. She had given up the struggle to join the conversation and was instead leaning against the corner between the back seat and the door. Her legs up were up and her knees bent as she faced Danny.

"I wonder if he would leave his wife behind," Danny said.

CHAPTER 39

Tyler was nose-to-frame with the automatic doors at the hospital's entrance until they glided open, and he flew through. The seconds had felt endless. He jogged past the elevators and through the door to the stairs. Three by three, he hauled up them to see Jean. He stood in the doorway, staring at an empty room. The bed had been stripped of the sheets and blankets. All surfaces had been cleared. His heart pounded harder as the fear heated his entire body. Horrible scenarios played in his head, all of which ended the same way. Jean had died alone. Tyler was dressed in his prior day's clothes, unshowered, unshaven, and weak from exhaustion, both emotional and physical. He had spent the night trying to figure out what to do with Raina and distraught over abandoning Jean. Never before, since they met, had he gone this long without seeing her. His promise to her was broken. He had left her alone, and see what had happened.

A familiar nurse greeted him. "Are you okay, Mr. Jenkins?"

He was frozen in place. He felt the nurse rest a hand on his shoulder as she repeated her question.

"Where's my wife?" he asked.

His tone was cold and his manner frayed since he was unable to think about anything except the emptiness he felt. It was mixed with regret, sorrow, and a strong sense of failure.

Only two hours earlier, Tyler had received a call from the head nurse that Jean was conscious and asking for him. His hands had immediately begun to sweat and shake. As a result, he had lost his grip on the phone, and it had smashed on the ground. His mind had gone blank, except for his thoughts of his wife, lying in her bed, unaware of all that had happened, asking for him, and he wasn't there for her. All the time he spent promising her he would never leave her alone, and she would think that was exactly what he had done. Left her. The whole drive back, he imagined how scared she must have been, not knowing where she was or why, and he hoped that no one had told her about the loss of the baby. He fled the Southampton house without any regard for Raina or thought to the future beyond his need to get to Jean. How could things have changed so fast?

"Right this way," the nurse said and walked with him down the hall.

"Why has she been moved?"

"She's fine. They moved her down to the end of the hall. It's quieter there." She placed another supportive hand on his shoulder as they walked.

It took a few seconds for him to process that. Although there were very few staff on the floor, Tyler took some comfort in the familiar environment with its distinct smell and bright lights. As he and the nurse approached the last room, the nurse stopped and silently raised her palm, presenting Jean to her right. There existed the illusion of a private corner with mostly empty patient rooms. Tyler thanked the nurse and gazed in at Jean. She was facing away from the door on her side under a sheet. Her blonde hair cascaded behind her, and fewer tubes were attached to her. Anxious to speak with her, he contemplated waking her. Then, another thought struck Tyler that panicked him. Since his wife had regained consciousness, they would be able to begin to determine if there was any brain damage. For many weeks, he had been told they wouldn't know the extent of it until she was awake. When they called, he was told that Jean had asked for him, and that meant at least some of her brain functions were working. She could speak, and she had memory. All that mattered was that she was alive and that she remembered him. She had said his name, and that was enough for the moment.

The nursed urged him in. "It's okay."

He stepped towards the bed, placed his hand gently on her thigh, and whispered her name. Worry was overtaken by excitement. It had been so long that it almost felt strange to expect an answer. What would his first words to her be? How would she feel? The blanket moved as she folded it back and sat up slowly, hanging her head down. His body trembled. He moved around to her, pushed her hair behind her ear, and she raised her head. Stunned by her face, he peddled backwards and hit the wall behind him. This woman was not his wife. In one motion, he bounced forward and sprang for the door. Two large figures blocked the way. His heart raced, he was trapped, and he froze in place like a rabbit. The woman rose from the bed and pulled the pulse monitor from her index finger. Together the two men flashed their FBI credentials without breaking eye contact.

"Mr. Jenkins, I'm Special Agent Blainey with the FBI. We need you to come with us."

Tyler glanced back. The woman who had posed as his wife made an apologetic face and presented her federal ID, "Special Agent Judith Bryant."

Blainey and a third agent stepped inside the room leaving the doorway unblocked, an opportunity that wasn't missed by Tyler. He kneeled down to retie his sneaker, pushed off, and bolted past them. He was surprised that they had fallen for that elementary diversion, took full advantage, and ran down the hall. Knowing the hospital better than the agents, he quickly turned a corner and disappeared into a stairwell. The door slammed behind him as he jumped down three and four steps at a time. Then he heard the stairwell door open. Blainey spoke into his radio alerting the officers at the front entrance of Tyler's escape. He picked up speed, jumping the last five steps of each landing, pounding the floor and angling for the next set of stairs. As the heavy beat of footsteps continued above him, he exited the stairwell, crossed the building on a different floor, and rode a service elevator down. It let out at the back of the building. He hid behind a group of green dumpsters to plan his next move. The smell was awful. He wasn't sure what the extent of the FBI plan had been. The part that haunted him was that he didn't know if his wife had regained consciousness or if that was part of the ploy. Did she really call for him? Was the staff in on the trap, or did the FBI gamble that he would show up at some point? It made sense, he realized, given his attendance. The exit door opened slowly, and Tyler slid further between two dumpsters. He held his breath to keep from choking from the stench. He crouched down when a small-framed man with a full head of grey hair and wearing scrubs came out of the hospital. The man reached into his front pocket and pulled out a cigarette and a lighter. Tyler was anxious for him to go back inside. After the man's last puff, he discarded the butt on the ground and dragged a giant bucket and mop back inside.

It was time to execute his next move. His car was in the visitor parking lot and surely under observation. That was not an option.

He scanned the lot and spotted an old Mustang convertible parked a few rows over, top down. No one was in sight, so he jogged over to the car. With one hand on the car, he easily hopped over the door and landed in the driver's seat. Sweat formed between his shoulder blades as he reached under the steering wheel and yanked a bunch of wires. He tried various combinations until a spark flashed, and the engine started. He raised the convertible top and powered down his cell. As his foot hit the gas, memories flooded his mind. When he was a young teenager, the thrill of stealing cars had given him a sense of power. It was a skill learned from one of the other foster kids, but it didn't take long for it to become second nature. This time there was no rush, no thrill, no feeling of satisfaction. This time it was only adrenaline that kept him going since he was tired, worried, and flying without a plan.

CHAPTER 40

Raina swallowed and then managed her first word since her rescue. "Danny," she whispered in a hoarse voice.

Codis' ears rotated in Raina's direction, followed by his head. She reached over to pet him, and his tongue caught the heel of her hand.

Danny reacted as quickly as Codis. "How do you feel?"

"I'm sorry, I should have called you." She swallowed again. Danny handed her a bottle of water. She drank some then continued, "...to let you know what I was doing."

"No, *I'm* sorry." He gave her a kiss and an endless hug.

"Hey, get a room," Stone said as he glanced at them in the rearview mirror.

Danny smacked him on the back of the head. "Check in with Hawkeye, would you?"

He took Raina's hand, kissed it, and kept it in his. "I'm sorry, but right now I need to know what happened and everything you know about Tyler."

Stone started the engine and continued around the circular driveway until they were back onto Little Plains Road headed north. Raina started at the beginning of her investigation, going all the way back to *Mission Bottle*. She told them how Tyler aided in the mission to get Harvey's DNA and how they followed him around for a while and carefully collected the evidence.

"Inserting yourself into the investigation is a common thing for serial killers. I should have realized that at the time," she said.

Stone responded, "You asked him for help, right? He didn't offer. And he doesn't fit the rest of that profile."

"He jumped at the chance," she said.

"He's not an attention seeker, never contacted the media or left intentional leads. Never any indication that he thrives on recognition either," Danny said.

She continued to hit the highlights of her investigation, how she followed Harvey to the bar and to the club.

"When I found the remote in Tyler's car, it didn't set off any bells." She paused, and her face immediately flushed as she let her hair cover part of her face. *No, I couldn't have been so wrapped up in Tyler that my detective skills were dulled.*

She forced herself to refocus. "It wasn't until I saw the remote again in my bag that it clicked. Then we planned *Mission Remote Verification*. When we confirmed it, I did initially go home." She stopped for a moment, her thoughts scattered. "I need to let Sloan know I'm okay."

"Stone," Danny said.

"On it." He reached for his cell to call Sloan.

"Can't you drive any faster?" Danny asked.

"This isn't your C5 Corvette with the V8 350hp."

"His what?" Raina asked.

"Never heard about Danny's racing days?"

Racing days? How could she not know he had racing days? When she thought about it, there was a photo at his house with him standing next to a racecar. She had never imagined it was his. He likes country music, and he once had a racecar. Was her New York cop really from New York? She began to doubt she knew anything about him.

"Babe, you never told me about that," Raina said.

"There's lots about me you don't know." He raised one eyebrow seductively.

Dimples aside, she was slightly disturbed.

"Keep going with your story, and never mind Stone trying to start trouble," Danny said.

She wondered what else she didn't know and why was Danny classifying that information as trouble. Too wiped out to deal with that right this moment, she accepted his mysterious side for the time being and continued.

"I put it all together. His wife, you know Jean, she's blonde and about the age of the victims. Her coma may have pushed him over the edge. He always kept a positive front, but inside he must have felt helpless. Symbolically putting Jean out of her misery, painlessly killing the women who resembled her, might have been an outlet for him. Then she lost the baby and that was another trigger." She stopped for more water.

"Damn, she's good," Stone said.

"You know my trigger spreadsheet?" she asked.

"Yeah, but you said…" Danny started, but she interrupted.

"Before each murder the news reported a drug overdose. Each OD was a woman leaving her children without a mother. I'm not sure how that fits with Tyler, but it has to. Basically, he's using drugs to OD his victims. It has to be the trigger that sets him off. Somehow the drugs and his wife fit together."

"That's my girl," Danny said.

Her body stiffened at the possessiveness of that statement, not sure how to respond, not sure where their relationship stood. The expression on Danny's face suggested regret. Regret for that comment, for walking out, for not returning her calls, she wasn't sure. Neither said a word until crackling came through the police radio. The reception was poor, and they couldn't make out all the words. They heard 'Escape sssssss sssss stolen sssss FBssss'. The hissing from the radio interested Codis. He touched his nose to it and waited for a reaction. The radio didn't move, so he poked it again with the same result, and once more for certainty's sake. When he was confident the radio wasn't a threat, he curled back down in the front seat.

"Call in and see what's going on," Danny instructed Stone then turned to Raina. "So let me get this straight, Agatha," he started.

"Agatha?" Stone asked.

"Agatha Christie? Hello?" Danny said.

"Hello yourself, I know Agatha. How old are you, man?"

Danny continued without responding to Stone. "You realized Tyler was a serial killer, and you decided to go after him anyway?"

"With no back up," Stone jabbed.

"I realize how careless I must have appeared, but I wasn't afraid of Tyler, and I never believed he would ever harm me. I still don't. And he didn't, I'm alive. And most of all, I knew I could get close to him and get the proof you needed."

"You should have called me." The words seemed to slip out before he could stop them, but she was interrupted by her own thought before she could react to him.

"Proof!" she said. "He had a bag filled with vials of morphine and needles and tubes."

"Where is it?"

She rubbed her temples. "The last place I remember seeing it was his house." She hesitated. "He must have had it in Southampton. How else did he keep me sedated?"

She described the bag.

"I know," Stone said before Danny could ask, "calling Hawkeye."

Raina backtracked on her story. She told Danny about *Mission Bag* and explained how they got back to his house and how the bag left on the floor caught her eye because it was the only thing out of place in his entire house. She withheld her feelings and, of course, the sex part. As she got to that point in the story, she took a breath and forced herself not to think about it. She also didn't mention the headlock. None of those things would help Danny capture Tyler or help repair their relationship. Regardless of the murders, she felt bad for Tyler. She knew the situation with Jean and the baby had changed him and made him kill. That didn't make it acceptable to end the lives of innocent people and devastate their families and friends, but her desire to help him was still intense and unstoppable.

A loud thud came from the front seat as Stone slapped the top of the dashboard. "Yeah! They found the bag and they lifted prints."

Raina's eyes lit up. "The banking department has his prints on file, and so does the FBI. It's a requirement to become a licensed mortgage loan officer in New York. They can compare the prints."

"Pull over," Danny said.

"Why?"

"I'm driving. She's obviously fine."

Stone obeyed the lieutenant's command and stopped the car. Then he gave Codis a shove towards the back seat. Stone moved around to the other side, and Danny took the wheel, leaving Raina with her dog.

"We have a victim's necklace found in Tyler's house. We also got a sample of his DNA and ran it over to the lab," Danny said.

"Is that public knowledge?" Stone asked.

Danny curiously avoided the question. "Once Tyler's caught, a sample would have to be taken directly from him to be admissible in court."

"Can I please talk to Sloan myself now?" Raina asked.

From a pocket somewhere, Danny produced her cell phone and handed it over the seat. As he let it drop into her hands, she wondered what had gone through his mind when it was found at Tyler's.

"You found it at his house?" she asked, feeling heat rush to her face again.

"Yeah."

The phone had been set on silent mode and showed twenty-three missed calls.

Danny drove west on the Long Island Expressway while Raina tried Sloan. Her call was answered with tears. The conversation only lasted long enough for Raina to assure Sloan that she was okay and to give her the basic details. She needed to speak to her brother and pacify him as well. Half of the missed calls were from him. The last was a threat to call their parents, a call that she really wanted to avoid.

"Shane," Raina said to her brother.

"Sloan explained everything. I was really worried though."

Sloan hadn't prepared her for this, and Raina didn't want to mess up whatever story Sloan had told him. The only way to prevent that debacle was to call him back later. Later, after she got the story straight. No way would he have been so calm if Sloan had told him that she tracked and got kidnapped by a serial killer.

Raina was shocked as Danny filled her in on Tyler's childhood. When Tyler had spoken about his mother, it had always been in the most loving way. Thinking back, she realized it had all been abstract. Raina couldn't recall one fact about her. She had always assumed that she was deceased by the way he spoke about her in the past tense, but she had never imagined that hers had been such a horrible death. And a horrible life. She struggled to understand his feelings and actions and how his past had led him to become a killer. The combination of the publicized drug related overdoses and his wife's condition were too close to his past. Those were his triggers. Her feelings intensified, and the drive to help him became overwhelming.

CHAPTER 41

At home Raina paced and then checked her answering machine. The light was blinking *15*. Instead of listening to her messages, she checked the call log on the phone. At least half of the calls were from out of state from area codes that she didn't recognize. Her curiosity got the better of her. She pressed the button and listened to calls from Madison who gradually became frantic, calls from Sloan who tried not to say anything incriminating in case someone else heard, calls from her brother who was worried, and finally one call from her grandmother.

"You guys need to execute Raina's plans better," Stone said to Michael and Charlie who had followed them in.

"Maybe on the next mission," Michael replied.

Raina retold her story starting at the point at which she had left them at the vic's house. This time she expanded on her escape attempt.

"Wow," Michael said. "Weren't you afraid he was going to kill you?"

"I know it sounds weird, but I wasn't."

"He drugged you and then kidnapped you? That's not scary?"

Raina glanced Danny's way. He was across the room and listening intently, so she halted the conversation.

Everyone's attention turned to Stone when his phone buzzed. His eyes widened as he listened. He was bursting with information.

"The prints are a match," he said after what seemed like an eternity.

Suddenly Raina could hear the hum of her refrigerator and the summer insects from outside. If a pin had dropped, she would have heard that, too. The TMM had been positively identified, and they knew him. Raina knew him - intimately. Tyler: a serial killer. Her friend, her co-worker, someone she saw everyday: a serial killer. This was the first time she truly understood the definition of "surreal."

"Danny," Raina said and stepped closer to him. "Let me call him. I can help."

Danny shook his head emphatically, but she didn't give up. "He'll talk to me, and I think I can get him to turn himself in."

"It's worth a try," Stone said.

"Absolutely not," Danny said.

It was a good idea, the only one they had at the moment, and Stone backed up her proposal. "We'll have eyes and ears on her at all times. We'll put extra men on the task, and she'll be totally safe."

"No extra men will be needed. She's not going to meet him," Danny said.

"She's not going to talk him in over the phone," Stone argued.

"Oh yes she is."

"I'll be fine. This time you, the police, and the FBI will be protecting me," Raina said.

"Danny," Stone began.

Danny held his hand up to Stone to prevent further protest. "Okay. *Mission Tyler* begins."

Danny alerted Agent Blainey of their plan, and in return Blainey warned him of the risks of getting civilians involved. His respect had grown for the FBI after their plan saved Raina's life by luring Tyler away from her. Tyler may not have wanted to kill her then, but he would have realized at some point that he had been left with no choice. She was a loose end that needed to be tied up. The thought that Tyler would get back to that consumed him.

In the backyard, Danny half listened as Blainey analyzed the inner thoughts of a serial killer. Not just any serial killer, but the one who had captured Raina, the one that they were about to apprehend. He remained on the deck and digested the whole situation while he listened to the rest of the group discuss their plan. Stone was intoxicated as he planned the capture of a serial killer. The fact that he was involving Raina didn't seem to bother him a bit. It wasn't *his* girlfriend. Danny winced at the whole situation. It wasn't the right time, but he had to somehow fix things with Raina. He tuned out the chatter inside as he watched three, brightly colored butterflies flutter around the flowers. *What do they know?* he thought.

"You should get in there," Stone said as he went by with the phone pressed to his ear.

Danny acknowledged his suggestion but stayed on the deck.

Stone moved further away to continue his phone conversation. "As soon as this case is over, let's go away for the weekend?" he said. "Yeah, Montauk sounds perfect."

As Stone headed past Danny again, he smiled. "Lacey."

"Good," Danny said and followed Stone back to join the crew.

Raina updated him on the plan and advised him that it was already in motion. He wasn't surprised, and he let them know it by the expression on his face.

"Babe, don't go off without us this time. Please," Danny said.

"I promise," Raina said.

"So what did I miss?" Stone asked.

Charlie spoke up, "Oh, not much, dude. Raina left a voicemail for Tyler on his cell. Now we wait for him to call back."

"Did it go straight to voicemail?" Stone asked.

Everyone realized where he was heading with this question. If his cell phone was on, they could track it. If it went straight to voicemail, it was probably powered off.

"No, it rang a few times first," Michael said then reacted to Danny's puzzled look. "She called on speaker phone."

Danny shook his head and turned to Stone who had already called in the trace.

"It registered in Dix Hills seventeen minutes ago. Seems to be powering it on and off."

"It was worth a try," Charlie said.

"Better than a try," Danny said. "We know he's still in town or at least he was seventeen minutes ago. Not a big head start if he's left. And we know he has his phone, and he might even call Raina back."

"What if someone else has his phone?" Michael asked.

"Unlikely they would turn it on and off," Stone said.

"Unless they didn't want to get caught with a stolen phone."

"Anything's possible. We've seen stranger."

They all sat around and waited for the phone to ring except for Charlie who had slipped out the back door to place an order with

Francesco's for a couple of pies, garlic knots, and soda. Danny pulled
Stone aside to give him an abbreviated version of the information he
had received from the FBI. Several conversations were occurring at the
same time when they returned to the living room or, as Raina had
begun to call it, *Temp HQ,* short for temporary headquarters. Raina had
Sloan on the phone and headed for the back room. Danny had caught
a few words and wanted to hear the rest. Maybe he would find out
what she was thinking. He waited until he heard her plop on the bed
and then snuck up as close as he could get without being seen.

"I'm not sorry I called Danny, but I hope you're not mad at me,"
he heard Sloan say.

"I could never be mad at you."

"What about Danny? You and Danny?"

"He apologized in the car. I'm not sure for what."

"He's proven his love. He's your knight in shining armor. If he
hadn't rescued you, who knows what could have happened. Now
what?"

"I don't know what, we'll see."

Danny's stomach twisted. Now what *was* a good question. Raina
sounded hesitant, not like in the movies when the girl falls immediately
for the hero.

Before Danny could retreat to Temp HQ, Raina sped past him,
holding her phone out in front of her.

"It's him! It's him! Can you see his location on the screen?"

Stone gave her the signal to answer the call. In a panic, she hit the
send button before the phone was close enough to her ear.

Speakerphone was on so that everyone was able to listen, but she
quickly pulled the phone close to her ear. "Tyler, are you alright?"

"I'm sorry you got dragged into this," he said.

"I want to help you. Can we meet?" she asked.

"We've been friends a long time, Raina. I know you want me to
surrender myself," he answered.

"It's only a matter of time before they find you. Let Danny take
you in peacefully."

They could hear him weeping faintly. His tears and the pain in his
heart came through in his voice.

"Tyler?"

"Look what I've done to Jean. She's alone. And if I go to prison,
she'll be alone forever. I vowed to be with her forever, in sickness and

in health, in good times and bad. I'm supposed to protect her. We promised each other."

"Tyler, we'll figure something out. Please come to my house. Danny's here, and he'll help you."

The voice on the other end of the phone belonged to Tyler, but he sounded like someone else. He had had a horrendous childhood, one that no child should ever have to endure, but Danny couldn't let any emotion be assigned to the killer. When he was behind bars for life, then the system could assign him psychiatric help. For a moment, Danny felt a twinge of jealousy. Until now, he had never considered the bond that Raina shared with Tyler. Or was it that their target had contacted her and not him?

There was a long silence before Tyler responded in a weary voice. "Okay."

"Okay?" As she repeated the word, mimed victories filled the room in the form of fists pumping, touchdown hand signals, and punctuated nodding.

"It will be okay, I promise. You're doing the right thing."

The call ended, and Danny crouched in front of the laptop.

"What are you doing?" Raina asked.

"Tracking Tyler on the Internet. We can watch his route."

"So you'll know exactly when he'll be here?"

Danny waited to see how Stone was going to respond. Stone could tell what Danny was thinking because he was thinking it, too. The hospital was Tyler's destination, not Raina's house. There was no way he was leaving Jean alone in this world. He had made that perfectly clear.

"Tyler isn't coming here," Danny said. "He's going to the hospital."

They all thought they had understood, but they hadn't. Blainey had explained it to Danny who had relayed it to Stone. Tyler was trying to recreate the death of his mother, biological and/or foster, so he could assure it was painless, to relieve his guilt. They knew that Tyler couldn't leave Jean alone for fear that she might suffer as his two mothers had.

Everyone watched the laptop screen as the green, blinking dot travelled beyond the point where it should have changed direction to come to Raina's. It continued, heading northbound towards the hospital. Danny motioned to Stone. They walked to the other end of the room and spoke in low voices.

"I'm heading there. You stay here and keep them out of our way," Danny said.

Raina spoke from her seat at the table. "Stone doesn't have enough handcuffs for that."

"Raina, like it or not, he's a killer," Danny reminded her.

"Sorry, Lieutenant, I can help," Raina said.

"You and your..." he paused to come up with a word, "unit stay here."

With that he glared at Raina and left Stone to deal with her and her friends. Danny knew it wasn't a job Stone was thrilled to have since babysitting was not on his top ten list. It wasn't on his top one thousand list either. Stone wanted to be on the front line in the center of the action. Danny had to go, but he second guessed his decision to leave them together.

CHAPTER 42

The front end of Danny's Denali wasn't off the driveway before Raina started with Stone.

"Are we under arrest?" Raina asked.

"Come on Raina. I don't want to be here any more than you, but he gave me an order," Stone said.

"He's not *my* boss."

"Raina."

"Either you can come with me, or I can go without you. Which do you think your lieutenant would prefer? Huh?"

He considered her words, "Let's go. The dog stays."

She smiled with satisfaction. "Fine."

Just in case, Michael and Charlie were assigned to remain at Raina's.

Stone checked the monitor to note Tyler's location, almost to the hospital, and then Stone and Raina left the house.

Michael tossed her a bottle of water. "Doc said you have to keep hydrated."

As they reached the bottom stair, Stone turned to her. "Saabs aren't standard issue police cars, but it'll have to do," he said.

"Maybe it doesn't have lights and sirens, but it's turbo."

"I'm driving," he said.

She lobbed him the keys.

"Buckle your seatbelt."

Stone blasted out of the neighborhood and onto the main road. He drove right through stop signs, red lights, and only slowed slightly at the major intersections.

"When we get there…" Raina began.

Stone cut her off and shot her a look. "You do what I say," Stone said looking at his phone. "Shit."

"What?"

He punched a speed dial. "Rainman, the deal is going down. Meet me at Kelly's."

"What's going on?" Raina asked.

"We're taking a detour, and when we get there, you stay in this car with the doors locked. I'll just be a minute."

The car fishtailed as Stone rounded the last corner. He threw the car in park and bolted inside Kelly's. As soon as he was out of sight, Raina climbed into the driver's seat, parked the car legally, and headed for the bar. Danny had told her about Hawkeye's obsession. Stone had received a message and had called Hawkeye to meet him there. It didn't take a genius to figure out something was about to happen. She cupped her hands around the outside of her eyes and peered through the window, but there was no sign of Stone or Hawkeye. There was a moment when she thought better of it, but she grabbed the handle and opened the door. She walked straight along the side of the bar to the other end and heard the commotion. Some sense of self-preservation kicked in, and she backed into a corner where she was out of the way but could hear everything from the other room. There was a lot of yelling and cursing and what sounded like movement of furniture and bodies as they crashed into the wall. The bartender paid no attention to the ruckus. Finally, she heard Stone reading someone his rights. The door opened. She stayed glued to the wall.

Hawkeye came out first with a man in cuffs. His head was covered with a hood, and his jeans were ripped. He was muttering something about a deal and jarring his shoulders back and forth to make leading him out more difficult. In all her time with Danny, she had never seen a real arrest, and she felt an equal mix of excitement and fear. Stone followed with another man in custody. This one was calm and quiet and wore a suit, and Raina was startled when she saw his face. It was him, Levy, the first victim's husband. Why was he under arrest? And, more importantly, how was she going to get back to the car without Stone seeing her?

Stone went ahead of Hawkeye and kicked open the front door. As they stepped outside, two marked cars pulled in front, lights flashing and sirens blaring. Raina moved closer to the entrance. As Stone handed Levy over to an officer, she slipped by and got back into her car. He had seen her, but what did it really matter? It didn't. The rush had distracted her from her real desire to get to Tyler. They had to get to the hospital, only a half-mile away. If Tyler was already there, she might have missed her chance to see him, to help him, to make sure no one hurt him. She felt sick and worn out and energized all at the same time.

Stone jumped back into the driver's seat and peeled out of the spot without a word. She plugged in her seatbelt and held on.

"What was that about?" Raina asked.

"Loose ends."

"What was Levy arrested for?"

Stone's head whipped towards her so fast that his shoulder followed and the car jerked to the right. "You know him?" he asked, then wrenched the wheel back to straighten the car, jarring Raina in her seat.

She couldn't understand why Stone was surprised. The victims' identities had been released.

"What's going on in that bar?"

She continued to prod him for information, but Stone clammed up. *Fine*, she thought. *I'll find out without him.* The rapid beeps from her keypad continued until she filled Sloan in on the latest.

They approached the building moments later, and Raina remained quiet. Stone sprang from her car, leaving it in front of the entrance but away from the emergency vehicle area. It was not legally parked, rendering it likely to be towed. He flashed his badge on the way in. Raina asked the guard to keep an eye on her car with the promise they would be quick as she scooted behind Stone. They sprinted to the elevator, and Raina struggled to keep pace. Stone pounded the up arrow button repeatedly.

"Stay behind me at all times."

Danny had helped Blainey secure the area while Tyler was in with Jean, stroking her hair, apologizing, and promising never to leave her. This time there was nowhere for Tyler to go, so they agreed to let Tyler continue. The IV had been temporarily disconnected in anticipation of Tyler's next move. It would be better psychologically for Tyler to believe he had accomplished what he set out to do, and then easier to secure him. They watched him tilt her head to the side, adjusting it to a specific position, and gather her hair. Blainey hushed Danny with a nod when Danny began to question the delay in capture. Tyler turned around.

"You don't understand. I have to help her," he begged.

"I understand, but that's not helping her, mate. Put the needle down and place your hands behind your back," Blainey said.

"Tyler, we want to help you and Jean. Take a step back," Bryant tried with a softer approach.

"It's too late. I know what I have to do." He plunged the needle into the IV, held her hand, and whispered in her ear.

As Tyler emptied the vial, Bryant took a step closer. Tyler heard the approach and spun around, stopping her in her tracks as he drew a gun. Within seconds, Danny and the agents had their guns pointed at Tyler.

"Don't come any closer," he said.

"Please, Tyler, we can help you. Let us help you," Bryant said.

She reached out to him for the gun. Instead, he held it firmly and released the safety. While Bryant was trying to negotiate the situation, Danny had spotted Stone running down the hall.

When Stone and Raina were almost to the door, Danny swung his arm across her chest and tried to stop her. Raina pushed through, but the sight of Tyler pointing a gun stopped her in her tracks.

Blainey stepped towards Raina.

"I thought it was going to be a peaceful capture. I thought he would say goodbye to Jean and surrender," Raina said with tears streaming down her cheeks.

No one had shared the full FBI profile with Raina, or she would have known that Tyler had intended a murder suicide combo. That was his solution: he and Jean would be together in eternity. He would protect her there.

She reached for Tyler.

"No, Tyler, no. Wait!"

Tyler's arm relaxed for a second as he looked to Raina with a tortured look in his eyes. Bryant took advantage of that second and fired a shot. Tyler fell to the floor, and the gun spun out of his hand. Stone jumped in, kicked the gun across the room, repositioned Tyler's arms, and cuffed them behind his back. Blainey motioned for the staff waiting down the hall on standby.

CHAPTER 43

One month after the capture of the TMM, Danny led a toast. Glasses and bottles were raised to welcome the newest member of the Detective Squad. Detective John "Hawkeye" Lorenzo had earned his gold shield. They were celebrating outside on the bulkhead at Mug Shots on a cool, late summer evening. The sinking sun backlit the waterfront homes and the edges of the Long Island Sound. Boats gently rocked on the water, and the outgoing tide filled the air with its scent.

"Congratulations, Rainman. You worked hard on the TMM case," Stone said.

"You don't believe that," Hawkeye said wiping wing sauce from his fingers.

"Do your mindreading shit on someone else."

"He's right, Hawkeye. You were invaluable on the TMM case. You deserve it. Helping Stone bring in the drug dealer didn't hurt either. His information led to the arrest of important players in a pretty big drug ring," Danny said. "Watch out or DEA might try to recruit you, too."

Stone's head whipped around. "What? He's lucky I was there to cover his ass."

Hawkeye contorted his face. "You're lucky I showed up when I did. Otherwise your informant would have successfully escaped."

"Yeah right," Stone said. "What about the time you dragged the drunk around while we were hunting for a killer?"

Hawkeye ignored Stone and turned towards Danny. "Thanks, Lieutenant. I'm truly honored to serve as a detective."

"Danny to you."

"Come on Stone, admit I was right," Hawkeye said.

"Right about what?"

"I knew there was a connection between Levy and Kelly's."

"He's right," Murphy said. "He did. Raina figured out that Levy was supplying the drugs to the women that OD'd, and Sloan matched their phone records. And," Murphy turned to Hawkeye, "that explains why Levy had such a sophisticated security system. Did you see that safe he had hidden in the bedroom closet? After his arrest, we executed a warrant to have it opened. One guess what was in it."

"Raina had made the connection between the drug ODs and the TMM. She was the first to tag that as his trigger," Danny said. "And thanks to Hawkeye and his gut for keeping on top of it."

"Yeah Rainman, you're not just a hat rack," Stone said.

The team congratulated him with hardy pats on the back, handshakes, and another round of drinks. It was a good time, but Hawkeye was anxious to get home and celebrate the good news with his wife. After an hour or so, everyone went their separate ways. Hawkeye drove straight home. He bolted through the front door with a smile as wide as his face, arms extended for a hug. Kathy walked towards him. He produced his gold shield.

"You got it!"

"I did."

"This is my proudest moment," she hesitated then shared more good news, "until the baby is born."

The Lorenzo household was a happy place. They ordered in dinner and talked about how much their lives were about to change.

Early the next afternoon, the sun was shining bright and hot. There was no breeze or relief in the shade.

"Dude!" Charlie yelled across the pool as he punched the volleyball over the net.

"Are you thinking what I'm thinking?" Michael asked.

"Are you thinking end of summer party blowout?"

Charlie scored as the ball went into the net on Michael's return shot. "Yeah! Party!"

They climbed up the tiled steps from the pool and hit the lounge chairs. Michael dried his hands and grabbed his phone from the table. He dragged his forefinger along the screen, and his contact list scrolled before him.

"Lots of numbers in here," he said.

"Are we inviting Harvey this time?" Charlie asked.

"He's a party animal, why not?"

"I can't believe his wife hasn't left him yet. She knows what he does, and she stays with him."

Michael shook his head in agreement. "He's got a successful business. Maybe she likes his money."

"Dude, she can take that in a divorce."

"Speaking of divorce, I don't think Raina has seen Danny in weeks."

"You think after a few weeks she's already over him?"

"It can't hurt to try. Maybe she's ready for a real man."

"You're crazy, dude. What would she want with you? You're not a one-woman man."

"I could be, for her."

Michael caught himself before he responded to Charlie's eye roll. Maybe Charlie was right, but she was worth a try. He would call her after Charlie left.

"I'll call DJ Sean, and you order the food. I'm sure they have a record of our last party order. Tell them to duplicate it," Michael said.

"Then we call the hot chicks."

"Lots of them!" Michael said, but he wanted just the one.

With the biggest case of his life behind him, Stone felt sullen. The excitement, the rush, and the hunt were all over, and he was headed to Lacey's to pick her up for their first vacation. One week together, trapped. Packing was torturous. He hadn't had a serious relationship, nor had he spent any length of concentrated time with one person in years. The thought of it suffocated him.

As he neared Lacey's neighborhood, his breathing became irregular, and he was gasping for air. He sucked in a deep breath and strangled his shaky hands to regain control, as he pulled in front of her house and contemplated fleeing. He would run across her at work, but he wouldn't have to deal with the weekend. He could send her a text saying that something had come up at work, apologize, and move on. He threw the car in drive, but before he could escape, Lacey opened the door. Too late, she had seen him. He put the car in park, turned towards her, and the strangest thing happened. The sight of her standing inside, smiling, waiting sent a warm calm through his body. Somehow her presence was all he needed to get past his anxiety. He could do this. He was going to be fine.

The drive out East was nostalgic for Stone. He had taken the trip many times before, but the last one had been during the race to rescue Raina. The whole case flooded back into his mind, and he hit the gas for a short sprint on the open road.

"Hang on," he said with a big grin.

When they arrived at Lenhart's Cottages, they were led to a one bedroom cabin with a view of the ocean across Old Montauk Highway. The cabin had a fireplace in the living area with cozy couches around a rustic, wood table. A full kitchen was at the other end of the living room, and the bedroom was in the back. Lacey placed her bag on a chair and gave Stone a big hug.

"This is going to be a great weekend," she said.

"I know." He kissed her. "Did you know that I was on vacation before the TMM case erupted? I came back early to get on the case."

"Doesn't surprise me, Cowboy. You always want to be where the action is."

"Speaking of action..." He leaned closer to kiss her again and stripped her of her clothes.

After a marital blowout, the hospital and Paul agreed to release Sloan from custody as she had begun to call it. The doctors couldn't find anything to be overly concerned about, and Sloan was feeling fine.

A week before Labor Day, Sloan was ten days past her due date, and her patience had run out. She had spent hours on the Internet searching for natural ways to induce labor. The choice suggestion was to walk. She had recruited Raina to keep her company in case walking had an immediate effect. Armed with cell phones, they set out to make many quarter mile circles around the neighborhood, never too far from their cars.

"Walking makes your hips sway from side to side and helps rock the baby into the correct birthing position," Sloan said.

"Feel anything yet?"

"Not really."

"I don't think she wants to come out."

"Look." Sloan cradled her stomach with two hands as she waddled down the road. "I'm going to burst. She has to get out."

"All that time in the hospital for nothing. It must kill you," Raina said.

"Can you believe they kept me practically strapped to the bed for so long, and now they want me to walk? Right now, I just want this baby out."

Raina grabbed her cell and connected to the Internet. "Says that sex helps induce labor, too."

"Paul's been all over that. It's not so easy these days, you know," Sloan said.

Yeah, I bet he has, Raina thought.

She slowed her pace each time they passed the corner where they would turn if they were heading back to Sloan's.

"Keep walking," Sloan said. "Are you ever going to return Danny's calls?"

"I will when I figure out what to say."

"Why don't you hear what he has to say?"

"He's going to say the same thing he always does: that things were good the way they were. I want more, he doesn't. We have to want the same thing, or neither of us will be happy."

The scent of barbequed meat distracted Sloan as she turned her head in its direction. Raina took full advantage and changed the subject.

They hit the two hour mark on the fourth day of trying to walk the baby into being ready for the birth. Sloan was hungry, and Raina called in for a lunch delivery.

They walked a while more, and when they made it back to the house, the delivery car had been waiting by the gate. Raina handed the guy enough cash to cover the bill and the tip in exchange for two generic, brown paper shopping bags of food.

Raina spread the Chinese food containers on the table. "This might help: Spicy Tangy Chicken, General Tso's shrimp, Kung Pao Beef, and eggplant and broccoli with garlic sauce. Everything had a little red pepper symbol next to it."

"I've tried the spicy food thing."

"Well, try it again."

After scooping in large amounts, Sloan stopped. "Is there any word on Tyler and Jean?"

Raina's expression adjusted to the new subject. "Jean's the same. The doctors still can't say much. And Tyler," Raina took a deep breath, "the FBI still has him in some federal holding facility. He's under 24-hour suicide watch."

"It's so hard to picture him like that. The guy we knew seemed so happy with life."

"I know." Raina stared at the floor.

"Don't even go there, Raina." Sloan put her hand on Raina's arm. "This is not your fault in any way. You should be proud. Who knows how many more he'd have killed if you hadn't helped stop him."

Raina nodded, but Sloan could see in her face that the sad feeling remained.

On her way up the stairs that evening, Sloan grabbed her abdomen and doubled over before she made it to the top. She held onto the iron railing and screamed for Paul.

Twenty-two hours later, she and Paul had their baby girl.

CHAPTER 44

The stove clock read a quarter after eight. Calculated in Danny-time, that gave Raina another fifteen minutes before he would arrive to pick her up. It would be the first time they had spent an evening together socially since the capture of the TMM.

Danny had called her regularly to check in, but he never brought up the day he walked out, and neither did she. She questioned whether it was worth talking about. Their relationship appeared to be over. Why open old wounds? She didn't take his calls and had returned them intermittently. When she did, they were both brief and business-like. He was buried under endless reports, the FBI, and the attorneys on both sides, and she was healing emotionally, or at least trying not to make cause for more internal turmoil. His calls confused her. He didn't appear to want anything, but he kept calling.

When he had asked to see her, she had initially declined. The invitation was strangely ominous. She had spent the last month dealing with her mixed bag of feelings. Between Danny and Tyler and all that occurred, Raina had a lot to sort out. She had resigned herself to the fact that it had all been beyond her control, and she was working to move on. Danny was persistent though. Over the past week, he had called every night asking her to go to the beach with him like old times. She was still haunted by her relationship with Tyler and sometimes doubted her worthiness of Danny. In the end, she agreed to go.

"Relax," Sloan said. "Call me if you need anything. It will be fine."

"I should be saying that to you. Maybe I can stop by later and see the baby."

Raina threw on her favorite jeans, the ones with the hole in one knee, a light pink T-shirt, and her favorite flip-flops. She tossed a sweatshirt next to her bag and waited for Danny. To her surprise, her wait was short, and Danny pulled into the driveway on time. Maybe he's trying to change. She could feel the excitement bubbling up inside, knowing that she was probably setting herself up for another let down.

Codis stood on the love seat waging his cropped tail and followed Danny with his eyes as Danny approached the door.

"Ready?" he asked.

She forced a smiled and scooped up her stuff. Danny whistled at Codis. He ran to the car and hopped in through the rear door that Danny had left open for him. Codis was seated, waiting for his chauffer to take him somewhere. It was a smart, calculated move on Danny's part as Raina was happy to have her dog with them. The ride to the beach was quiet. Raina asked Danny about his part in the pre-trial preparation, but he wasn't supposed to share that information. It was odd for Danny to not tell her anyway, and he was unusually quiet. Given the delicateness of their relationship, whatever that was, she didn't press the issue. She sat tensely in the passenger seat, not sure what to say or how to feel. So much has transpired, she thought as she twirled her Tiffany bracelet.

Raina scanned the empty lot at the beach and appreciated the vastness of it as they parked close to the entrance. The three-quarter moon was bright, and the air had the coolness about it that came every year with the onset of fall. Danny took her hand, and they strolled through the tunnel under the beach parkway, along the well-landscaped walk, and onto the boardwalk. They sat on a stone bench while Codis took a flying leap to the sand and began sniffing furiously. Danny leaned against the metal railing on the far side, giving them the view of the moonlit ocean. He guided Raina in front of him, and she leaned her back against his chest. It used to be her favorite place, but she felt uneasy in his arms. He wasn't quite hugging her. She wasn't quite relaxed. There were more than a few awkwardly quiet moments.

"So, Raina." He spoke in a choppy manner.

She felt his heart pound against her back as he took a deep breath. He had always been the calm one. How bad could it be that he's nervous? She thought he had taken her to the beach to keep her calm. What did he want to say? He wouldn't have dragged her here for closure, would he? She waited patiently and hoped it was something good.

The extended silence felt like an eternity. She tried to push him along with a gentle squeeze of his knee and then a comforting rub on his leg.

He swallowed and struggled to speak. "We've been through a lot the last couple of months. I almost lost you. It scared me and made me realize that I don't want to lose you."

Raina's heart raced with excitement. Could he possibly be ready to take the relationship to the next level? That thought lasted less than a second. Several times before, she had mistakenly thought he was going to give her a ring for her birthday or Valentine's Day. She wasn't going to let that happen again. She was smarter now. Maybe he wanted to live together or plan a vacation. That would be a big step for Danny, but was it enough for her?

He continued on with forced effort. "You mean so much to me, and I need you."

Raina swung her leg across his and twisted her body around to see his face. How was she going to tell him whatever he wanted wasn't enough? Maybe it would be better if she didn't let him even ask.

"Danny."

"Let me finish," he said.

His serious look stopped her from continuing. She decided that it was best to rip the band-aid off and get it over with. Let him say what he was there to say.

"I'm listening."

"Babe, I love you."

She felt him reach into his pocket, and her heart dropped so hard that it felt like it collided with her stomach. It had to be. He had to be reaching for a ring box. He sneezed and pulled a tissue from his pocket. A tissue? He was reaching for a damn tissue? The tension was making her shoulders ache. He shoved the tissue back in his pocket, then took a deep breath. Her stomach was tied in a knot, her heart pounded against her chest, and she tried to hide it all and prayed he'd hurry up and spill it already.

"I want you to marry me," he blurted.

In an instant, everything was different. Her whole world changed. A smile spread across her face as he presented an open ring box to her. Nothing else was important at that moment. She didn't hear the people walk by or the waves crash against the shore, only Danny's words that echoed in her head.

He pulled the ring from the box and slid it on her finger.

She flung her arms around his neck. "Yes!"

The diamond sparkled in the moonlight, outshined only by Raina's happiness.

The End

When LJ KING isn't defending her position that she is not an eccentric recluse but a focused writer, she is out of her office at the beach, playing tennis, gardening, and doing things *with* people. She has a degree in Literature and Art and serves on the Board for the Long Island Authors Group.

For more information visit www.ljking.net

CPSIA information can be obtained at www.ICGtesting.com
Printed in the USA
BVOW040919050612

291697BV00001BA/13/P